Praise

HOUSE OF HUNGER

"Gorgeous and lushly dark. . . . A nightmare vision that will pull you into its terrifying grip."

—Simone St. James, *New York Times* bestselling author of *The Book of Cold Cases*

"A gory gem of a story that sinks in its teeth and won't let up, *House of Hunger* proves that Alexis Henderson is one of the best Gothic writers out there."

—Hannah Whitten, *New York Times* bestselling author of *For the Wolf*

"A Gothic masterpiece that demands to linger like the coppery scent of blood in the air long after the final page is turned."

—Eric LaRocca, author of *Things Have Gotten Worse Since We Last Spoke*

"Readers will devour every page. . . . A chilling, atmospheric tale shrouded in mystery, indulgence, deceit, and dangerous consequences."

—N.E. Davenport, author of *The Blood Trials*

"Bloody and atmospheric . . . will lull you into a false sense of security just before baring its teeth."

—Genevieve Gornichec, national bestselling author of *The Witch's H*

"Cements Henderson's place as one of the great Gothic writers of our generation. Readers will be absolutely spellbound."

—S.T. Gibson, author of *A Dowry of Blood*

ALSO BY ALEXIS HENDERSON

The Year of the Witching

HOUSE

of

HUNGER

———————— ◆ ————————

ALEXIS HENDERSON

ACE
NEW YORK

ACE
Published by Berkley
An imprint of Penguin Random House LLC
penguinrandomhouse.com

Copyright © 2022 by Alexis Henderson
Readers Guide copyright © 2022 by Alexis Henderson

ISBN: 9780593438480

The Library of Congress has cataloged the Ace hardcover edition of this book as follows:

Names: Henderson, Alexis, author.
Title: House of hunger / Alexis Henderson.
Description: New York: Ace, [2022]
Identifiers: LCCN 2022014354 (print) | LCCN 2022014355 (ebook) |
ISBN 9780593438466 (hardcover) | ISBN 9780593438473 (ebook)
Subjects: LCGFT: Novels.
Classification: LCC PS3608.E52548 H68 2022 (print) |
LCC PS3608.E52548 (ebook) | DDC 813/.6—dc23
LC record available at https://lccn.loc.gov/2022014354
LC ebook record available at https://lccn.loc.gov/2022014355

Ace hardcover edition / September 2022
Ace trade paperback edition / September 2023

Printed in the United States of America
1st Printing

Book design by Daniel Brount

To those whose stories are often told in whispers

1

To bleed is to be.

—VANESSA, FIRST BLOODMAID OF THE HOUSE OF HUNGER

BEFORE SHE WAS FIRST bled, when she still had the name her parents gave her, Marion Shaw was a maid at a townhouse in the South of Prane. On that morning—the morning she would later come to identify as the beginning of her second life—she knelt on the hard wood floor of the parlor, sleeves rolled up to her bony elbows, a scrub brush in her hand.

Across the room, in an upholstered armchair, Lady Gertrude sat, watching her work. She was a shrewd woman, blue-eyed with silver hair and a pinched aristocratic nose, spattered with age spots and freckles. While other nobles preferred to leave their maids to their labor, Lady Gertrude preferred instead to preside over them, watching with a falcon's eye as if to ensure that her help earned every penny she paid them.

"You missed a spot," she sneered, seizing her cane to point at a minuscule stain on the floorboards.

Marion batted a dark curl out of her eye. She did what little she could to mind her tone. "I'll be more careful, milady."

"You ought to be. There's girls more handsome and less sluggish than you who'd be happy to have your position," she said, and she bit down on a brittle tea cookie, spitting crumbs when she spoke again. "You've grown slow . . . and lazy. I can see it in your eyes. The little light there was in them has long gone out, and now you expect to drag yourself through my halls on your hands and knees like a common drunk. With your hair unkempt and your apron stained—"

"Rest assured this floor will be spotless by the time I'm through with it," said Marion, cutting her short. She could feel the rage pooling in the pit of her belly like bile. "You have my word."

At this, Lady Gertrude merely frowned, the slack skin of her brow wrinkling like fabric. Marion couldn't help but think that she was rather lonely. Long widowed, without children of her own, or companions or family to speak of, she had no means of social stimulation apart from Sunday mass. Thus, every day she followed Marion from room to room, watching her scrub the floors and polish the silver, sometimes (if her health allowed it) going so far as to trail after her into the kitchens, where she'd remain until her aching knees drove her back to the comfort of her parlor.

Marion polished the floor until she could see her own reflection in it—wide-set eyes gaping back at her, a firm nose and full lips slightly parted, tongue tucked behind her teeth, skin a deep tawny, hair a mess of curls. She frowned at herself just as the church bells rang twelve. With a ragged sigh, Marion peeled her gaze from her own reflection, dropped her scrub brush into the bucket with a splash, and pressed slowly to her feet.

In accordance with the new labor laws, all workers were promised an hour's rest at the top of their seventh hour of work, a precautionary measure enacted after no fewer than six girls worked themselves to death after twenty-hour shifts in a cotton mill. And while Lady Gertrude was not a particularly kind woman, she was a great adherent to order and strict regulation, regardless of whether it was a benefit to her. Thus, when the clock struck noon, she was quick to dismiss Marion.

Unlike many of her set, Lady Gertrude couldn't afford to buy herself a townhome more than a spitting distance from the more . . . *unsightly* corners of Prane, and it took Marion only a few minutes to reach the cusp of the slums. Here, Marion's pace quickened and she felt her spirits lift, if only slightly.

Gradually, the fine brick townhomes gave way to shanties and warehouses, cast in a pall of smog. Marion shouldered down the crowded streets of the stockyards and adjoining meat market, trudging through half-frozen manure and past the racks of cattle corpses that hung, swinging, by the hooves. Instinctively, she rounded her shoulders against the blast of the coming cold. Fall had only just begun, but it was unseasonably chilly that day and the streets were thick with snow and slush.

Outside, the crowds spread through the stockyards, rounding the corrals where the cattle huddled—shuddering from the cold or the fear of the coming butchery or both. Marion trained her eyes on her boots as she passed them by. Almost ten years of walking every day through the stockyards and she still couldn't bring herself to look those beasts in the eye.

Marion kept walking. The seething smog was low-slung, and so thick that the sun could barely shine through it. The streets were thronged, as they always were at midday. Crowds gathered around the vendor stalls, and if Marion had coin to spare on a bit of roast eel or herring, she might have joined them. But she didn't, so she went about her way, navigating the crowds and icy streets, snow slush leaking into her boots as she walked.

A vicious wind circled down the alleys and ripped at her coat as she neared her favorite place to sit, a dark doorstep at the back of an abandoned warehouse, on the cusp of Prane, overlooking the trenches and the long scar of the northern railroad beyond them.

It began to rain, and Marion retreated into the shadow of the awning, fishing a pack of matches and her last cigarette from the back pocket of her coat. She lit the smoke and nursed it, cupping her hand to shield it from the wind. Between draws she wheezed and shivered, blowing smoke through her fingers to warm them.

The cigarettes did wonders to calm her hunger pangs, and at a halfpenny a pack they were far cheaper than the offerings of the roadside food vendors, who, as far as Marion was concerned, always overcharged.

"If it ain't the jewel of Prane."

Marion turned to see Agnes wading toward her through the thick of the crowds. She raised a hand and Marion greeted her with two raised middle fingers in turn. Agnes was a gaunt, jaundiced matchstick girl with pale brown eyes and thinning hair that she wore in a braid that hung, like a rat's tail, down her back. Like Marion, Agnes had spent the early years of her childhood pickpocketing on busy street corners. In fact, that was how they'd met, and they soon learned that thievery was a trade better suited to two. Agnes would act as the distraction—chatting nonsense with their targets, keeping them occupied—while Marion crept up from behind to nab a coin purse or slip a silk handkerchief from the breast coat of a passing lord. But at age ten, when the legal repercussions of thievery became too steep, Agnes had taken up honest work on the factory line where she made matches—dipping wooden sticks into sulfur—from dawn until dusk. Soon after, Marion secured a position as the scullery maid of Lady Gertrude.

Still, despite their new occupations, every day at noon the two girls made a point to converge at the same street corner where they'd first met. But Marion and Agnes weren't friends, because Marion didn't *have* friends. The way she saw it, friends were a luxury reserved for people who had the spare time to spend with them—like the girls who wandered Main Street with their parasols and bone-white gloves, retiring to their parlors in the afternoon to take a bit of tea and talk. No. Girls like Marion and Agnes had no use or time for companions. They were simply fixtures in each other's lives, a part of Prane's habitat, like the reeking miasma and the crows and the rats that roamed the streets in packs at night.

Marion passed Agnes the nub of her cigarette and slipped both hands into her skirt pockets, doing what little she could to keep herself warm. She had another five hours of work ahead of her, and it was hard to scrub floors with cold-stiff fingers.

Agnes pulled on her cigarette in silence, the smoke leaking through the gaps of her missing teeth. She looked haggard from the time she'd spent slaving away on the line, breathing the toxic phosphorous fumes day in and day out until the chemical stench filled her up like a second spirit. That was something Marion's mother used to say. That folks in Prane had two souls—one made of the stuff of the heavens, the other from miasma.

Agnes took a final pull on her cigarette and flicked the butt into the trenches. "Ugly day, isn't it?"

Marion shrugged. "No worse than the others."

"But it is. The days are shorter than they ever were before, the nights are longer. And the sun, it doesn't rise as high as it used to. I swear it. The summers aren't as warm. Fall is shorter. The winters are colder." Agnes shook her head. "I can feel the change."

"Prane doesn't change," said Marion, and it was true. Prane was the northernmost city of the South. It existed in the rift between the worlds—the arctic North and the punishing heat of the industrial

South. And so, Prane was never one thing or another. In the night, the light of the city was such that it seemed the sun never fully set; in the day, the gray pall of smog made it seem like it never fully rose. Thus, the slums of Prane felt much like a realm caught between, in perpetual indecision, as if the skies couldn't decide what they wanted to be.

Never fully day. Never fully night.

Never anything at all.

And though she knew nothing else, Marion had come to hate that indistinction . . . and most everything else about Prane too. She sometimes wondered if there was a single person in the slums who found something, anything, to love about the place. Agnes, for her part, seemed resigned, even content. But begrudging contentment was not the same as happiness. At best it was familiarity, and at worst defeat. It certainly wasn't the same as true fondness.

Marion lowered herself to the stoop beside Agnes, wincing a little as the snowmelt seeped through her skirts. Her gaze drifted north. In the distance, she could just make out the night train's station on the cusp of Prane—a beautiful structure of glass and iron with its own clock tower that only ever called the hours of the night. Marion had visited the station only once, on her eighth birthday. She had begged her mother to let her see it, in lieu of a proper birthday gift. And so, that evening, they had ventured down to the station.

Marion's mother had lifted her up onto her hip to peer into the night train's windows, and she had caught the briefest glimpse of its cabin—its seats upholstered with red velvet, its windows draped with brocade and dyed silks. Each cabin was lit by the shimmering chandeliers that dangled from the ceilings. They didn't care that the men in the three-piece suits scowled at their presence, or that the women clutched their skirts and coin-fat purses closer at their approach.

Marion and her mother had merely laughed and smiled and watched in awe as the northerners (you could tell them apart from the touring southerners based on their fine clothes and the way they tilted their chins, just so) boarded the train and settled themselves for the journey north. There was a bloodmaid among them, a black-haired girl with a fine mink muff who smiled at Marion through the window. At seven past twelve, Marion and her mother watched from the platform as that great, black-iron beast roared to life and charged into the dark of the night.

Every time she heard the keen peal of the night train's horn, she felt the same stirring in the marrow of her bones that she had as a child, standing on the platform alongside her mother. She loved the sound and the feeling of the train's approach. Sometimes she imagined herself onboard—sitting among the northern nobles and men of Parliament—a gilded, one-way ticket in her pocket that cost more than ten times what a maid like Marion earned in a year.

Agnes eyed her through a cloud of cigarette smoke. "Still looking north?"

"Nothing else to look at."

"Then I suppose you won't be wanting this." Agnes reached into the shadows of her coat and withdrew a folded newspaper. She stole one every day, in a kind of unspoken agreement, an important part of their ritual. Agnes brought the stolen paper, and Marion the cigarettes, and together they made the most of what little time they had to spare.

The wind tore at the edges of the newspaper as Agnes opened it and spread it flat across their thighs. They didn't bother with the headline stories—long articles about taxes and tariff wars and cholera outbreaks in the slums. Instead, they skipped to their favorite section, the matrimonial advertisements at the back of the paper.

It was the top of the week, so there was a large selection of adverts to comb through. One for a respectable physician seeking a maiden wife. Another for a widowed cleric with a parish in the country in want of a wife of "impeccable morals" and a mother for his *nine* children (he requested that the lucky woman be no older than two and twenty). At the bottom corner of the page, an advert for a self-described spinster, aged thirty-eight, seeking a bachelor of fortune to receive with "kindness and affection."

Marion and Agnes read each of these adverts in their best mockery of a posh accent, illustrating the postings with wild imaginings about the appearances of the subjects, their homes and lives and favorite proclivities.

"He might be a fit for you," said Agnes, with a sly smile. She tapped an ad for a navy officer in want of a "wholesome" maiden, and Marion laughed aloud. She was many things, but wholesome she was not. Virtue, in the conventional sense, had never become her. At twenty, she'd shared beds with several women, and she enjoyed indulging readily in the delights of the flesh. She and Agnes had had a brief tryst one summer, but there was no real feeling between them, and things had ended badly. They'd since decided they were better smoking companions than lovers.

Agnes squinted down at the paper. "At a salary of four hundred a year maybe he'd be a fit for me too. I could be a maiden."

"Somehow I have a hard time picturing that," said Marion, turning the newspaper's page. And it was then that she saw it, an advertisement in the midst of the matrimony column. Unlike the other postings, it was printed in the most peculiar shade of scarlet. And the letters were different, larger and filigreed, the dips and curves of each one sweeping into the next like cursive. It read:

WANTED: *Bloodmaid of exceptional taste. No more than 19. Must have a keen proclivity for life's finer pleasures. No references required. Candidates will be received by mail at The Night Embassy, 727 Crooks Street, Prane, or personally from 10 to 12 in the evening hours. Girls of weak will need not apply.*

Below the posting was a crest—the crude face of a frowning man with olive branches in his hair—the seal of the House of Hunger, one of the largest, and most feared, in the North.

Agnes hissed through her teeth at the sight of it.

In Prane, bloodmaids were regarded as symbols of opulence and depravity in almost equal measure. They were said to spend their days as the cosseted charges of their noble, northern masters—strumming harps, powdering their upturned noses, studying arts and languages, stuffing their cheeks with frosted tea cakes and chocolates and other delightful confections to sweeten their blood to the taste.

The worst of their job was the bleeding, which bloodmaids did frequently to satisfy the carnivorous appetites of the nobles, who relied on the healing properties of their blood as a lavish remedy for their varying ailments. According to the newspapers, blood was purported to cure a number of diseases including, but not limited to, tuberculosis, rubella, measles, syphilis, rickets, and arthritic pains. Some even believed that blood contained youth-preserving properties, especially when taken directly from the source and consumed while still warm.

But the way Marion saw it, work was work, and the work of a bloodmaid was far easier than that of the average factory hand in Prane. Besides, Marion had heard it rumored that upon the end of their tenure bloodmaids were rewarded with lavish pensions that ensured they'd live their remaining days in accordance to the same standard of luxury they'd been accustomed to during their time as bloodmaids. Marion had heard stories of retired bloodmaids being gifted seaside villas, even entire estates, in the Southern Isles, complete with full households—footmen, drivers, stable hands, and even bloodmaids of their own.

Agnes glowered down at the newspaper. "They've got some nerve to advertise a posting for a blood-whore in the matrimony column, of all places."

In the South, the prejudice against bloodmaids ran deep, and Agnes was far from the only person in Prane who harbored ill feelings toward the blood trade. Some girls, even beautiful ones, refused to consider the position of bloodmaid as a matter of principle. Such was the stigma against the profession. Marion had heard it said, many times over, that mothers would rather see their daughters become harlots on the streets of Prane than bloodmaids in the North. And many a southern priest had preached from the pulpit about the immortal dangers of bleeding, the toll that dark work took on the body and soul. There were ample rumors about girls drained of blood and spirit, returning to the South penniless and pale after years of bleeding with nothing but their scars to show for it.

"Where else would you have them place it? A bloodmaid could hardly be called a servant."

"Well, they're far from wives," said Agnes, and when she spewed the words, she flecked the newspaper with spit. "Whoring for a night lord is nothing like a marriage."

Marion saw little difference between the two. Both the act of becoming a bloodmaid and the act of becoming a wife were a kind of amalgamation of fealty and flesh, blood and fidelity. And why sell yourself to a penniless man when you could sell yourself to a lord of the North? "I don't see how the two are so different. I'd rather bleed to sate the appetite of a night lord than bleed on the birthing bed, bearing the children of a man I hardly love."

An ugly wind ripped down the alleyway, so violent it nearly snatched the newspaper from Marion's hand. But she held fast, folding it quickly and slipping it into the inner pocket of her coat for safekeeping.

Agnes studied her with a furrowed brow, and Marion could see the silent accusation in her eyes: *traitor*. But before Agnes had the chance to open her mouth and say it, to warn Marion of the North and all its horrors, the dull toll of the church bells echoed down the alley, beckoning them back to their work.

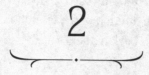

2

We are all alike in the fact that our great life's work is
deciding who and what we are willing to bleed for.

—OLIVIA, BLOODMAID OF THE HOUSE OF FOG

AFTER A LONG DAY'S work, Marion limped home at half past six, her feet swollen in her boots, her arms aching. The slums of Prane welcomed her back with their normal fanfare—a chorus of catcalls and street hounds barking, hooves on cobbles, a baby's squall—the din of a long day finally at its end. She felt no comfort as she approached the crooked, slate-brick shack that she called home. It was an odd structure, crushed between a horse stable and the town poorhouse, with a twisted chimney that belched clouds of thick, black smoke when the stove fire was lit. But there was no smoke coming from the chimney that evening.

Marion shuffled through the courtyard to the threshold and stepped inside.

The space was sparsely furnished. There was an iron bed pushed against the far wall, the same one that Marion had been birthed in, and that her parents had died in just a decade later. By the fire, the cot where she slept every night. In the middle of the room was a table

with two chairs; all of the other furniture had been chopped to bits
and pieces and burned for tinder last winter in the height of a nasty
cold snap.

Shivering at the chill in the room, Marion wondered what they'd
burn to stave off the cold in the coming winter, now that most of the
furniture was gone. The stove in the far corner was doing little to
warm the room, and in the cold months, when tinder grew scarce,
coal and wood went for a steep price. Which meant that they might
have to make do with dried cow pies, and the reeking stink of them
as they burned.

Marion shut the door gently behind her. The sickly perfume of
maudlum hung on the air, the smoke moving in lazy tendrils about
the room, riding some phantom wind. Marion cringed at the scent
of it, squinting a bit as her eyes adjusted to the dimness.

Across the room, her older brother, Raul, sat where he always
did, on the edge of the bed, before the fire—which in truth was less
a fire and more a pile of ash with a few stubborn embers glowing
dully from the shadows of the stove. She could tell he was high on
maudlum, caught between dreams and reality. He was a sad figure—
pale-skinned for his race, with bruise-dark bags beneath both of his
eyes. He was thin to the point of being gaunt, and he wore his hair—
dark and half-matted—in a thick braid at the back of his head.

But the most startling aspect of his appearance was the angry
rashes that cropped up—all over his body—and left mottled scar
patches behind when they healed. The doctors Marion consulted
about his deteriorating condition offered few answers, and nothing
more than grim, speculative prognoses when she pressed for more.

The last man she'd seen—a physician in a fine borough of Prane,
who had claimed several weeks' worth of wages as payment for his
care—claimed that Raul's symptoms were the result of an "illness
caused by things done in darkness." When Marion demanded a

formal diagnosis, he said that some things weren't fit for the ears of a young woman and were better left unsaid. But, in truth, Marion didn't need him to explain. She knew the name of Raul's affliction. Had known for some time, though she didn't dare admit it to herself. In the slums they called it the grippe. It was a disease most often transmitted through the passions of lovers.

There was no cure for it.

"Are you awake?" Marion asked, not knowing because Raul often dreamed with his eyes wide open. As a child, when he slept that way, his eyes were always wide with wonder. But now, as a grown man, his eyes seemed to be flung open in horror. As if he had gazed into the dark maw of a hungry god.

Raul stirred with a sudden start at the sound of her voice, then nodded and raised his pipe to his lips, his hand shaking so badly that some ash spilled from the bowl and scattered across the floor. He was smoking the cheap stuff that day; she could tell by the cloying stench on the air. "You're home late."

Marion kicked off her boots. "No later than usual."

Raul's eyes narrowed. He had been handsome before he fell ill. A tall boy with a firm jaw and fine features that looked almost noble. If he dressed the part and kept his mouth shut, he could easily pass for one of the businessmen from the southern boroughs.

But his sickness had remade him. His bones had begun to soften, eroding his posture, so that his shoulders bowed inward, his chest caving so severely he couldn't snatch a single breath without a struggle. Sores pockmarked his cheeks and arms, and he was always scratching at them.

But despite the severity of his illness, Raul managed to drag himself to the taverns in the northern boroughs or the smoke dens where he liked to spend his days squandering Marion's hard-earned money and dreaming himself into oblivion and out of the reality of his own impending demise.

But Raul bore his worst wounds on the inside. The sickness had gotten to his mind before it did anything else, and it was there that the true damage was done. He'd been ill for years, growing worse every day, and in that time he'd developed their father's temper, a kind of cruel, cagey way about him, like a hungry dog tethered. But as the sickness grew within him, he became worse and worse. Marion wouldn't call him dangerous—she refused to do that—but she knew full well that there had been little kindness in her brother to start with and the sickness had only made him worse. Still, as terrible as he was, he was all she had left in the world. And she loved him for it.

Marion took off her cap and hung it on a hook in the wall by the door. It was too cold to strip out of her coat, but she tore her gloves off with her teeth and shoved them into the pocket of her apron. She crossed the floor to the porcelain basin in the corner of the room. The water had frozen over, and Marion cracked the ice crust with the backs of her knuckles and scrubbed her hands clean, the water going dark as she rinsed the ash and grime away.

Drying her hands on her apron, Marion turned and set about the task of putting on a kettle of tea. It took her a few moments to coax the cold coals of the stove into a fire again. And once the task was done, she filled the kettle with water from the pitcher and waited for it to boil.

Save for the racket of the streets, the slum house was silent. Raul sat sprawled in front of the now crackling flames, legs thrown out in front of him, sucking on his pipe, one of the few things he'd inherited from their father. They'd sold the other bits and bobs for coin years before. Apart from a few small items—the threadbare quilt tossed over the bed, the maudlum pipe, the kettle, the bed frames, and the little portrait of their mother pinned above the stove—the slum house was devoid of all fixtures that would have made their rented shack seem like a proper home.

The kettle began to whistle, and Marion retrieved two tin cups and a wooden box of tea from the cupboard. She was measuring the leaves when she felt Raul materialize behind her, his long shadow stretching across the walls as he rose and crossed the room to her side. He hovered over her as she made the tea, swaying a bit on his feet, lurching forward then back again, steadying himself on the hot stove only to snatch his hand away with a barked curse.

Marion didn't turn to face him. Didn't look at him. He didn't like to be looked at, not in that state anyway. "Is there something you need?"

He didn't answer. Instead, he lurched forward a half step and sniffed, his nose wrinkling in disgust. Marion stiffened, her hand folding around the tin cup in a vise grip so firm its sides dented a little. The hot metal burned her palm and fingers, but she didn't let go.

"You reek of piss," Raul murmured. This was his regular refrain. The piss smell he referred to was the stench of the ammonia-laced solution that Lady Gertrude insisted they use to scrub the floors, claiming it would stop the spread of cholera or typhoid, which she greatly feared.

"I'll wash when I can."

Silence.

Marion reached for the butter knife.

Raul caught her by the wrist. "I need a favor."

Marion faltered, felt something close to anger stir within her. "What now?"

"A few coins, that's all."

"I don't have any coins to spare. We've got rent to pay at the top of the month, and if we're late again we'll be thrown to the streets."

Raul exhaled hard. His breath stank of stale beer. His fingers—bony and cold—gripped her wrist. "You're lying. I know you keep coins squirreled away."

She turned on him then, with so much force he staggered back and crashed into the cupboard. A few tin plates clattered to the floor. "You spent every coin I gave you on dreams in the smoke dens. I have nothing left to offer you. Not if we want to keep a roof over our heads."

Raul's eye twitched. His hand didn't leave her wrist.

As children they had never really gotten along. They fought often, in a series of vicious, sometimes bloody brawls. But it had been years since they'd had a proper fight with their fists. Which was not to say they didn't have their scuffles—like the time when Raul shoved her into the wall so hard a protruding nail carved deep into the soft skin between her shoulder blades. Or the night when, in a drunken rage, Raul ripped her from bed by the ankles and dragged her halfway across the room and out of the shack, into the muck of the streets. Raul locked the door behind him, and Marion had been forced to spend the night out on the street, picking splinters from her hands and knees to pass the hours.

Marion knew she should've left him then. But the sad truth was that she was loyal to Raul, not as he was then, but as he was as a boy, before their parents' death. In the early years of their childhood, he had been softer, even close to kind sometimes, on the good days. But after their parents died—back-to-back after a grueling bout of tuberculosis—Raul took to the street corners in the dark of night, returning in the early morning with bruised lips and enough coin in his pocket to cover a loaf of bread to split between the two of them.

Even then, he had been so pretty. Marion often thought, had he been born a girl and not a boy, he would've made the loveliest bloodmaid—with his wide and watery hazel eyes, his full lips and trim figure. But men were never chosen to bleed. The position was filled only by women.

Though he never spoke of it, what Raul did to earn them money began to rot his soul so thoroughly that every day he became a little less of himself and a little more . . . cruel. He began to drink, and rage, and break things. As his sickness worsened, he grew increasingly paranoid and blamed Marion for all of the ills that plagued him. But even when Raul was at his worst, Marion couldn't help but see that fifteen-year-old boy, limping through the darkened alley by the spare light of dawn, the boy who had done what he deemed unspeakable to keep food in their bellies and a roof over their heads, even though it was killing him.

"You know there's no point to it," said Marion, half-pitying, half-firm. "You can't just waste your days on dreams."

"They're my last days," said Raul. "Don't you think I should be able to do with them what I please?"

"Don't say that."

Raul narrowed his eyes. "The *money*, Marion."

"No."

Raul paused at that, cocking his head like a dog begging for scraps at the dinner table. But he wasn't looking at her. His eyes—bloodshot and glassy—came to focus on the pocket of her coat. He snatched the scrap of newspaper before she had the chance to stop him. A range of emotions passed over his face as he read through the advert requesting a bloodmaid—first fury, which was what Marion feared the most, and then, to her immense relief, amusement. "Is this what you dream of at night? Lifting your skirts and spilling your blood for some pitiful northern lord starving in the ruins of a House that was once great? Helping him cling to the vestige of his dignity, the ghost of his power, while the rest of the world moves on?"

"There's still power in the North," said Marion. "There's still money."

"And soon that, too, will be squandered." Raul was right.

The North, sparsely inhabited by nobles, had once been the world's bastion of power. Its Parliament, composed entirely of the reigning counts of the twenty-seven noble Houses, had single-handedly charted the course of the modern world. But in recent decades, the seat of power had shifted from the North to the industrial South and its democratically elected Parliaments, composed almost entirely of politicians and factory owners, oil barons, and their heirs.

Since then, the once great Houses of the North had fallen to vestige and ruin. There were few of them left now, and most were inhabited by wealthy southern heiresses (and their offspring) who married into northern families in want of a title. Their ample inheritances lined the empty coffers of the ancient estates of the North, keeping the Houses from falling into squalor.

Now, of the twenty-seven Houses, only four held any real power: the House of Hunger, the House of Fog, the House of Locusts, and the House of Mirrors. These Houses—established centuries ago by the North's founding and most formidable families—were the last relics of the North's golden age. And soon—to industry and modernity and the shifting sands of time—these, too, would fall.

Marion tried to snatch the paper back, but Raul didn't let go and the column ripped clean down the middle. He gave a drunken laugh that dissolved into a fit of coughing.

"Give it back," she said, the tattered shred of the newspaper column fluttering in her hand.

"Tell me why you want it," he said, and he edged a bit closer, forcing Marion's back to the stove. She could feel the heat of the iron seeping through the folds of her coat, nearly hot enough to burn her.

"I don't want to play this game, Raul. Give me the paper. Now."

She waited for his protest, for an outburst or a curse, or perhaps a well-placed shove that would send her sprawling. But to her surprised and immense relief, Raul simply slipped the tattered papers into the pocket of her coat and lumbered across the flat, collapsing into his seat in front of the fire, his legs thrown out in front of him. He raised the pipe to his lips again, spitting smoke rings at the ceiling.

"You and I, we're blood," he said, mumbling around the stem of his pipe. It was only then that she noticed the coin glinting in his left hand. He'd slipped it from her pocket so deftly she hadn't even noticed it was gone. He rolled it between his knuckles—back and forth, again and again. Then he closed his eyes, smoke billowing from his nostrils. "Leave me and you'll live to regret it."

———— • ————

THAT NIGHT, AS RAUL SLEPT SOUNDLY IN HIS BED, MARION LAY wide awake. She held the crumpled scraps of the newspaper in either hand and pieced them back together, read the words of the advert once more by the light of the dying embers: WANTED: *Bloodmaid of exceptional taste. No more than 19. Must have a keen proclivity for life's finer pleasures. No references required. Candidates will be received by mail at The Night Embassy, 727 Crooks Street, Prane, or personally from 10 to 12 in the evening hours. Girls of weak will need not apply.*

Across the flat, Raul shifted in bed and the iron frame groaned beneath him. He wouldn't stir for another ten hours, when the sunlight grew bright enough to drag him from his nightmares. Marion stared down at the tatters in her hand once more, moving the ragged pieces of the advert together so that they became one again. And then, silent as a street cat prowling down an alley, she stood up, snatched her coat from the nail on the wall, and slipped into the night.

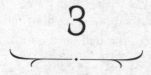

3

The first bloodletting is a kind of unbecoming,
wherein a girl dies and a bloodmaid is born.

—JOYCE, MOTHER OF THE HOUSE OF NOON

MARION WALKED BY THE spare light of the streetlamps, traversing the back alleys on her journey to Crooks Street, on the southern side of Prane. A wet snow was falling fast, and the cobbles were so slick with ice it was hard for her to find her footing. The slums were all but deserted save for the odd street dog or the rats that scuttled through the shadows. And Marion was grateful for that. Those who walked the night rarely meant well.

She picked up her pace a little with each stride, ever aware that time was against her. She should've left an hour earlier if she planned to make it to the embassy by ten. As she approached Groveshire, the most expensive borough in Prane, the snow came down harder, giving way to a heavy sleet that soaked through her cap and coat, impeding her view of the fine houses.

This neighborhood was the great pride of Prane, the place that nobles, businessmen, and even a few retired bloodmaids called home. Tall trees, which were a rarity in the slums, lined the cobbled streets on either side. In the springtime they flowered with blush-red buds that smelled of honey. As a child she remembered walking for hours just to pick a few fallen blooms from the grass and steal away before the patrolling constables chased her off, as they did all of those that dared to venture up from the slums.

But there were no constables patrolling on that night. Marion guessed that the cold had forced them to retreat back to their stations and was grateful for it. She knew if she was spotted in such a place at such a late hour she'd likely be thrown into a jail cell before she had the chance to explain herself.

Doing her best to keep to the shadows and avoid the glow of the streetlamps, Marion traveled the long roads of the upper district. She passed rows of redbrick townhomes and snow-frosted mansions with sprawling lawns and courtyard gardens. She wondered which of the townhouses and city estates were owned by former bloodmaids.

From Groveshire, it was a short walk through Magnolia Park—a well-groomed orchard in the center of the upper district—to the Night Embassy. It stood on a square of its own, encircled by an iron gate that crawled with ivy. Like the other mansions around it, it was an imposing structure—with a pillared entryway and a grove of live oaks that grew on either side of the marble-cobbled walkway, forming a kind of canopy from the street's edge to the front door.

But despite the impressive facade, the embassy was, in a strange way, inviting. The windows were warm with the glow of firelight, and the wind made a soft *hush hush* as it moved through the trees.

Marion stepped beneath the canopy of the branches and out of the falling snow. She hurried up to the doorstep just as the church bells struck eleven. The door was painted a glossy black, and in its center was a brass knocker forged in the shape of a raven's skull. She knocked twice.

Moments later, the door creaked open, and Marion was surprised to see a woman standing in the foyer. She wore a black dress and a white pinafore starched stiff. Her hair, which was a lovely shade of red, was pulled back into a neat bun at the back of her head. Her neck was long and thin and wrapped with a thick black ribbon. She looked to be no more than a few years Marion's senior. At once, Marion knew her for what she was: a bloodmaid.

She was one of the few that Marion had seen up close since the evening of her eighth birthday, when her mother had taken her to the night train. And she was only a little less beautiful than the one she'd encountered that night—a pale, raven-haired girl with rosy cheeks and blue eyes. Both bore the kind of beauty that made Marion's head go empty with awe. She couldn't imagine how anyone, man or woman, could spend more than a few hours in their presence and not be madly in love with them by the end of it.

The bloodmaid surveyed her with a little frown. Marion didn't blame her. She knew she was a sorry sight. Her boots were caked with mud and manure, her coat was soaked through with icy slush, and her hair hung in wet ringlets about her face.

"What brings you here?" the girl inquired. And when she did, her mouth, red as an overripe raspberry, pursed into a pert little smile. She almost appeared to be . . . *flirting*. This shouldn't have been entirely surprising to her.

Agnes had often told her that she had a way with women. Or, perhaps more aptly, that women had a way of being drawn to her, like moths fluttering in the halo of a streetlamp. Marion had always attributed this to her natural boyishness, the fact that she liked women as much as women liked her, so it only made sense that she so often found herself entangled with them. But the bloodmaid simpering before her now was *far* too good for the likes of her.

Marion fished the sodden tatters of the newspaper posting from her pocket. Under the roving gaze of the bloodmaid, she felt small and out of place. Perhaps she was a fool to even consider the idea that she could one day ascend to the same rank as the girl who stood before her now. "I-I saw your posting in the paper," Marion said, flushing with embarrassment as she slipped the clipping back into her pocket again.

The girl raised a plucked eyebrow, and for a moment Marion was quite certain she'd slam the door shut in her face. But to her surprise, she stepped aside, drew the door open, and motioned her in. As soon as Marion stepped into the foyer, the bloodmaid stripped off her coat and disappeared to put it away somewhere before she had the chance to say thank you. So Marion stood, shocked and alone, sodden and muddy in the beautiful foyer—a slum rat in a House fit for a king. She almost laughed aloud at the absurdity of it.

Moments later, the bloodmaid returned empty-handed and motioned down a long, candlelit hall. "This way, if you will."

Marion followed her. A part of her was surprised the security in such a place was so lax, given that tensions between the North and South had heightened in recent years.

They walked down a wide corridor with markings on both walls: faint shadows and suggestions of human bodies, frescoes covered with a thin layer of paint. The bloodmaid led Marion down a series of hallways, most overlooking the sprawl of the inner courtyards, which were glassed over so that fruit trees and flowers could still bloom and grow despite the cold. They passed a large, empty parlor, lit by a roaring fire, and what appeared to be a dining room, though there were no chairs to be seen and the mahogany tabletop was almost as high as Marion was tall.

Finally, after they scaled a flight of stairs at the back of the manor, they stopped at a set of double doors.

The bloodmaid turned to Marion again. "You will speak only when spoken to. When you are asked to leave, you will go without complaint. Your belongings will be waiting for you by the door."

Marion nodded.

"Your hat."

Flushing, Marion snatched it off her head. She opened her mouth to thank the bloodmaid when the door opened, just wide enough for Marion to slip through sideways.

She entered into a dim room with a vaulted ceiling. The walls were windowless and lined with bookshelves so high that even the tallest man would have trouble reaching the top shelves. There were armchairs scattered throughout the room, which appeared to be a kind of den or study, all of them empty.

Standing by the hearth, a man smiled at her. "Good evening."

He was handsome, dressed in a dark topcoat, fitted with a string of brass buttons that resembled human eyes. He wore rings on every finger, thick metal bands that were carved and studded with pearls and stones. A froth of lace peered out from the cuffs of his coat sleeves.

"Hello," said Marion.

The man reached into his vest and withdrew a small timepiece that caught the light of the fire. It ticked to the speed of a mouse's heartbeat, as if counting the seconds in double time. He studied its face for a moment, then slipped it back into its place. "Come into the light so I can see you fully."

Marion stepped forward, tracking slush and mud across the carpet.

The man examined her carefully, nodded to the cap in her hand. "That's a nice hat you have there. Did you knit it?"

She nodded, a little sheepish. Her talent with knitting needles was abysmal at best.

"Charming," said the man, and Marion might have thought him

sarcastic if it weren't for the genuine warmth in his eyes. She didn't even know a night lord could *be* warm. All of the northerners she'd met, admittedly in her very limited experience, had been proud and distant, as if they barely deigned to acknowledge anyone from Prane. "What's your name?"

"Marion Shaw."

"Age?"

"Twenty."

"I would have thought you younger," he said. "Well, my name is Thiago, and I am a Taster. I travel the world looking for potential bloodmaids, whom I then place with great Houses of the North. You could consider me a kind of . . . connoisseur. A blood sommelier, if you will."

"It's a pleasure to make your acquaintance," said Marion, because that was the sort of thing she felt she was supposed to say to fill the silence.

Thiago smiled. "Tell me, what brings you here, Marion?"

"I-I want to apply for the position of bloodmaid," she said, confused. She'd thought that much was obvious.

"Yes. I understand that, but what *brings* you here? Why do you want to be a bloodmaid?"

The question caught her by surprise. There were a thousand answers to it, but all of them boiled down to one simple truth: "I don't want to die in the slums."

Thiago's brows drew tight together. "Do you have family?"

"It's just me and my brother, and I think he'd just as soon be rid of me."

"What of your parents?"

"They died when I was ten."

Marion could tell that this piqued his interest. "What did they die of?"

"Tuberculosis. They were dead within a fortnight of the day they fell ill."

"I see . . ." Thiago reached into his breast coat and removed a folded leather flap. He opened it and Marion saw that sheathed within were an assortment of needles, maybe eleven of them, in varying lengths and widths. "I do ask a small favor of my applicants."

"What would you have me do?"

"Bleed," he said, and he motioned to the teacup on the table by the armchair. It was small and painted with a tangle of naked figures who seemed to be dancing in a forest of sorts. "But only if you're willing, of course. I promise it'll only hurt for a moment."

"All right," said Marion, nodding, and Thiago beckoned her closer. In three short steps she crossed the parlor and extended a hand with some reluctance. She'd thought it would be easier; she was never one to shirk at the idea of pain. But it felt startlingly unnatural to give herself over to be bled, and her every instinct balked at the notion of making herself prone to the man, the stranger, who stood before her now.

Thiago took her hand gingerly and flipped it palm side up. He drew a small golden needle from its leather sheath. Its point caught the firelight and flickered brilliantly. Thiago's pupils narrowed to catlike slits as he lowered the needle to the vein just above the knuckle of Marion's middle finger.

There was a sharp pain that radiated down her finger and through her hands, and then the blood began to flow, just enough to cover the teacup's bottom.

Thiago produced a small slip of red ribbon and tied it like a bandage around her finger. Then Marion watched as he raised the teacup to his lips, closed his eyes, took a sip, and swallowed hard, as if he were downing a stone.

Marion watched as a series of expressions passed over Thiago's face—sadness, then anger, delight, pain, pleasure—in quick succession. He drained the cup down to the dregs. Licked the last of Marion's blood from his lips. "Exceptional taste indeed."

"You . . . like it?"

"Like it?" Thiago scoffed like she'd told a particularly funny joke. "Marion, your blood is unlike any I've tasted before. It would be my honor to offer you a ticket on the night train to the North. I think you'd be a perfect charge for Lisavet, the Countess of the House of Hunger. Her palate is incredibly discerning and there isn't a doubt in my mind that she'll accept you into her household upon tasting you, as I have tonight." Thiago reached into the shadows of his vest and withdrew a thin, pale envelope in the same mottled flesh tone as human skin. He extended it to her. "Your ticket . . . if you will?"

Marion was tempted to take it, then and there, no questions asked. But her intuition told her to stay her hand. "What's in it for you?"

"Should Lisavet indenture you, and I do believe she will, I'll receive a small finder's fee of two thousand pounds for securing you, selecting you, and transporting you to the North. Consider it an industry standard."

"And what will I receive?"

"Contracts vary, depending on the girl. But the House of Hunger is . . . particularly generous. Usually they extend seven-year appointments to their bloodmaids. In addition to room and board during your tenure, upon the completion of your contract, you'd receive an annual pension of no less than six thousand pounds."

"*Six thousand pounds?*" The number was even higher than she'd imagined. It would be more than enough to afford her a villa in the Isles by the sea, complete with an entire household of her own. It seemed far too good to be true. "What happens if I fail to complete my contract?"

"You're free to leave whenever you like. But should you fail to complete the years of your indenture, you could return to Prane with part of your pension, or perhaps court another House in hopes of securing a new placement. As a bloodmaid, your opportunities are limitless. There would be no luxury beyond your reach."

It was an offer beyond her wildest imaginings and yet . . . she hesitated to take it. Some part of her balked at the idea of leaving Raul and Agnes, of allowing them to fade into the dusty recesses of her mind the way that her parents had. But a greater part of her feared herself, and the person she'd become should she leave Prane behind. Seven years she would likely spend in the North, and when she emerged from her indenture, would she still belong to herself? Could she call herself Marion, or would the title of bloodmaid demand a sacrifice so great that no vestige of her former self remained? Would she be better for it?

Of course.

Marion staggered forward to take the envelope. Sheathed inside was a crisp and gilded one-way ticket north by night train. "Thank you."

Thiago laughed outright, a harsh sound, like church bells tolling. "Is that all you have to say?"

"Am I expected to say something else?"

"You could give me an answer. You could tell me that tomorrow evening, at eight, you'll be waiting on the platform to board the night train alongside me. You could tell me you accept the position."

It was so strange, to hold everything she'd dreamed of for years in her grasp—a life of luxury without a want for anything. And yet . . . she faltered. "My brother. He's sick."

"Leave him. Leave all of it. This is your moment to make a choice, Marion: the North or the slums. You said yourself you don't want to die here, and I'm delighted to offer you a way out. Don't be a fool. Take it."

"I don't know that I can."

"Well, you have a day to decide. But by moonrise tomorrow, I expect to see you at the night train's station," said Thiago, and he took Marion's hand and crushed his lips against her knuckles in a firm kiss. "Until then."

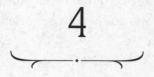

4

The night I was chosen, I believed myself most highly favored.
A goddess among girls. I was not wrong . . . but I know
now that there are greater goddesses than me.

—MARCIA, BLOODMAID OF THE HOUSE OF EMERALDS

MARION DIDN'T SLEEP THAT night, or in the morning that followed it. She returned home just long enough to wash up, eat a quick breakfast of stale bread, and hide the envelope given to her by the night lord beneath a floorboard in the kitchen where Raul wouldn't find it. She walked the slums and through the stockyards in a daze until she reached Lady Gertrude's house.

For hours, she scrubbed the floors of the kitchens under Lady Gertrude's watchful eye, her hands burning from the ammonia solution, the calloused skin sloughing off her palms as she toiled. The hours rolled by, one after another, too fast for Marion's liking, and all the while her mind raced with dreams of the night train and the North and the fate that lay in wait for her if she chose to accept the Taster's offer.

"You missed a spot," said Lady Gertrude through clenched teeth. Her leech jar—a large ceramic urn, gilt and filigreed—stood on a small table beside her. Her physician hovered over the leech urn, removing the writhing creatures with a pair of long-tipped tweezers and applying them to the pale expanse of Lady Gertrude's forearm. There they suctioned themselves, growing fat and bulbous with her blood. "Did you hear me, girl?"

"I did," said Marion, squeezing her rag so hard all of the reeking ammonia solution drained out of it. "I'll get to it."

Lady Gertrude knit her thick brows together. "Mind your tone."

Marion looked up at the woman, and the woman looked down her pinched nose at Marion, as though she were a roach she'd like to crush beneath the heel of her slipper.

"You take after that drunken brother of yours," said Lady Gertrude, sneering, her upper lip curled to reveal the ghastly gray of her gums. She picked up her fan and glared at Marion over the top of it. "Must run in the family. You know, I've heard the other servant girls whispering about how he staggers the streets, begging for coin like an overgrown waif."

Marion felt something violent and nasty stir within her. She hung her head, willed herself to take deep breaths and let the anger pass. But beneath the anger was something worse: shame, and then hurt after it. The open wound of her pride gaping and raw.

"Could that be so, Doctor?" Lady Gertrude inquired, with faux innocence. A thick stream of blood slipped down her wrinkled forearm as the physician pried one of the leeches free. "Can these afflictions of the spirit be passed down through the blood?"

The doctor applied another leech, just below the crook of Lady Gertrude's elbow. It latched there and began to suckle. "Well, I could hardly—"

Marion dropped the rag back into the scrub bucket and pressed to her feet, pausing only to smooth the creases out of her apron. She walked across the parlor, and the physician staggered back. Lady Gertrude straightened in her seat, eyes flung wide open. "And what do you think you're—"

Marion seized the pot of leeches by both handles, raised it high above the woman's silver head, and overturned it. Water and leeches gushed over the woman, soaking her fine petticoats and her shawl, her hair falling from its coif. Lady Gertrude began to scream and thrash, kicking her feet and very nearly tumbling out of her chair as the physician looked on in horror.

Smiling, Marion stepped back. Released the handles of the leech jar. It shattered on the floor, ceramic shards skittering across the parlor. Then, without a word, she turned on her heel, stalked out of the parlor and down the narrow hall of the foyer and through the front door.

As soon as she emerged from the townhouse, Marion bolted, tearing off her apron and running through the streets of high town with a desperation she hadn't felt since her days as a pickpocket, racing away from the constable. She smiled, then laughed, as she tore through the streets, her curls falling free of her bun, dancing on the wind behind her.

As she rounded a corner, she collided headfirst with none other than Agnes. She hadn't even realized it was noon. Upon impact, Agnes dropped her steamed salt herring, and the fish hit the cobbles with a wet *smack*.

"Goddamn it, Marion," she cut through her teeth, then plucked the fish from the ground and brushed it clean with her sleeve. "Thought your days of thieving were over." She extended the fish to Marion, but she shook her head.

"I'm leaving. I've got to go."

"What—"

"I emptied Lady Gertrude's pot of leeches—"

"No harm done. Go to the wharf to replace them. Water's filled with leeches there—"

"On her head, Agnes. I overturned it on her head."

The girl's eyes went wide.

"But it's all right, because I have new employment," Marion said, rather hastily. "I'm taking the night train north. I'm going to be a bloodmaid. Least, I think I'm going to be a bloodmaid. The Taster said I'm likely to be snapped up."

"That advert in the paper," said Agnes, as the full truth dawned on her. "You *answered* it?"

"I had no choice. I can't keep living like this. Scrubbing the floors for the likes of Lady Gertrude until I grow too old and they cast me out and I'll be lucky to scrounge up enough coin for food and firewood—"

"And you think that selling your blood to the noble leeches of the North is a better fate?"

"Yes. I do. I would bleed, and for that matter whore myself to any lord in the North before I would spend another day scrabbling for survival in the slums of this godforsaken city."

"I thought you had too much dignity to lower yourself to this."

"Don't be such a prude."

"It's not prudish to cling to some semblance of common decency," Agnes snapped in biting retort. "You have an honest job. No children. You have your beauty yet. You could find your way out of Prane if you wanted to. You could marry a farmer and escape this city. You have options I don't, and still they aren't enough for you. You want more than an honest life. Is that it? You want splendor and luxury and all the vices that come with it. I can see it in your eyes. The greed. The want for things you were never meant to have. The way you watch the women of high town hold their parasols and tilt their chins just so. Even as a child you'd try to mimic them, walk heel to toe the way they did. Turn up your nose."

"I make no apologies for my ambitions," Marion snapped. "But to say I mean to rise beyond my station is a lie. I have no intention of turning my back on my past or pretending to be something more than I am." Even as she said it, she wasn't sure it was the truth. "After I'm placed at a House in the North, I'll write to you—"

"Will you?" said Agnes, eyes wide with mock delight. She pressed a grubby hand to her chest. "Marion the Bloodmaid will grace *me* with a letter? How charitable of her ladyship to bestow such a gift upon the lowly likes of me."

"Agnes—"

"This will ruin you," she said, and when Marion attempted to reach out to her, she slapped her hand away. "Mark my words."

———— • ————

RAUL WAS STANDING ON THE SLUM HOUSE STOOP WHEN MARION finally returned home. He stood with one shoulder braced against the doorframe, his maudlum pipe smoking in his hand. A new rash had cropped up just below his left eye, which was swollen and half-closed.

"What are you doing here?" he demanded.

Marion avoided his gaze. These days, it hurt to look at him. And it wasn't the sickness, the symptoms of it, it was the resentment in his eyes, flat and cold. "I got off early."

"You're lying," he said, and he caught her by the arm. "Last night, I heard you come home late. You're not as quiet as you think you are, and I'm not half as stupid as you believe me to be."

"I don't want to fight, Raul." And then, with her eyes on his, she said, "Please. Let me go."

Raul released her, but only so he could reach into the shadow of his coat and withdraw the envelope with her ticket north. He'd found it. He must've seen her hide it when she'd thought him asleep. "Who gave you this?"

Something stirred in her then; it felt like a small starvation burning in the deepest pit of her belly. It made her fingers twitch. "Give it back, Raul."

"I asked you a question."

"I asked you to return what belongs to me first." She grabbed for the envelope, but Raul snatched it back.

"It was that posting, wasn't it? The one in the paper? You're hoping to lift your skirts and whore for some night lord?"

"Just because I want something more than a life of waiting on you hand and foot doesn't make me a whore or a traitor." She nodded to the courtyard and the reeking slums beyond it. "Who wouldn't want something more than this? This world is *killing* us all. Can't you see that? If I take this position as bloodmaid, once I have my pension I can pay for you to receive the care you need to get better. I'll be able to cover the costs of medicines and the finest doctors. I won't turn my back on you, I promise. I'll send money home, to Prane. I'll care for you better there, as a bloodmaid, than I have here—"

Her brother worked his jaw, the muscles at the corners of his mouth twitching with the motion. "I'm burning this ticket."

"Raul, no—"

He started to shut the door on her, but Marion sprang forward, and it closed on her hand. She staggered, ripped her throbbing fingers free, her knees going soft beneath her. Raul charged to the stove and tossed her ticket to the flames.

A shriek tangled in Marion's throat, and her legs gave way. Desperate, she crawled across the floor to the oven, but with a well-placed kick to the ribs Raul sent her sprawling.

"I told you not to go," he said, his voice shaking. "I told you not to leave. Your blood is *mine* along with the rest of you. We're kin to one another; that means we belong to each other. It's all we have, Marion. I'm not going to watch you board that night train and bleed for another. If you want to bleed, you do it here, where you belong. With me."

Marion sat on the floor, shaking, her throbbing fingers cradled to her chest. Her vision came and went in glimpses. The envelope and ticket writhing in the flames. Raul's tear-filled eyes. Her own hand bruised and swelling fast. That strange and vile feeling stirred in her stomach again. Behind the cage of her ribs, her heart began to race.

Raul dropped to his knees in a crouch before her, wiping her tears away with the back of his hand. "We need each other," he said, and he ruffled a hand through her curls. When he spoke again she caught the flowery reek of maudlum smoke on his breath. "And I know it hurts, but the hurt is good . . . do you know why?"

Marion shook her head.

"Because it's waking you up. It's making you see. You've got to have your eyes open, and yours were closed, and in a world like ours that's dangerous. You've got to see everything for what it is. Right?"

Marion remained silent.

"Answer me."

Again, Marion said nothing.

He seized her arms then, pinning them to her sides, his fingers pressing through the muscle and down to the hard bone beneath. Marion's head snapped on its axis with the violence of his shaking. Pain shot down her neck and her skull connected with the wall, once, twice, three times over. The room seemed to fracture before her eyes. She saw stars, then black after them.

With a cry of pain, Marion shoved Raul with so much force that he staggered back, stumbled over his own feet, and crashed into the stove, his head snapping against its edge with a sickening *crack*.

Raul slumped to the floor, twitching. Blood leaked through his hair and slicked his forehead, pooling around his left eye. He tried to shape Marion's name, but his tongue betrayed him, and he mumbled incoherently. He was too weak to crawl, so he dragged himself, whimpering, across the floorboards and collapsed at her feet.

And Marion saw it then, the bloody gash where his skull buckled inward. A sliver of white . . . of bone and the pink meat beneath it. Raul kept pleading and bleeding on the floor, his hand a finger's length from Marion's feet.

But she didn't move to help him. Instead, she turned her back on him, on the slum house and the only home she'd ever known—which was, in earnest, no home at all—took to the streets, and ran.

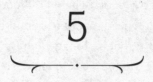

5

The calling of a bloodmaid is that
of pain and luxury in equal part.

—ROSA, BLOODMAID OF THE HOUSE OF BRAMBLES

MARION STAGGERED DOWN THE night station's platform, clutching her throbbing hand to her chest. The patrons of the night eyed her with disgust as she shouldered through the crowds, searching in vain for the night lord, Thiago. The station's clock tower struck seven-thirty, but there was no sign of the Taster, or the night train.

Marion found a bench to sit on in the shadow of a brick awning, away from the wandering eyes of the constables who patrolled the platform. It was only a matter of time before one of them spotted her and shooed her away, taking her for a beggar. And with no ticket to prove that she belonged there, they'd likely toss her in a jail cell and leave her there to rot until the morning. By that time, the night train would have long departed, and her only chance at escaping Prane's slums along with it.

But there was no help to be had for that. And she still had some luck on her side. After all, the night train hadn't departed yet. She thought about venturing to the liquor store a few blocks away and stealing a small swig of brandy to ease the pain of her throbbing hand, which had begun to swell and blacken. But she thought better of it. It was better to take the pain. That was what her mother always taught her. If you cheated your way out of life's hurts, you wouldn't be ready for the next blow. And the next blow was *always* coming.

"Aren't you a sad sight."

Marion looked up to see Thiago appraising her, and a kind of head-spinning relief washed through her. "You're here."

"Where else would I be?" he asked with a raised eyebrow. Then his gaze fell to her bruised and swollen hand. "Do you need a doctor?"

"I need to leave," she said, and began to cry with a series of brutal, racking sobs. "I want to go with you, please. I accept your offer."

"Your ticket?"

She shook her head, tried to explain herself but couldn't talk through the tears.

"I told you to keep it close."

"And I did, or at least I tried to"—her voice broke as she choked on another raw sob—"but . . . it was taken from me. I'm sorry."

"I see." Thiago considered her for a moment, and his eyes softened some. He encircled her in his long arm, pulling her to his chest like a child. He was warm, and to her surprise he smelled of pipe smoke and maple—a good wholesome scent, if a little strange for a blood lord.

Together they walked the platform to the ticket booth, which was housed in the station's looming clock tower. They waited in line for a few minutes, behind a series of wealthy patrons. There were women in mink coats with trains so long they trailed behind them. Men with waxed mustaches smoking golden pipes. And then, at last, it was their turn.

They approached a short countertop of black marble. Above it was a red stained-glass window, and the man behind it looked less like a clerk and more like an army officer. He wore a black uniform and pins on his lapels. His cap was smart, with a short, stiff brim that cast a hard shadow across his face.

"One ticket to the North," said Thiago, and he withdrew a check from the pocket of his vest, which he quickly signed. It seemed strange to Marion that she could hold—in one hand—a slip of paper worth more than a decade of her former wages. "First class for the eight o'clock departure."

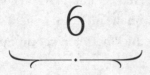

6

The locomotive is the bridge between two worlds:
the dark obscure and the dawning contemporary.

—ALFRED S. BRADFORD, ENGINEER OF THE NIGHT TRAIN

THE NIGHT TRAIN MADE its grand arrival soon after Marion procured her second ticket and began boarding shortly thereafter. With no bags or belongings to speak of, Marion walked empty-handed to the boarding queue, trailing behind Thiago like a little duckling in the shadow of its mother. This seemed to amuse Thiago, who periodically gazed back at her with a fondness Marion had only glimpsed in the eyes of her blood kin, and only very rarely at that. She couldn't fathom why Thiago had taken such a liking to her, but she suspected it had something to do with her blood, the taste of it, and all of the things its taste provoked in him. He seemed to think her a valuable asset, and she could only hope that her prospective mistress shared his opinion of her.

Upon boarding the train, Marion took her seat on an overstuffed red velvet bench alongside the window. Thiago settled himself opposite her, crossed his legs, slipped a timepiece from the breast pocket of his vest, and frowned at it.

"Are we running late?"

The night lord nodded, slipping his timepiece back into his pocket once more. "Seventeen minutes and counting," he said, and Marion could have sworn he muttered something about a blood fuel shortage, though his thick northern accent made it impossible for her to be certain.

Thiago pressed a small golden button on the wall beside the door. Moments later, a train attendant dressed in an evergreen suit—complete with a small cap, red as a drop of blood—materialized behind the door. Thiago said something to him—and yet again his accent made it impossible for Marion to distinguish what, exactly, he had said—but the attendant left and returned moments later with a bearskin blanket folded on a golden tray, which he extended to her, perched precariously on the tips of his fingers, in the way of a well-trained footman.

Once comfortably nestled beneath the blanket, Marion turned her attention to her surroundings. The cabin was immaculate. Prane's cathedral could not match its splendor. The walls were cushioned and upholstered in leather and gold-spun brocade. The floors were a burnished mahogany. But the ceiling of the cabin was what took her breath away. It was painted with frescoes that depicted the fiery lakes of hell filled with naked women and fork-tongued men, serpents that laced between bare legs, and leaping flames that burned red and brilliant blue.

The train's horn shrieked into the night, and its engines began to roar with a sound that was not unlike that of summer storm winds. The cabin began to shudder, the windowpane rattling in its casing, and with a violent lurch that very nearly threw Marion off her perch on the bench, they started off into the night.

For a long while, Marion sat in total silence, watching the black blur. She craned in her seat to catch a final glimpse of Prane, the lights of the slum city winking in the distance until they died, consumed by the shadows of the night.

"Beautiful, isn't it?" said Thiago, watching her watch the dark. "I sometimes think there's nothing more awe-inspiring than the night. *True* night, that is."

"This isn't true night?"

Thiago shook his head. "This isn't true night, child. True night is black too thick to see through. It's a crescent moon and starless skies and the kind of cold that kills. You'll know it when you feel it."

Marion squinted at the window, trying and failing to distinguish the black plains from the starless skies above them. It was like a sea of darkness, and there was no end to it. At least not as far as Marion could tell. If this wasn't true night, she shuddered to think what was.

As their trip wore on, Marion sat awake, watching the black landscape smear past. As they journeyed on, the darkness thickened, and a gentle rain spattered against the windows. The cabin shuddered a little as the winds picked up. Marion heard the storms before she saw them, a great roar that made the windowpanes rattle in their casings. As they neared the northern border, a bolt of lightning split through the sky, and for a fleeting moment she caught sight of the storm shelf, a dark and churning cloud bank that seemed to cleave the sky in two.

"Have you been north before?"

Marion pulled her eyes from the storm's edge to look the Taster in the eye. He sat with a handkerchief pressed to his nose, the fabric soaked with a sharp orange essence. It seemed like a silly question, given how few people in Prane could afford to travel north.

"Never."

He smiled above his handkerchief, his eyes twinkling. "Well, I daresay you're in for quite a show."

Just then, a roll of bone-rattling thunder shook the carriage, and even a few of the more seasoned northerners startled. Conversation died into silence, and Marion—peering through their cabin's port-hole window and into the aisle beyond—noted that the passengers braced themselves on the handrails that ran along the walls.

The train listed to the left, its wheels screaming against the track spitting sparks that danced wildly on the wind before dying into the night. The temperature dropped suddenly. Marion's ears began to pop, and she had to work her jaw constantly to ease the pressure.

And then, all at once, the winds picked up again, and this time they blasted so hard that the train actually slowed. The wheels screeched in protest again. Overhead, the chandelier swung like a pendulum, tossing light and shadow across the walls of the cabin, its crystals clattering together so violently Marion feared they would shatter.

The rain came, then the hail just after it. It battered the train's roof and windows, striking so hard Marion was surprised they didn't shatter. The train began to pick up speed, as though its conductor was trying to race against the storm raging outside.

The thunder was so loud it sounded like the bones of some great eldritch god breaking. Every few moments, bright gasps of lightning illuminated the storming heavens and rain-wrapped windstorms that tore across the distant plains.

"What nasty weather," said Thiago, with remarkable ease. He sat with his eyes closed, sipping the wine the clerk brought him, which splashed against the sides of his goblet and threatened to spill over onto his pants with every violent shift of the cabin. But if he was at all concerned, he gave no indication. "We're safe here, but I pity the poor bastard who tries to cross the plains on horseback. Can you imagine?"

Watching the cyclones that snaked down from the clouds, Marion could not—in fact—imagine anyone foolhardy enough to attempt such a journey, much less survive it. "Are the storms always this bad?"

"No," said Thiago. "They're normally much worse than this. In the height of the summer even the night train doesn't dare cross these plains for fear of being sucked into the skies and spit back out again. A few years past there was a terrible accident of that sort and they found the remnants of mangled train cabins scattered across the plains, miles apart." Marion swallowed dry, and Thiago opened his eyes to smile at her. "Never fear, we're safe here, the night train has never had an accident like that. It runs on blood fuel, sourced from cows, I hear, and that makes it fast enough to outpace almost any storm."

The cabin gave another violent lurch as if the wheels had lifted from the tracks. Marion gripped her seat to steady herself. "I thought that was just a rumor."

"Just because it's a rumor doesn't mean it isn't true," said Thiago, swallowing the last dregs of his wine. "I'll let you in on a little secret that will serve you well in the North: The whole world runs on blood. Who has good blood. Who has bad blood. Whose blood is shed and whose isn't. That's what it all comes down to in the end. And you southerners like to pretend that isn't true, but you're just as bloodthirsty as the rest. Blood is everything in the South. It's everything everywhere."

Gradually, the storm winds died to a gentle howl, and the hail began to abate and gave way to rain showers. Across the aisle, fellow passengers drew the curtains back from the windows and unfastened their seat belts, allowing themselves to relax now that the worst of the storm had passed.

"Sleep," said Thiago.

And Marion, too tired to disobey him, did just that.

————— • —————

IN THE DARK, QUIET HOURS IN THE AFTERMATH OF THE STORM, Marion fell into a thick and dreamless sleep. She woke to Thiago's hand on her shoulder, gently shaking her awake.

"Dinner," said the night lord.

Marion gave a stretch and yawn, shaking her head to clear it from the fog of sleep. She pressed out of her seat and stumbled into the aisle. She found it hard to stay on her feet while the train was moving; every step sent her stumbling, so Thiago kept a firm hand on her elbow, keeping her aloft as they walked down the center aisle.

The dining car was three cars from them, so they made their way slowly, taking care to mind their steps and cross slowly from one car to the next, stepping out into the cold dark of the night, the wind ripping around them, the train tracks a sickening blur in the wide gap between one car and the next. But Thiago kept a firm grip on her arm, and Marion found that with him guiding her, she wasn't afraid.

The first cabin they entered was thick with cigar smoke, and mustached men sat at marble countertops, smoking and sipping small glasses of cognac and brandy, snacking on olives between drinks.

In another car, a lovely parlor had silk-upholstered chaises that ran along the walls, where women took their tea at little tables. The patrons of the cabin were stunning. They wore mink furs and velvet dresses, and pearls in their hair, and held lace fans to their faces and spoke in whispers as Marion moved through the cabin.

The third car was the most beautiful; Thiago called it "the viewing room," but it seemed too simple a name for such a stunning place. The car was made almost entirely of glass, like a greenhouse on wheels, so that you could see the passing landscape from almost every angle. Marion tipped her head to look outside, and what she saw stole the breath from her lungs.

There were stars, and not a simple smattering of them either. The sky seemed to arch overhead like a cathedral's ceiling, and it was spangled with constellations and the bright, churning storms of galaxies she'd never seen before. In the distance, a red crescent moon like a small paper cut sliced into the black night sky.

"I've never seen a moon like that," said Marion. In the slums the smog clouds were so thick it was a wonder the moon was able to shine through them at all, and sometimes it didn't. And in the night, when the mills and furnaces purged the waste of the day, the fog only got thicker, clogging the sky so that not a glimpse of star or moon glow could be seen.

If left to her own devices, Marion might have stayed in that car, staring at the stars for the duration of their journey, but with a gentle hand at her back Thiago urged her onward to the dining car, which had the look of a fine restaurant. On either side of the car were round tables, draped with white cloth and set with porcelain plates and heavy silver cutlery. The napkins were carefully folded into abstract animal shapes—swans and cranes, fish and butterflies, and creatures of the North that Marion didn't know by name. The entire place smelled of burnt spices, roast meat, perfume, and, below that, a gamey warm-blooded stench that reminded Marion of the slaughterhouse.

To the chagrin of a few of the other passengers—who glared or even scoffed at Marion as she passed them by, wrinkling their noses at the stench of the slums that clung to her clothes, her scummy boots, and her tangled hair—Thiago claimed a table at the center of the car that was lit by a beautiful candelabra, bolted to the table to keep it from tipping over when the train moved. A clerk materialized beside them, pushing a four-tiered cart that displayed an array of appetizers, many of them delicacies like goose-liver pâté, small tins of caviar, and expensive cheeses. The clerk stared at the two of them, expectant. If he was taken aback by Marion's presence, he gave no indication of it. "What would you like?"

Thiago paused only briefly to study the contents of the cart and rattled off the twisted names of a few of the cheeses, which the clerk promptly served on little porcelain plates that were painted with a similar design to the one that adorned the teacup Thiago first sipped her blood from. In addition to the cheeses, Thiago selected a miniature chocolate cake—expertly frosted and garnished with paper-thin slices of what appeared to be candied fig, a crusty slice of black bread that looked like it was made with a mix of flour and powdered charcoal, wine, several dishes of olives, a tin of caviar that looked like dark river pearls, and—of course—a decanter of blood wine.

Then, as if these refreshments weren't already enough, Thiago made his final selections from the menu on the table, ordering for both of them without bothering to consult Marion about what she'd prefer. But she didn't mind. The food on the table was already enough to last her more than a week, if she rationed it properly. And besides, most of the offerings on the menu were foreign to her anyway, and what little she did recognize she didn't like the sound of.

When the waiter moved on, pushing his cart down the aisle, Thiago nodded to the cake on the plate in front of Marion. "Go on, then. Have a bite."

Marion tried to oblige him, but she struggled with her fork. She'd never been schooled in the proper arts of dining, and because Raul had crushed her right and favored hand in the door, her limited skills were hindered to the point of sheer ineptitude.

But while some of the other patrons of the night train laughed and scoffed at her incompetent attempts at dining, Thiago didn't laugh or smile, he didn't poke fun. He even helped her a bit, steadying the tall and precarious pedestal her cake was perched on with his hand, so she could slice it into bite-size pieces.

At last, she prevailed, ushering a single forkful of the cake into her mouth.

The taste was unlike anything she'd sampled before.

Bitter as burnt coffee, but buttery and a little sweet. With hints of rum and cherry. The icing was sticky, but it melted in her mouth the instant it touched her tongue. It was a far cry from the stale spice cakes she'd bought from street vendors to share with Agnes, whenever she had coin to spare.

"Isn't it divine?" said Thiago as she closed her eyes. "The best cake you've ever tasted, no?"

Marion nodded. "The very best."

"That's just the complimentary refreshment. There's much more to come. There'll be wine and chocolate, roast and truffle, fruit and bread, and more cheeses than you could possibly count."

"I don't know how to repay you."

Thiago waved her off with a flourish of his hand. "Let your new mistress handle the grave business of bills and repayment. All that you need to do is bleed."

A different clerk returned, not with food but an array of cigars. And Marion, now confident that she would not owe Thiago any debt for these luxuries, selected one of the thumb-thick cigars she'd seen the night lords smoking in the pub car. The clerk cut it for her, but Marion leaned forward to light it on the candelabra herself.

"That's not a habit becoming of a bloodmaid," Thiago remarked, and while she knew he was teasing, there was a vein of seriousness beneath his voice.

"If I am expected to stop smoking, then you might as well turn this train around and dump me back in the slums of Prane where I belong."

"Your vice runs that deep?"

"Deep enough," Marion said simply, and she turned the cigar to examine the band around its wrapper. It was green and it simply read *The Golden Opus* in gilt letters, some northern brand, she assumed. "The smoke reminds me of home."

"Well, I'm afraid you'll have to leave home behind you," said Thiago. "There's no place for nostalgia in the North. What you're to become will require you to forsake everything you were before. In time you will purge yourself of all that you were in order to become all that you must be. That is the way of the bloodmaid. It's your great sacrifice." Thiago delivered this warning with the kind of fervor typically employed by street preachers or the corrupted, tithe-hungry priests that scuttled the aisles of Prane's cathedral.

"What if she doesn't like my blood?"

"She will. Lisavet is something of a sommelier in her own right. Her palate is incredibly discerning. She'll be able to appreciate the complexity of your blood's . . . robust flavor profile."

"What if she doesn't like *me*?"

"Then you will learn to make her like you."

Before Marion had the chance to press him more, the train waiter returned with the last of their food on a golden tray. He placed a bloody rack of lamb in front of Thiago, with a little dish of chunky apple and mint jam, and a large, golden puffed-pastry pie before Marion that filled the air with steam.

Marion tucked into her dinner eagerly, quickly forgetting the conversation she'd held with Thiago. She lifted her heavy spoon and shattered the pie's golden crust to sample the rich wine-gravy within. The pie was filled with tender bits of rare meat, sliced leek, and truffle mushrooms that bled when Marion sliced them with her knife, but despite their startling appearance they were fragrant and delicious. And after her third bite Marion was not only certain that it was the best dinner she'd ever had but the best one she *would* ever have. But as she cut through a cube of rare meat—saw the pink innards, the blood seeping across her plate—she thought of Raul on the floor of their cottage, bleeding from the nose and ears, his head caved at the crown.

"The life of a bloodmaid is a sacred indentureship," said Thiago, rekindling the previous topic of conversation. "The bond between a bloodmaid and her master is almost spiritual in nature."

"Is that why the position was advertised in the paper's matrimony column instead of with the other job postings?" Marion asked, thickly, through a spoonful of pie. She knew, in vague terms, that the position of bloodmaid was an indentureship, not a normal job like the ones she'd worked in Prane. But the particulars of the arrangement were still something of a mystery to her. As they were to almost all southerners.

Thiago nodded. "Smart girl. You're correct. The station of bloodmaid is more akin to a marriage than a job, which is why it's always advertised in the matrimony section of the paper. To be a bloodmaid is to commit yourself, body and soul, to one's master or mistress, as the case may be."

Marion was quiet for a moment. "What's she like?"

"The Countess?"

Marion nodded.

"Lisavet"—her name alone was enough to make Marion stiffen—"is capricious and . . . reclusive. Her bloodmaids come and go, but she almost never leaves her House, or the island that it stands on. Her health is poor, which is why she employs so many bloodmaids. I've heard it said that she needs at least four to supply blood for her medical regime. If she doesn't get enough, she'll die. She buys each day with the blood of girls like you."

"Do you know what she's sick with?"

Thiago swirled what little wine was left in his glass. "A hereditary disorder of the blood, I fear. That's why she needs yours. I'm told her condition is so severe she hasn't left her House in more than seven years."

"Do you think she's lonely?"

"No. She has her bloodmaids and she keeps a small court, but I know little more than that. Lisavet and the company she keeps is something of an enigma."

"Why is that?"

"Nosiness is not a becoming trait for a bloodmaid," said Thiago, in firm correction. "You'll meet your new mistress soon enough. Perhaps you can ask her yourself."

That night, while Thiago disappeared to another train car to make conversation with his fellow night lords, Marion retired to the viewing car. Given the late hour, and how little there was to see, the cabin was totally empty. And Marion was grateful for it. It allowed her to lie back on one of the benches and stare up at the stars and moon as they shifted slowly past.

She didn't recall falling asleep, but when she opened her eyes there was a blanket draped across her lap and Thiago sat close beside her. He was watching her, with a kind of grim expression that made her shiver, despite the blanket's warmth. She was surprised to see him there. It was less than proper for a man to be left alone with a lady who was not his wife. But then she remembered that Thiago was not just a man, he was a Taster, and she was far less than a lady, she was a bloodmaid-to-be. The typical protocols and social observances that dictated proper conduct didn't apply to the likes of them.

Her gaze shifted. The sky was the deep lapis of early dawn. Beyond the train tracks, the marshes stretched, on and on, into what seemed like eternity. They were covered with a high, dark grass that rolled like water when the wind breathed through it.

Marion sat up, disoriented, a little dizzy, unsure of where she was or why she was there. But then the memories flooded back to her—the night train's station, the embassy, her blood at the bottom of Thiago's teacup, the ad in the paper, the night lords, Raul on the floor of the slum house, bleeding from the gash in his head. He would be dead now. And he would've died alone, on the floor in that reeking house, or perhaps in the street if he'd had enough strength to drag himself out to it. She hated herself for leaving him there, but had she stayed she knew she would've hated herself even more. Perhaps, in death, Raul could forgive her for her sin. But Marion knew that in life, she would never be able to forgive herself.

Tears came to her eyes, and she squinted through them and out the window, where she saw the lights of small villages in the distance. But they were no slums like those in Prane. This was, after all, the open country of the North, wild and yet untouched by industry.

"Come now," said Thiago. "It's time to wake up. Our journey's at its end."

7

Consumption is the highest honor.

—SELINA, BLOODMAID OF THE HOUSE OF HUNGER

THE NIGHT TRAIN GROUND to a slow stop in what appeared to be the wilds. Marion could hear the gentle *hush hush* of wind stirring through the marsh grass as she stepped off the night train and onto the platform below. Staring out into the open dark, Marion shuddered violently and pulled her knit cap down over her ears. The cold air smelled of sulfur, and the chill was gnawing. She gritted her teeth to keep them from chattering and studied the station where she stood.

To her surprise, it was far smaller than the one in Prane. On the small platform, a wrought iron bench sat in the halo of a lamppost that burned just bright enough to keep the shadows at bay. Just beyond it was a one-room cottage that appeared to function as the depot, though there was no signage to declare it so. Marion scanned the ticket window for any sign of a clerk but saw no one.

A shrill chorus of seagulls shrieked into the night. Marion detected the scent of salt and sulfur on the air. She realized she could hear the rhythm of waves breaking against a distant shore. This came as something of a surprise to her. She'd had no idea they were so close to the coast. On a narrow road adjacent to the cottage depot stood a black carriage hitched to two long-legged steeds that looked like the racehorses that ran the tracks back at Prane.

"We're expected," said Thiago, appraising the awaiting carriage, and for the first time since he'd sampled her blood, he seemed surprised.

Marion shoved cold-stiff fingers into the pockets of her coat in a vain attempt to warm them. "Expected by whom?"

Thiago only smiled, and with a snap of his fingers he motioned the carriage driver off his bench. The man assisted the night train's porters with Thiago's luggage. There was a lot of it: crates and trunks, a number of leather chests—all of them fastened shut with chains and padlocks—and paper-wrapped parcels that Marion couldn't distinguish the contents of by shape, jars containing different and varying wet specimens (a pig fetus, an eyeball, a long-legged bullfrog), a taxidermied elk head so large it took two train porters to carry it, and a birdcage big enough to comfortably house an eagle that was draped in a bone-pale sheet.

Marion waited, silent and shivering, while the clerks loaded the carriage with Thiago's strange array of belongings. A violent wind swept inland off the sea, carrying with it the reek of brine and sulfur. The gnawing cold made Prane's worst winters seem as temperate as a warm summer's day. Shivering, Marion hoped her indenture at the House of Hunger would include a complimentary coat . . . and perhaps a pair of boots too. Otherwise she'd spend her days freezing until she could scrape together the coins she needed to secure new clothing.

When all of Thiago's goods were safely loaded on top of the carriage and carefully secured with a webwork of ropes and chains, both he and Marion settled themselves in its cabin and then they were off, down the narrow road that snaked into the shadows. Thiago was strangely quiet for most of the drive, picking at his nails or risking a glance at the windows to watch the moors roll slowly past.

"Do you have a bloodmaid?" Marion's question cut straight through the quiet, and Thiago startled slightly, as if, for the first time in a while, he was remembering she was there.

"I do but she doesn't travel with me."

"I thought all night lords kept their bloodmaids close."

"I'm not a night lord," said Thiago, laughing. "As I told you, I'm a Taster. An acquirer, one could say. I work with several Houses of the North, venturing south in search of remarkable new blood."

"But I thought you were noble?"

"I am, in the sense that I'm the son of some poor wench who fell in love with a House lord. I have little to do with my father, which is fine because between the two of us he's the poorer. All he has is his title and the ruins of a House that was once occupied by men far greater and far richer than he." It seemed like a rather petty thing to say, but if Thiago noticed the gracelessness of the statement he didn't seem to care. "But I have no title to my name. I'm simply Thiago of the North, the same way you're Marion of Prane, though that's soon to change."

"What do you mean?"

"Well, when you become a bloodmaid, that will be your new name and title. Marion, Bloodmaid of the House of Hunger, Ward of Lisavet Bathory."

"That's a long title to tack to one person."

"You'll learn to wear it well."

Marion considered this for a moment in silence. "Are you sure the Countess will have me?"

"I'm certain of it," said Thiago, and he slipped his pocket watch from the shadows of his vest and squinted at it. "I've staked my time on it, and when you're as busy as I am there's no gamble so big as that."

They journeyed in silence again. There were few sounds save for the carriage wheels grumbling as they rolled over the gravel, and the low hiss of the wind moving through the swaying grass of the distant marshland. These were the northern wilds she'd heard about in rumors and legends: the plains that were haunted by strange and shifting creatures, where the spirits of the gods drifted, low-slung, close enough to stroke the earth with their fingertips. Even in the darkness, its beauty was vicious and staggering. It was a world yet unclaimed, unlike Prane with its cut roads and factories, where the hands of humankind had forced nature into submission.

Their carriage stopped at the edge of a wooden dock. The driver loaded Thiago's belongings on a small boat that was tethered there. By the time they boarded—Marion stepping gingerly into the belly of the vessel, as it listed and bobbed beneath her boots—she was quite certain it would sink.

The carriage driver, now boatsman, dragged on the oars. Here, the fog lay thick over the water, so that it was hard to see anything more than a few yards past the prow of the rowboat. Marion could hear toads croaking somewhere far off in the dark and overhead; the gulls were still shrieking their nighttime dirges. Gradually, the fog began to thin. Through it, Marion could just make out small lights dancing in the distance, the crude shape of what might've been an island jutting up from the murky marsh water.

"There she is," said Thiago, pointing out through the pall. "The House of Hunger."

It was a fearsome thing. At least six stories tall, it seemed to crouch on the distant horizon like a spider lurking in wait of its prey. Its windows, too, were arachnid; candlelit and glowing, they seemed to gaze like eyes, all-seeing, into the vastness of the marshland and the open ocean beyond it.

"It's huge," Marion whispered, and with the words her breath made soft shapes on the air.

"It was once called the jewel of the North," said Thiago, and Marion was certain she heard a note of sarcasm in his voice. Bitterness, even. "It's the first and largest of all of the Houses. They say it took two hundred years to build; more than six generations of architects spent their lives raising it from the dust of its foundation only to die without ever seeing it finished."

They docked at a small beach on the south edge of the island. While their chaperone struggled to unload the boat, Thiago and Marion climbed the narrow gravel path up to a small courtyard at the side of the House. Here, there was a dying garden, choked with ivy and shadowed by a canopy of willow trees so tall they loomed several stories high. Thiago approached a small red door flanked by gargoyles that were half-devoured by moss.

"Are you ready?" he asked, turning to Marion.

"No."

"You likely never will be. I've been a guest at this House many times in the twenty years since I first entered it, and each time I approach its doors, I feel so painfully small in the shadow of it."

Thiago knocked on the door. A few minutes later, a tall woman opened it.

She was dressed in the northern fashion, her gown dark and her head covered by a long, black veil, the slack fabric draped over her shoulders like a shawl. The woman's gaze shifted to Marion. Her eyes were a muddy gray. "What have we here?"

Thiago put a hand to Marion's back, urging her forward by a few steps. "This is Marion. She's ventured north to serve. Marion, this is the House Mother, Demelsa. She presides over all of the bloodmaids who dwell here."

"I don't recall a request for a new bloodmaid," said the woman, knitting her brows, and Marion felt her heart plummet into the depths of her stomach. Had Thiago led her so astray? Had she come this far only to be turned away at the doorstep of her one chance at a new life?

Thiago, for his part, did not seem perturbed. "Marion is exceptional," he said, and he extended a hand to Marion and drew her matted curls back to expose the bare curve of her neck. "Taste her yourself if you don't believe me."

"You know that the first taste belongs to the Countess."

"So Lisavet *will* have her?" said Thiago, smiling now, with an eyebrow raised.

"I said no such thing. But if she is as exceptional as you say—and that is a very large 'if'—I would not have her spoiled. She will see the Countess tonight, and if she doesn't please her she'll be relinquished back into your care. Am I clear?"

"Perfectly," said Thiago, sidestepping as two servants brushed through the door, burdened with his cages and jarred wet specimens, floating in their chemical brine. "Just allow us a moment to freshen ourselves—"

"That won't be necessary," said the House Mother, motioning for them to follow her down the hall. "The Countess would see you as you are."

The House Mother ushered them through a series of hallways and galleries to a grand archway where two columns carved in the shape of naked men stood stooped, seeming to bear the full weight of the House on their shoulders. They passed between the columns and down a long, mirrored hallway that was lit by what seemed to be a thousand candles, their flames reflecting and refracting as to triple their brightness.

As they walked, Thiago and the House Mother spoke of northern news—a new opera that graced the ballrooms of several neighboring Houses, and the tariffs the northern Parliament was soon to impose. The two were just broaching the topic of elk hunting in the northern moors when Marion heard the soft traces of music winding through the halls. They traveled deeper into the House, and Marion caught the rich aromas of roast meat and coffee beans, cakes baking in warm ovens, yeast and sweets and chocolate. But just below those tantalizing aromas, something wet . . . and faintly fungal.

Marion was grateful when they slowed to a stop at the end of a drafty hallway, before a pair of double doors that were painted with the landscape of a meadow so realistic it seemed like the window to another world that one could merely step into. But on the other side of those doors, Marion could hear music and dark laughter, the slurred snatches of drunken conversation and boisterous political debate.

There, in the shadow of the door, Thiago turned to Marion and put a hand on her shoulder.

"This is the last time in your life you will be Marion of Prane. The moment you step past that threshold you are a bloodmaid. Am I understood?"

It was the first time Thiago had been even remotely severe. "But what if she will not have me? Will you send me south again?"

"Marion—"

"I can't go back," she said, panicking a little at the thought. Her memories dragged her back to her last moments with Raul, when he'd fallen, struck the floor, the blood that had leaked from his ears . . . his eyes even. "If I go back to Prane I—"

"Lisavet *will* have you."

"You shouldn't make false promises," said the House Mother, chiding him, though there was no malice in her eyes. Only pity, as she gazed upon Marion.

"I do no such thing. I promise that Lisavet will have her because Lisavet *will*." With that, Thiago squared his shoulders and nodded to the footmen who stood—glaze-eyed and stoic—on either side of the doors. "We're ready."

In tandem, the footmen shifted and heaved the doors wide open, revealing a large parlor packed to capacity with a throng of northern nobles. The walls were painted a gory burgundy, though a few of them were devoted to erotic frescoes, depicting orgies and other gruesome acts of pleasure. In the far corner of the room, a stringed quartet played a lapsing arrangement—all long low notes and deep bass that reverberated through the room in waves and echoed through the eaves.

Overhead was a brass chandelier fashioned in the shape of a naked man, with his legs drawn up to his stomach and his hair fanning out behind him like he was frozen in the midst of a fall. In each of his hands and tangled in the brass curls of his flowing hair was a lit candle.

Thiago managed to lead Marion through the throng of the nobles who milled about between card tables, smoking thin cigarettes that smelled, sharply, of myrrh and clove. All of them moved with the kind of intrinsic grace Marion had come to identify as a defining characteristic of pureblooded northerners. A few women sat in the laps of nobles, laughing loudly at witticisms that Marion couldn't hear. In an adjoining parlor, a group of four lay tangled on a chaise in various states of undress. By the hearth, two men kissed each other between deep draughts of blood wine staining their lips and chins red.

Few of these drunken revelers registered Marion's presence at all, but those who did gazed at her with a kind of famished curiosity, as if she were some jester come to slake their boredom. Entertain them. Never had she felt more out of place. The slums were crawling with girls like her—girls in muddy boots and patchwork dresses whose hair reeked of smog and ammonia—who knew nothing but a life scrubbing floors. But here, in the North, she felt like a caged animal in a zoo.

As Thiago stepped forward to the center of the room, edging around card tables and little clusters of nobles, pressing through the swollen skirts of the ladies, the crowds seemed to thin and clear, forming a kind of path to the far wall. There, flanked by a small crowd of nobles, with a blond bloodmaid in her lap, sat the Countess.

Lisavet was younger than Marion had expected her to be, appearing no more than a decade older than she, and at first glance she didn't appear sickly. She had high cheekbones, a small narrow nose, and bone-pale skin. Her eyes were green and so faint that when the candlelight touched them, it appeared that she had no irises at all. Her hair was black, straight, and cut short like a boy's. She wore a dress of black velvet, strung shoulder-to-shoulder with a thick golden chain. On the middle finger of her left hand, she wore a thick signet ring, dark silver wrapped around a crude-cut ruby that was the largest gem Marion had ever laid eyes on. Upon closer scrutiny, she realized it was hewn into the visage of a man's face.

The bloodmaid perched on Lisavet's knee was her opposite in most every way—fair-haired, full-bosomed, and totally naked save for the black ribbon around her neck. There was something vacant, and vaguely feral, about her eyes as she studied Marion, as though there was no real spirit behind them.

Lisavet eyed Thiago impassively and ignored Marion completely. "Thiago, it's been some time."

"I don't rush my acquisitions, but I can assure you they're well worth the wait." Thiago stepped aside with a theatrical flourish of his coat and motioned to Marion. "Allow me to introduce Marion Shaw, who has come north to serve in your court as a bloodmaid."

The Countess didn't bother to dignify Marion's presence with so much as a passing glance. "I don't recall requesting new blood."

"Marion is exceptional."

"I *have* exceptional bloodmaids," said the Countess, and the girl on her lap beamed with pride.

"None like this one. Marion is . . . *refined*."

A few of the nearby nobles laughed outright, but the Countess silenced them with a raised hand.

"Taste her yourself and you'll see," he said, and he reached back, motioning for Marion to give him her hand. "The girl has no equal. The flavor of her blood is unlike that of any I've tasted before. I would compare it to that of a wine aged over several centuries. There are notes of plum and cedar . . . even smoke. But moreover, there is an ineffable quality, as if one is tasting things that could only ever be felt—jealousy, rage, passion, the full spectrum of one's own carnality as experienced not in the heart and mind but on the palate."

It was a stirring endorsement, and Marion couldn't imagine she was worthy of such high praise. A part of her wanted to taste her own blood, just to see if it was all that Thiago professed it to be. The Countess seemed to share in her skepticism. Unmoved, she summoned Marion forward with a flicker of her fingers. At once, she knew what was being asked of her. She extended her hand to Thiago, her fingers shaking. The Taster attempted to wipe her arm clean with a pass of his handkerchief before drawing a thin golden needle from the inner pocket of his vest.

"I'll take it from the source."

Thiago stopped, with the needle just an inch from Marion's wrist, and swallowed thickly, dropping his hand. With no small amount of trepidation, he stared down at Marion, then nodded to the Countess, who sat before them. "It'll only hurt for a moment," he assured her.

Shaken, but trying her best to hide it, Marion started forward, her old work boots scuffing across the glossy marble floors, leaving muddy tracks behind them.

"Your cap," said Lisavet, addressing Marion directly for the first time.

Flustered, the girl snatched the knit cap off her head, tucked it into the pocket of her coat, and hastily attempted to tame her curls to little avail.

As Marion approached, the Countess softly ordered her blood-maid to leave her lap. Frowning, the girl stood and stepped just a pace away. As she brushed past her, Marion was surprised to discover that the bloodmaid was even taller than she was, but so thin she looked almost starved.

Marion stopped just short of the Countess, unsure of what to do.

"Hasn't anyone taught you to curtsy?" the bloodmaid demanded.

"Hush," said the Countess, and then, to Marion: "Where are you from?"

"Prane."

Thiago stepped forward to elaborate. "It's an industrial town on the cusp of—"

"I'm familiar," said Lisavet, still eyeing Marion. "Did you live alone?"

"No, milady." She thought of Raul's head, cracking against the edge of the stove. Thought of him dragging himself across the floor on his belly, scrabbling at her feet, begging her not to go. "I lived with my older brother."

Lisavet's expression remained inscrutable. "What happened to your other hand?"

Marion peered down at it. Her fingers had swelled more than she'd realized, and her knuckles bore the bright beginnings of nasty bruises. "Shut it in a door."

"Spoiled goods," said a woman seated at a card table a few paces away, summoning another chorus of laughter. Marion realized then that they didn't see her as human. At least, not in the way they saw themselves as human. Bloodmaid or not, the way they regarded her was akin to the way Lady Gertrude once had—staring down the bridges of their noses, their lips drawn away from their teeth in disgust.

Lisavet's expression remained unchanged. If she shared in the contempt of her peers, she didn't show it. "You haven't seen a doctor?"

"I don't need a doctor," said Marion, with a defiant tilt of her chin, that dogged, street rat pride stirring up in her, despite the circumstances. "Pain is pain."

Lisavet's eyes narrowed. "What was your previous employment?"

"I was a maid."

"And how did you like that?"

Marion merely shrugged. "It was honest work that kept food on my table. At the time that was enough."

Seemingly satisfied with her answer, the Countess leaned forward. "Your wrist, if you will?"

Marion extended it and Lisavet took her by the hand, leaning forward so that Marion could feel the heat of her breath. The Countess ran her tongue along her bottom lip, eyeing Marion's veins, her pupils narrowing to pinpoints as she primed for the bite. When she opened her mouth, Marion saw that both of her canines were capped with golden crowns that were sharpened and hooked into vicious points. She'd heard that a few of the northern nobles made such . . . adaptations. Metal nails honed to knifelike tips; gold-capped canine teeth so sharp they had to take care not to slit the tips of their tongues when they spoke. These modifications made it easier for them to pierce the skin and suck the blood straight from its source. The Countess opened her mouth so wide that Marion swore she heard the soft *pop* of her jaw unhinging, then snapped it shut around her arm.

Marion expected pain, but in that instant there was none. In fact, the rest of the world—Thiago, the nobles, the nearby bloodmaid— seemed to shrink out of existence, until there was nothing but her and the Countess at her wrist, her teeth sinking deeper, a single trail of blood leaking from the punctures at the points of her gold-capped teeth.

The Countess hunched over Marion's arm, her jaw locked around her wrist, her eyes unseeing. Her throat bobbed up and down as she swallowed. After a few long moments, she released, tearing her teeth free of Marion's flesh. Lisavet collapsed back into her chair, limp and breathless but . . . *laughing*, with all of the carefree mirth of a child. The court looked on as she wiped her bloody mouth clean on the back of her hand and, grinning, gazed at Marion, as if the two of them shared in some unspeakable secret. "Welcome to the House of Hunger."

8

They say there is honor in the calling of a bloodmaid.
If so, I have never known it.

—LYONA, BLOODMAID OF THE HOUSE OF DAY

MARION HAD NEVER HAD a room of her own, but in the aftermath of her formal introduction to Lisavet and subsequent acceptance as a bloodmaid, she was quickly ushered through a series of corridors to a private chamber on the west wing of the House. The room was stunning. There was an alcove bed, cut right into the wall, with a thick curtain to separate it from the rest of the chamber. It was dressed with fat, down-stuffed pillows, embroidered quilts, and pale bearskin furs so large they all but engulfed the mattress.

The hearth fire was lit, burning high and bright, by the time Marion entered. There were wide windows on three of the four walls, and they were framed with rich green draperies that pooled on the floor. Between the windows, the walls were hung with a series of paintings, bloody warscapes, grotesque portraits—all smeared oil paint and heavy brushstrokes. The kind of impressionistic abstractions that made prudish southerners turn up their noses in disgust and claim that anyone could call themselves an artist if that was the sort of thing that passed for a masterpiece. But Marion found the paintings compelling, intriguing to the eye as if every time her gaze passed over the images, they were a little different.

Across from the bed, a wardrobe taller than Marion stood in the far corner of the room. A night table by the bed housed an oil lamp and silver bell, which Marion realized, with a start, was to summon a servant. And though she didn't ring it, a servant came anyway. She was a pretty girl with full cheeks, her hair braided modestly, two ringlet curls bouncing at her temples.

"Morning bells ring two hours from now, at nine. But you've had a long journey; would you like to sleep for a little while?"

Marion nodded, suddenly aware of her own exhaustion. Her limbs felt leaden, her head thick, as if stuffed with cotton. She wanted nothing more than to crawl into bed, which was exactly what she did upon stripping out of her dress and stockings, kicking off her mud-crusted boots.

"Sleep well, milady," she said, tucking Marion into bed, drawing the thick, down-stuffed comforter and quilts up to her chin. She snuffed out the candles on either nightstand, pinching them between index and thumb without so much as flinching.

It was a strange thing, Marion thought, to go from waiting on people to being waited on. Just weeks before, she had been the girl who had tucked Lady Gertrude into her bed, rubbed her feet through her stockings, combed her long, yellow-gray hair. How quickly she had transcended her station, the very circumstances of her birth. "What's your name?" Marion asked.

"I'm called Ebba," said the girl, and she drew the heavy curtains of the canopy closed, smiling down at Marion as she did it. Then she walked slowly across the room, her footsteps echoing. "Do sleep well."

The door groaned shut and Marion swore she heard the soft *click* of a lock's bolt sliding into place. But she wasn't certain. As soon as the servant was gone—the echo of her footsteps fading—Marion kicked off her covers and slid out of bed. The thick, patterned carpet was plush beneath her bare feet. She stepped into the center of the room on her tiptoes, not daring to walk flat-footed, as though she feared if she made too much noise—or so much as stepped too heavily—the ruse of her new good fortune would shatter, everything would be ripped away, and in the blink of an eye she'd find herself back in the squalor of Prane.

Tentatively, and by the flickering light of the hearth fire, she explored the room. She opened the wardrobe first, saw the dresses hanging there. At the vanity, brushes, combs, rouge, face creams in crystal bottles, and compacts of paper-pale talcum filled the drawers. Beside it, a mahogany chiffonier, stuffed to capacity with pale linen undergarments—petticoats and slips, chemises, and the like.

There were windows across the room, and when Marion spread the curtains open, she could see northern marshland cast in fog, its grasses rolling with the sweeping ebb and flow of the wind. Beyond them, the vast expanse of the ocean, licked by the pale light of the rising sun.

Marion began to cry then, looking at all of the beauty before her and thinking that there could be no one less worthy of it than she. She had *killed* her brother to achieve this, left him bleeding on the floor of their home. She wondered if his body had been discovered yet, and if so, who would bury him? With no present or living family in Prane to claim his corpse, would he be buried at all? Or would his body simply be surrendered to the fire to burn? Through her tears, Marion attempted to choke out a short little prayer to ease the passing of his soul but forgot the words and stopped halfway through.

Eventually, Marion managed to drag herself from the mire of her guilt and explore the rest of the room: rifling through the contents of the vanity, sampling the greasy, perfumed creams, smearing rouge onto her cheeks until she looked like she'd been backhanded twice. Stashed below the bed she found a chamber pot that was painted in an even more ornate fashion than Lady Gertrude's beloved leech jar. Marion spent several moments staring at the illustrations—the graphic depiction of an elk hunt, rendered in watery blue paint. Then she relieved herself, clutching the skirt of her nightgown to her chest, listening to the faint trickle of piss pooling at the bottom of the pot and feeling as though she wasn't worthy enough to defile such a fine object.

As she lowered the lid back onto the chamber pot and gingerly pushed it beneath the bed again, she spotted something in the shadows, a small pale object that she initially took for a pearl or pebble. But upon closer inspection, she saw that it was a small molar.

Marion examined the tooth. It still had the sharp and yellowing point of its root, the tip of it crusted brown with dried blood, as if it had been pried straight from someone's mouth and quickly discarded. When Marion peered into the shadows to see if there was perhaps another tooth there, she saw a word crudely carved into the underside of the bed frame's leg: *wretch*.

Puzzled, Marion pressed to her feet and placed the little tooth in one of the empty drawers of her vanity for safekeeping, with the intent of inquiring about its origins at a later date. Climbing into bed, she drifted in and out of fitful sleep. Several times she tried to rouse herself, but the gray hands of slumber stilled her limbs and dragged her back to her dreams . . . and nightmares.

In them, she saw Lisavet at her wrist, her mouth a bloody damson, and then the image became a reflection of her own face as seen in the window of the night train. Beyond her own eyes, the churning black of open night; storm clouds touched by tongues of fire and lightning; glimpses of the hungry, wind-tossed ocean. In the bellowing thunder, she heard Raul's voice calling to her from the dark, and when she snapped awake—in a fit of panic—she half expected to see him standing there at the foot of her bed, risen from the dead.

But it was not Raul who greeted her when she opened her eyes.

Rather, two girls. Bloodmaids, though unlike Marion, they both possessed the immaculate beauty their title implied. They wore the same uniform—dark velvet dresses, cut just low enough to expose their collarbones, black ribbon chokers, and matching bands around both of their wrists to mask the needle marks where their blood was taken from them. They stood shoulder-to-shoulder, backs to the open window, in a halo of morning light.

One was lithe with blond hair and eyes sharp and verdant. She had a poised but decidedly boyish way about her. Marion could see it in the way she sat, with one leg drawn up to her chest, the other dangling loose over the edge of the bed.

The second girl—and the more beautiful of the two—was dark-skinned with full lips and large eyes as black as the northern sky in the deep of night. Of everyone Marion had encountered in the North, she looked the most similar to Marion, which made her wonder if she was from the far South, like Marion's own mother had been.

Marion had heard it rumored that the Houses of the North liked their bloodmaids to be . . . *varied*. Some nobles swore that the blood of different ethnicities had markedly different flavors and healing properties. Thus—like the selections of a wine cellar—bloodmaids were often sourced from all over the world, with Tasters traveling across the sea and scouring entire continents in search of new talent. Thiago had said as much the night she first met him. As a rule, the more diverse the selection of bloodmaids, the more esteemed the House they served.

"Look, she's awake," said the dark-eyed girl, and she spoke as if Marion wasn't there to hear her.

"Finally," said the blonde, craning forward. A few of her loose ringlet curls skimmed the apples of Marion's cheeks. The girl gawked at her the way the pigeons flocking in the slums of Prane used to watch her eat her midday meal, lurking about in the hopes of a fallen crumb or perhaps a few fish bones to peck at. "I thought we were going to have to send for the smelling salts to wake her up."

Marion, bleary-eyed and confused, sat up in full and raked a hand through her hair, wincing as her fingers snagged through her tangled curls. She couldn't remember the last time she'd taken a comb to them and flushed with embarrassment at the thought.

"You slept like the dead," said the dark-eyed girl, and Marion could tell she was from the South by the way her accent pulled at each syllable she spoke.

"Do either of you have names?" Marion asked, in a hoarse whisper.

"I'm Irene," said the southerner, and she jabbed her thumb at the green-eyed blonde. "This is Evie. The House Mother has instructed us to escort you to the baths."

"And for good reason," said Evie, wrinkling her faintly freckled nose. "You reek of the streets. Do they not have soap in Prane?"

"Don't be rude," Irene chided, and already Marion could see that she was the mothering sort. Perhaps the elder of the two, certainly the more mature.

Evie merely rolled her eyes and pressed on, turning her attention back to Marion. "After you're bathed and groomed, we're to give you a tour of the House. And there's a lot to cover, so we ought to get started soon."

"Thank . . . you?" said Marion, less out of genuine gratitude and more because she wasn't sure what else to say. She had the odd feeling that she'd woken up to a life she didn't belong to. Her brain scrambled to recount the details of the days that had come before and assemble them into a narrative that explained why a street rat from Prane was sitting in a nest of silken sheets in one of the largest Houses in the North. But then, Marion remembered with a quickening of her heart, the Countess with her mouth fastened around her wrist.

She peered down at her arm and saw that it was freshly bandaged, Lisavet's bite wound dressed with strips of clean white gauze. Someone must've tended her while she was still fast asleep.

A sharp tug on the sleeve of Marion's dress dragged her back to the present. She looked down to see a little girl standing by the edge of her bed. To her shock, she saw that the child was no more than four or five. She was pretty, with alabaster skin and a shock of curly brown hair. As she gazed up at Marion with those distant, watery brown eyes, she reminded her of the porcelain dolls in the windows of the fancy toy shops that she'd always coveted as a child.

While Marion knew nobles preferred their bloodmaids young, she didn't know they liked them *that* young. The thought alone made her want to retch. "Is she . . . ?"

"A bloodmaid?" said Irene, perhaps sensing her concern. "Heavens no. It's illegal for children to be bloodmaids. By northern law, a girl must be six months past her first monthly bleed to even be considered for the role."

"We have to learn how to bleed for ourselves before we can learn to bleed for them," Evie muttered, picking at some invisible speck of dirt beneath her nail. "But who knows? Maybe Lisavet plans to bend the rules a bit."

"Her name is Mae," said Irene, shifting the conversation back on course. The little girl stared at Marion with her brows knit. "She's a ward of the House of Hunger."

"Which is a fancy way of saying she's a bastard of high esteem," said Evie, and it was enough to warrant a sharp pinch from Irene.

"Well, it's *true*. She's the illegitimate daughter of some southern lord whom Lisavet accepted in an act of good faith or political bipartisanship. And she's not the only one. I got my start the same way, and so did my sister, Elize, whom you'll meet soon enough. She's a bloodmaid too."

"Was she the one with Lisavet last night?"

"No, that was Cecelia," said Evie, making no attempt to mask her contempt. "She's First Bloodmaid of the House. The favorite."

Marion could've sworn she saw Irene flinch at the word *favorite*, a flash of pain registering across her face for the briefest moment. She stood up with an impatient wave of her hand. "Enough. The House Mother would have had you up hours earlier, and she'll be cross with us if we dally any longer. We should be on our way to the baths."

Nodding, Marion untangled herself from the silken sheets and slipped to the floor. When she stumbled to the wardrobe she was surprised to find her coat and dress gone, meaning the last memento of her life in Prane was the knit cap she wore on her head. She took it off and tucked it into the top drawer of her dresser for safekeeping.

The bloodmaids scampered from the room ahead of her, Mae following close behind them, and entered into a large, circular parlor that was windowless, save for the domed glass ceiling that flooded the room with pale, silvery sunlight. Four open doors stood along the walls in intervals, each leading to a chamber nearly identical in shape and size to Marion's. Another hall led to the entrance of the bloodmaids' quarters, and the corridors beyond them.

The parlor itself was furnished with an odd collection of velvet chaises and cluttered bookshelves, posted at intervals between the bedroom doors. The walls were hung with children's finger paintings and there were toys scattered everywhere—a porcelain doll with a shattered face perched upon a writing desk, a mink-fur teddy with a single glass eye (the other appeared to have been gouged out), a wooden train set overturned in the shadow of a writing desk.

A nursemaid wandered about the room, cradling an armful of these mutilated toys. The woman set them down on a nearby chaise, gathered the child into her arms (Marion thought she was a little old to be babied in such a way), and disappeared into a light-filled chamber—presumably Mae's bedroom—carefully closing its door behind her.

Irene kept a guiding hand on Marion's arm as they traversed the back corridors to the bathhouse, and Marion had to keep reminding herself not to cringe at her touch. She'd once heard that those in the North were more forward and effusive than their southern counterparts, always touching and grasping, standing close enough to exchange breaths and brush shoulders, clutching together to keep warm, some even going so far as to greet friends and acquaintances with the deep, openmouthed kisses that, in the South, were typically reserved for lovers.

But such were the strange passions of the North.

After a long walk, down a series of long spiral stairways that were empty of almost everyone except the odd servant, they entered into the baths beneath the first floor of the House. There was a stone door there, guarded by a footman who didn't so much as register their presence as the girls scurried past the threshold.

The bathing rooms were a kind of cave. The ceilings were of natural stone, stalactite-studded and painted white so that the baths bore the vaulted appearance of a cathedral's ceilings. There were six baths in total, each a different color and temperature. One crystal clear, another as black as soot, a third with a greenish hue that reeked so strongly of sulfur Marion's nose burned, and another, a milk bath dusted with rose petals, even a small circular pool that bubbled like a vat of water boiling on the stove. The air smelled of spiced salts and perfume, but beneath that there was the musty fungal scent Marion had first noticed upon entering the House—all earth and mildew.

Evie was half-undressed before they'd scaled the stairway. She stripped out of her slip and ran to the water, naked, and dove in. Marion feared she'd crack her head on the bottom of the bath (the image of Raul bleeding on the floor flashed briefly through her mind). But the water was deeper than it looked at a distance, and after a few long moments the girl surfaced, smiling and sputtering, unharmed.

"Don't be shy," said Irene, and she turned her back to Marion, so that she might help loose the laces of her gown. "You're of us and we're of you, now. We're bloodmaids and that makes us as good as family to each other."

So Marion took off her coat and waded into the cold and brackish water of the bath, only soaking for a few minutes before following Irene and Evie into another bath, and then another after that one. Her favorite was a small sulfurous bath she'd initially overlooked. It was a dark greenish blue and crowned with steam so thick it was hard to see the surface below it, though the pool was too small, barely wider than a well, so that if Marion went to the center and opened her arms spread-eagle she could almost touch both sides at once. But it was much deeper than the other baths. She couldn't feel, or even see, the bottom once she stepped off the ladder.

As they soaked—floating huddled together, so close their shoulders very nearly touched—Irene and Evie offered more thorough introductions, chatting rapidly above the lapping of the waves in the bathing pool. Marion learned that Evie and her sister Elize (whom she had yet to meet) were the bastard daughters of a famous opera singer. Both girls possessed their mother's talent and were often called to court to sing for the nobles.

Irene, in turn, was the daughter of a wealthy landowner on an island in the South who had been sent north to live with relatives after the death of her father and had, upon arriving, been sold to a Taster who later placed her with the House of Hunger. Irene informed her that her illegitimate grandfather—an aristocrat—believed there was no better use for a dark-skinned bastard girl raised on a sugar plantation, who had no virtues to recommend her apart from her blood . . . and her beauty. And Irene *was* beautiful. More so than Marion, Evie, or any other bloodmaid that Marion had yet seen.

"So your family just sold you off?" Marion asked, and she didn't mean it to come out as harshly as it did.

If Irene took offense, she didn't betray it. "As they do all of us. Every Taster collects his finder's fee."

The girls lapsed into silence then, and Marion let the gentle waves lull her into a thick stupor close to sleep. The warm water soothed her and eased the dull ache in her hand. Eventually Irene and Evie rekindled their previous conversation, gossiping about some low-ranking night lord who left his wife for his bloodmaid. Which, Irene claimed, was absurd because northern law prohibited bloodmaids from entering sacred matrimony with their keepers.

"Why aren't they allowed to wed?" Marion asked, studying her pruned fingertips. It seemed like a silly triviality, when bloodmaids so often filled the role of concubines and companions. Why shouldn't they be wives too? After all, Thiago had told her that the bond of a bloodmaid and her mistress or master more closely resembled holy matrimony than employment.

"Because we're little more than livestock by law," said Evie, flicking at the fat vein at the juncture of her elbow, which was already quite bruised from bloodletting. "They can't marry us any more than we could marry a dairy cow."

"That's *not* true," said Irene, with surprising sharpness. "And it's in poor form to liken our plight, a plight we *chose*, to that of those with no liberty to make that decision themselves."

Marion guessed it was a tender subject for her, given the nature of her birth. It was clear that, like Marion's own mother, Irene came from the Southern Isles, where the laborers who harvested spice and sugarcane had little to no ability to choose their brutal vocations. And while the plight of a bloodmaid was not an easy one, Irene was right in that it was at least a fate of their own choosing.

Just then, two servants entered and, on Irene's welcome, approached the pool. What followed next was one of the most painful and humiliating ordeals she had experienced yet. Under the care of the servants, Marion was scrubbed and plucked, prodded and shorn like a lamb. They smeared hot wax between her brows, grooming and shaping them. With little files and scissors they clipped her nails, picked out the dirt that was caked beneath them, and carefully shaped her cuticles.

Washing her hair was a two-servant job, but the process of combing out her curls required three. Tears sprang to Marion's eyes as the trio worked through the mats and the knots, starting from the bottom of her curls and working their way up to the roots until every strand was free of tangles.

But the servants' work was not done yet.

After they combed and trimmed her hair, one of the servants produced razors from the pockets of her smock and proceeded to shear Marion's legs of every hair on them. But by far the worst part of their ordeal was the waxing of her modesty, which was as excruciatingly painful as it was humiliating. It was then that Irene and Evie dismissed themselves, giggling, and retreated to the parlors again.

It was only hours later, when the gruesome task of her grooming was finally over, that they returned and immediately laughed at the stricken expression on her face.

"Well, she's starting to look the part," said Evie, and she touched Marion's thigh, which had been shaved as smooth as a baby's ass.

"Thank God for it," said Irene, cradling a folded bunch of cloth to her chest. "How do you feel?"

"Like a plucked chicken."

The two girls laughed, and Irene ushered a black bundle of clothing into Marion's arms. "Get dressed. I'm supposed to give you a tour of the House."

Drying herself on a nearby towel, Marion unfolded the black gown Irene had given her and dressed quickly, struggling a little with the heavy skirts and laces. She tied the black choker around her neck carefully. Once dressed, she caught a glimpse of herself in the run of mirrors opposite the bathing pools and was shocked to see a bloodmaid staring back at her. Albeit one with the poor posture and calloused hands of someone who'd spent years of her life scrubbing floors.

If only Agnes could see her now. What would she think? Would she even have recognized Marion if they'd brushed past each other on the streets of Prane? Would Marion even recognize herself, if she'd caught a glimpse of her own reflection in a storefront window as she passed it by? Scrutinizing herself in the mirror—the stranger, the bloodmaid staring back at her—she was certain the answer was no. It appeared that Marion of Prane was stone dead . . . and in her place, the usurper who stood before her now. A stranger.

"What a marvel you are," said Irene, staring at her reflection in the mirror. But there was something about the way she said it that made Marion think she was a little less than delighted. "You're already every bit the bloodmaid. Like you were born to it."

"Marion of Prane is dead," said Evie, with mock fanfare. She lifted a pink-frosted tea cake from the tray of refreshments the servants provided for them and raised it to Marion in a toast. "Long live Marion of the House of Hunger."

Marion smiled at the girl, the bloodmaid, in the mirror. "Hear, hear."

9

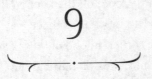

*Any bloodmaid worth her weight in gold (and every bloodmaid
should be worth at least that) should consider herself a student.
She is always the novice but never the fool.*

—FROM *A BLOODMAID'S PRACTICUM* BY ROSAMUND, FIRST
BLOODMAID OF THE HOUSE OF FERNS

AFTER THEIR TIME IN the bathing chambers, the three blood-maids embarked on an extensive tour of the House. They started with the kitchen on the first floor, a room that, according to Irene, was one where Marion would spend much of her time. The first floor was devoted to ovens, worktables, and a courtyard hothouse that contained a small vegetable garden and orchard, where the trees were budding with ripe plums and oranges and fat figs swarmed with wasps and bumblebees. On the second floor, in an open, loftlike space, was an extensive pantry complete with drying racks laden with cured sauces and aged meats, a cannery, and an extensive assortment of spices. In the basements below their feet, the ice rooms and wine cellar.

A tall, starved-looking man that Marion assumed was the head chef (based solely on the way he barked orders at the rest of the staff, who scurried around him like frightened mice) worked fervently, grasping the handle of a sizzling saucepan with two bloody hands.

"The chef often requires our . . . *talents* in the kitchen," said Irene, as if that was meant to explain the chaotic scene before them. She motioned to a little room off the kitchen that looked like a cross between a parlor and a physician's office.

In the room's far corner, in one of the six armchairs arranged in intervals along the walls, sat a bloodmaid that Marion knew at once was Evie's sister Elize. They were nearly identical, though Elize seemed more shapely than her sister, with full cheeks and the enviable curves of a woman. Her neck was encircled by a red ribbon (perhaps to conceal a bite wound?) and she wore her hair down around her shoulders as if she'd only just woken up. In her lap, a white cat slept soundly.

Her dress was of black velvet, and the left sleeve was folded back, exposing the soft crook of her elbow. Next to her was a silver plate stacked with chocolate-stuffed pastries, which she nibbled and nipped at, pausing every so often to lick the icing off her fingers. She didn't even wince when the servant at her side slipped the needle deep into her arm, and the blood began flowing into the bowl on the table beneath her elbow.

"It's not as bad as it looks," Irene assured her. "They fatten us up with pastries and cream to keep us from fainting and make sure we taste sweet. All you have to do is bleed, and the bleeding is easy enough once you get used to it. You'll see."

"That's because the hard part comes after the blood is spilled," said the girl being bled, so low Marion almost missed her words beneath the clamor of the kitchen. Her accent was slightly stronger than her sister's, and Marion liked the sound of it. "Just wait until you begin your etiquette classes with Madame Boucherie. I'd rather my blood be drained down to the dregs than spend an hour with that spiteful—"

"This is my elder sister Elize and her cat, Theodore," said Evie, gesturing to the girl in the chair. The cat fixed his wide and watery eyes on Marion and blinked. "And Elize, Theodore, this is Marion, our newest bloodmaid."

"Oh, I'm well aware," said Elize, biting into a cream puff. She dipped her finger into the pastry's whipped-cream center and let her cat lick it off the tip of her finger. "The whole House is talking about her. Apparently, Lisavet took quite the liking to your blood last night."

"I wonder if you'll unseat Cecelia and become the new First Bloodmaid," said Evie, and she plucked a blackberry from the corner of her sister's cake and popped it into her mouth. "Allegedly, it's been quite a while since Lisavet's favors shifted. And Cecelia looked quite perturbed upon returning to her chambers last night."

"We should be on our way," said Irene, firmly, and both of the sisters fell silent. As Irene led them away, Elize waved goodbye, her fingers sticky with pale buttercream, her blood still dribbling—dark and viscous—into the bowl beneath her elbow.

Marion followed Irene through the rest of the kitchen in silence, past roaring ovens and worktables, and racks of meat hanging to cure.

They entered what Evie introduced as the finishing room, which looked less like a kitchen and more like a salon. There were several tables, each adorned with a half-finished arrangement of food—a berry tart in a nest of flowers, a six-tiered cake half-frosted, and other dishes that had yet to be plated. In addition to these confections, there was a wide spread of meats: steaks (barely seared and still bloody), spiced sausages, baked fish with their heads on, their heat-shriveled eyes staring into nothingness.

A kitchen maid just across from them stood over a tiered tea tray, nursing a little cup and saucer. Marion watched as she took a little pitcher full of blood and set it on the tray next to the cream and sugar.

"The Countess takes her tea with blood," said Irene, by way of explanation as they ducked out of the kitchen and into a neighboring hallway. They took a flight of stairs up to the proper first floor, down a narrow hall, and into a wide loggia. A marble path led across a small courtyard and vegetable garden and into a glass greenhouse many times larger than the one housed in the kitchen's adjacent courtyard. Marion had read about those structures in the *Prane Gazette*. They were the favored attractions of the world fairs that took place in the capital, but Marion had never seen one in real life. Behind its glass walls grew date palms and fig trees and other flora native to the southern hemisphere. Marion couldn't imagine what it cost in both labor and fuel to warm a space like that in the midst of the bitter northern winters.

Irene led them past the greenhouse and the entrance of a large and overgrown labyrinth that rambled toward the distant cliff's edge. Its hedges were crawling with brambles, and the passages between them had grown so narrow they were barely wide enough to accommodate a single person walking sideways. They then reentered the House through a small side door and crossed into what Irene introduced as the gallery, a large room with cathedral ceilings that was crowded with dozens of marble statues, some so realistic they looked as if they might step off their pedestals at any moment.

"This is where Mae likes to play fox and hound. It's also the single most terrifying space in the House as soon as night falls. Every one of these creatures"—she flicked a nearby statue's nose—"looks like it's about to come alive."

Marion examined one of the sculptures; it appeared to be in the likeness of a young bloodmaid, wearing nothing but a choker around her neck. She stood with her arms extended, her upturned wrists prone and ready for bleeding. It made her think of the bloodmaids who had come before her, like the previous inhabitant of Marion's room. Had the tooth she discovered beneath the bed belonged to her? Was it she who'd carved that odd little word, *wretch*, into the underside of the bed? "Was there ever another girl, another blood-maid in my chamber?"

"Not during our tenure," said Irene lightly, coming to stand beside her. "Cecelia might know, though. She's been tenured at this House the longest. When she first arrived there might have been other girls here."

"What became of them?"

Irene shrugged. "I suppose their tenures ended. They retired to make room for the new blood." She gestured to the three of them. "Girls come and go. That's the way of bloodmaids. We don't keep our youth forever. And when our blood goes sour with age, our tenures end. Apparently, the blood of the young has more restorative properties than that of the old."

"And by old she means twenty-five," said Evie. She stopped to examine the sculpture of a naked man, paying particular attention to his marble-carved prick. "Do you suppose they're this big in real life?"

Irene chose to ignore that choice comment. "The Countess requires the highest caliber of bloodmaids, because of her ailing health. Her blood isn't thick enough, and it lacks the right properties to sustain life, so she needs to consume a steady diet of ours. Apparently, the disease runs in her family, passed down through her father's side. It's said that every direct descendant of the House of Hunger is sickened with it. But her mother, gods rest her, was said to be sick too. Though hers was an ailment of the mind, not the body."

"She was a bloodmaid. They say she went mad," said Evie. "The servants claim that her soul still walks the halls of this House every night. And when things go quiet, you can still hear her howling for the Count of Hunger. Made mad by her love for him."

"I see we're making friends." A thin voice rang through the gallery, cutting Evie short. Marion turned to see the House Mother. Today, she wore a sheer black mourning veil that stopped beneath her eyes. "I hate to interrupt, but I need to speak with Marion in confidence."

Marion turned to see that both girls, who had been chatty and smiling mere moments before, stood with their heads bowed, hands clasped behind their backs, knees bent into graceful curtsies. They looked deflated, like two puppets hanging limp from their strings. Then, without a word by way of parting, they dismissed themselves to the gallery doors.

The House Mother turned to Marion. "Do follow me."

10

We bleed for those we love most.

—ELMA, BLOODMAID OF THE HOUSE OF DUSK

THE HOUSE MOTHER'S PRIVATE parlor was a large room on the fourth floor, in the northernmost wing of the House. It was tastefully furnished—crowded with velvet-upholstered chaises, wingback armchairs, and dusty bookshelves. Its large bay windows overlooked the open ocean, the slit where sky met wind-tossed sea. One of the windows was slightly ajar so that when the breeze washed in—stirring the hearth fire and snatching at the flames of candles, sometimes snuffing them out—the room filled with the brackish reek of the marshes.

"I must say," said the House Mother, smiling at Marion through the steam rising from their teacups, "I was incredibly impressed with your performance last night."

Marion pulled her gaze from the horizon and took a sip of her tea. It was so hot it scorched her throat when she swallowed. Startled at the pain, she set her cup down in her saucer with a clatter. "My . . . performance?"

The woman nodded, sipping her own tea, seemingly impervious to the heat. "You bled well last night. Lisavet was quite taken with you."

Marion didn't know what it meant to bleed well, but she assumed it had something to do with the way Lisavet had looked at her, with her mouth locked around Marion's wrist, as if she couldn't bear to release it.

The House Mother stripped one of the furs off the back of the chaise they sat on and smoothed it across Marion's lap in a gesture that was surprisingly warm, given the fact that they were little more than strangers to each other. "Did Irene inform you about the rules of this House?"

Marion shook her head.

"Well, we'd better go over them now, because your future tenure depends, almost entirely, on your ability to abide by them. The first rule is to remember your station, always. You are a guest in the North, and you are a bloodmaid, which means you exist to serve this House. The second is that as a servant of this House you are expected to remain within it at all times. Should you depart without the written consent of the Countess, your tenure will immediately be annulled and your expected pension forfeit. The third is that after dinner you are to remain within the bloodmaids' quarters unless you're called to court or summoned by Lisavet. The fourth is that you are *never* to visit Lisavet unless a formal invitation is extended to you. The fifth is that your body is a hallowed vessel that belongs to this House and its presiding heir, Lisavet. You are never to share your blood or body with anyone other than Lisavet unless you are specifically ordered to do so by her. Thus, we come to the final and most important rule: In this House, Lisavet's word is law. Within this House, her authority is absolute.

"Should you break this code of conduct, your punishment will suit the severity of your transgressions. And I warn you that for a bloodmaid, disobedience is a *very* grave sin indeed. I keep careful records of every bloodmaid indentured to this House. All of your indiscretions, in detail, within them. In especially egregious cases, disobedience can result in dishonorable annulment, wherein a blood-maid is expelled without her pension. That's why it's crucial for you to abide by the laws of this House. Do I make myself entirely clear?"

"Yes, my lady."

"Mother," she corrected her, sharply. "In this House you will call me Mother."

"Mother," said Marion, testing the word. It had been years since she'd called anyone that. "Yes, Mother."

The woman smiled and appeared almost touched, as if Marion were a child spitting her first words. "Our bloodmaids are ranked first through fifth. Currently, Cecelia occupies the role of First Bloodmaid, followed by Irene, who holds the title of Second. The twins, Evie and Elize, often jockey for the positions of Third and Fourth, respectively. As our newest bloodmaid, you will occupy the role of Fifth, and your future rank will depend on your performance. Understood?"

Marion nodded.

"Wonderful. Now, on to the matter of compensation. Upon the completion of your indentureship, at the behest of the Countess Lisa-vet or at your request, you may annul your contract as bloodmaid, and you will receive a sizable pension in return for your years of service."

This came as no surprise to Marion, as Thiago had explained the particulars of a bloodmaid's indentureship before she'd arrived at the House. "When can I expect annulment?"

"Most bloodmaids serve no more than eight to ten years, until the blush of youth leaves them, and they retire to the courts of their masters or mistresses or take their pensions and go."

The woman put a dry hand to Marion's cheek and cradled her face for a long time in total silence. Then, rather abruptly, she removed it, opened one of her desk drawers, and produced a piece of paper. The House Mother handed the contract to Marion, along with a goose-feather quill and a squat little ink pot. "Sign if you will."

Marion studied the contract in her hand. It read as follows:

This contract is between Marion Shaw and the Countess Lisavet Bathory of the House of Hunger. Marion Shaw agrees to enter a sacred indentureship with the House of Hunger and its presiding Countess, Lisavet Bathory. According to this indentureship, Marion Shaw agrees to faithfully bleed, serve, and commit herself body and soul to the fulfillment of the Countess Lisavet. This commitment will be strictly observed for the duration of her tenure in accordance with the protocols of this House, as outlined and enforced by the presiding House Mother and the Countess Lisavet whom she serves. In exchange for her service, Marion Shaw will receive food, lodging, and a stipend of ten pounds per month to spend at her discretion.

This sacred agreement can be absolved in only one of two circumstances: dissolution or death. In the event of an honorable dissolution—wherein with the full, written consent of the Countess Lisavet, Marion Shaw retires from her duties as bloodmaid in good standing—Marion Shaw shall be awarded a minimum annual pension of six thousand pounds until the date of her death. In the event of a dishonorable dissolution—wherein Marion Shaw fails to fulfill the obligations of her station as a bloodmaid, thus breaking the terms outlined in this contract—she shall be immediately dismissed without pension. Should Marion Shaw die prior to dissolution, her remaining earnings will be distributed to her surviving next of kin.

In testimony whereof _____

The pension was as much as Thiago had suggested it would be. Upon receiving it, she would have more than enough money to secure herself a villa in the Southern Isles, perhaps hire a maid of her own, a few footmen, even a carriage and driver. Marion would live the rest of her days in comfort and freedom, never wanting for anything she couldn't afford to buy.

Thrilled by the thought, she took up the quill and dipped its tip into the ink pot. She moved to sign the contract but faltered . . . the memory of the tooth she'd found beneath her new bed stalling her hand. And then there was that strange word gouged into the underside of the bedframe: *wretch*.

A fat drop of ink splattered the paper just below the empty space where she was meant to sign. Marion lowered the quill. "Who used to occupy my chamber? Was there another bloodmaid before me?"

The House Mother's expression remained reticent. "There was one."

"What happened to her?"

"Her tenure ended," said the House Mother in the clipped way that people do when they're closing a topic of discussion. "That's precisely why I'm so happy to have you. I think you're quite special, and I know Lisavet feels the same. We share in our confidence that— with time and proper tutelage—you will become a fine bloodmaid someday. But it's not enough that we choose you. You must now choose us." The House Mother again motioned to the contract lying on the table between them. "If you will?"

Marion lowered the quill to the contract again, even as some timid instinct told her not to sign it. She wasn't sure what girl had come before her, but she was certain of this: Whoever she was had not been as strong or resilient as she. Marion had survived on the streets of Prane for years with no one but Raul to rely on, and he had become more a burden than a help. She had scrabbled and struggled for every penny, every crumb.

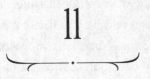

11

*My mother once told me beautiful was the worst thing
a girl could be. I'm now inclined to believe her.*

—MINA, BLOODMAID OF THE HOUSE OF HUNGER

AS YOU LIKELY KNOW, there are twenty-seven noble Houses of the
North," said Tutor Geoffrey, a lithe and wiry man with small
spectacles that glinted sharply in the sunlight. He gestured to the
map tacked to the chalkboard, outlining the Houses and their respective lands. Among them, Houses that were familiar to Marion—
the House of Hunger, of course, as well as the formidable House
of Fog and the House of Mirrors. As well as quite a few smaller
Houses that she wasn't familiar with, like the House of Doves or
the House of Brambles.

Marion made a valiant attempt to write down all of these names
in the thin, leather-bound notebook that she'd been given, along
with other supplies including personalized stationery and a wax seal
with the flourished letters of *M* for Marion and *H* for Hunger inter-
twined, a pale goose-feather quill and ink pot, and several thick,
leather-bound tomes she was expected to read as part of her studies.
But Marion found it difficult to focus.

It was Marion's second day at the House of Hunger. The gray morning had dawned into a bright and brilliant afternoon, rare for the North in that time of year. But the fine weather was wasted on Marion, who had been relegated to the library on the second floor of the House, a sprawling space that housed thousands of moth-chewed tomes and smelled, rather strongly, of horse glue and mold. Her tutor, a Mr. Geoffrey Harks, had spent the past hour dutifully outlining her future studies, which were to include the long, and at times violent, history of the northern Houses and their respective bloodmaids.

But Marion's attention was elsewhere. From her desk she had a good view of the window and the gardens beyond it where the other bloodmaids were taking tea. Marion couldn't help but feel that the girls looked like porcelain dolls that had come to life as they laughed and chatted, nibbled on the scalloped edges of shortbread cookies, ate finger sandwiches, and sipped exotic teas from cups so delicate they looked like they'd shatter at the lightest touch. Even Cecelia looked uncharacteristically cheerful, smiling coyly beneath the shadow of her straw hat. Behind the girls, the ocean rolled and swelled, the hungry, white-capped waves licking at the cliffs.

"Miss Marion?"

She snapped to attention, pulling her eyes from the window. "Yes?"

"Do stay focused. You will never count yourself among their ranks if you fail to do so. Irene, Cecelia, the twins—all of them are my former pupils. All of them devoted themselves to the arduous task of their studies. Contrary to popular belief, most bloodmaids are created, not born. The process of that creation can be . . . rather laborious, I'll admit, but there is no other way. You won't be called to court until your preliminary studies with myself and Madame Boucherie are complete. In light of that, it would be wise to fully devote yourself to your education."

"I understand," said Marion, and she felt a little ashamed for letting her attention slip. Here was a scholar who had devoted the bulk of his life to the study of the northern Houses—their cultures and histories, triumphs and downfalls. A man who had studied in the best libraries and colleges in the world. And here he was, lowering himself to lecture a girl from the slums of Prane.

The tutor offered her a curt smile and turned back to the chalkboard and wrote the names of four Houses: the House of Hunger, the House of Locusts, the House of Fog, and the House of Mirrors. "These are the principal Houses of the North. They are the oldest, the most powerful Houses. All of the other Houses, lower Houses, we call them, were born of these sacred four."

"How did the other Houses form?" Marion asked, in an effort to seem interested. She hadn't thought to ask any questions before then.

This seemed to cheer her tutor, who smiled widely, even stumbled over his words in his haste to explain further. "Well, some Houses fractured in schism. Others were traded and divided in wars and skirmishes. Occasionally a line of succession was disputed, two brothers each made a claim to the House, and the resulting tug-of-war caused a division. In rare cases, the illegitimate offspring of a bloodmaid has resulted in the fracturing of a House, wherein a distant but legitimate relative of the heir is contested by the love child of that heir and their bloodmaid. Such was the case here, when Lisavet—the daughter of the Count of Hunger and his bloodmaid Vanessa—inherited the House of Hunger after his death."

"I didn't know such a thing was possible," said Marion, still stunned that Lisavet was the daughter of a *bloodmaid*. As far as she knew, the highest rank a bloodmaid or her offspring could ascend to was retirement in a villa with a hefty pension. But to give birth to titled children, to become part of an aristocratic line of succession? That was unfathomable.

"I've found that a bloodmaid's potential is . . . near limitless should she fully devote herself to the rigors of her station. Those who are truly called to bleed may find themselves in the very seat of power, if they know how to claim it." The tutor paused for a moment before returning to his writings on the board. "Through the centuries of feuding and blood war, the four principal Houses have remained at the seat of the North's power. But in recent years, alliances among the lesser Houses—who have enriched themselves through investing in the industries of the South, have greatly diminished the power of the four principal Houses."

Outside, Marion could hear the bloodmaids erupting into fits of laughter. She risked a glance out the window and saw Evie, in a wide-brimmed straw hat, running around the table after Theodore, who looked utterly terrified.

"As you can likely imagine, these four Houses jockey for power. They are rivals, not allies, and alliances between them are fickle and prone to breaking. The Houses that fall beneath them operate as chess pieces on a playing board. You could think of this as . . . a war without a battlefield."

"Who's allied now?"

"For the past forty years, the House of Hunger has allied itself with the House of Fog. In turn, the House of Locusts has allied itself with the House of Mirrors. This has forced the North into something of a reluctant stalemate, though I doubt peace will hold."

Marion's quill stalled above her notebook. She'd been scrambling to keep up, scribbling down notes as fast as she was able in a vain attempt to remember everything. But in truth, she found the study of such things to be rather pointless. She'd never been able to understand why people who had so much fought over so little. What was the point of war when everyone had full bellies and more money than they could ever spend? What more could they possibly want?

As far as Marion was concerned, they were simply too rich and too bored and looking for violent ways to pass the years.

"The North has always been volatile," said Tutor Geoffrey, speaking quickly now that his allotted lecture time was very nearly over. "There's talk of alliances between the principal Houses being dissolved should the Countess take a husband. One can only imagine the strength of such a marital alliance. And I do wonder if it might be enough to rewrite the trade routes that are causing contention amid all of this talk of tariff war—"

"Will she?" Marion asked, rather sharply, frozen in her chair.

Tutor Geoffrey, who had already proceeded to the next topic of discussion, turned from his writings on the chalkboard. "Will she what?"

"Take a husband? Will Lisavet ever marry?"

The tutor considered the question for a long time in silence. Then he turned back to the chalkboard and wiped his writings clean with the cloth on its sill, signaling that their lesson was over. "No . . . I don't think that she will."

———————— ◆ ————————

AFTER COMPLETING HER LESSON WITH TUTOR GEOFFREY, MARION crossed the House (a trek that took her the better part of ten minutes) until she reached the parlor of Madame Boucherie. The study of etiquette, as it turned out, involved far more than table manners. Upon entering the dim, smoke-filled parlor, she saw a figure sitting in an armchair at the center of the room, back to the door, facing the hearth, which had no fire roaring in it. The curtains were drawn shut over the window, and what little light leaked through them was bluish through the cast of the smoke.

"Come here, girl."

Marion crossed the room and came to stand before the woman.

She was small, barely bigger than Mae, and wrinkled with raw, bloodshot eyes. Her hair was a silvery blond, plaited back, with several limp curls hanging from the nape of her neck. In her hand she held a small leather riding crop. She dressed in mourning black. On the table to her left, a cigarette smoldered in the detritus of an overflowing ashtray. She plucked it from the ashes and inhaled. "What's your name?"

"Marion."

"*Ma-ri-on*," said the woman, splitting the syllables as if her name were a tea biscuit she was snapping into little pieces. She examined Marion, top to toe. Her thin upper lip peeled away from her smoke-stained teeth in disgust. "Give me your hand."

Marion extended the same hand Raul had crushed in the door, thinking that the woman wanted to inspect it, as Lisavet had.

"Palm up."

Marion obeyed.

In a sharp movement, Madame Boucherie raised her crop and brought it down in the soft of Marion's palm with a smarting *snap*.

Stinging tears leaped to Marion's eyes. Her hand had been healing well, but it was still bruised and tender.

"You will curtsy when you make the acquaintance of a new peer. Let the pain make you remember."

"Yes, Madame."

"Extend your hand again."

Marion unfurled her fingers, extended her stinging palm.

"Curtsy."

Marion stole her hand back and bobbed into a graceless curtsy.

"Your hand. You will keep it extended to me, palm up, through the duration of this lesson until I tell you to lower it."

Marion extended it and Madame Boucherie struck her with the switch again.

"Why do you keep striking me?" Marion demanded through clenched teeth, rubbing her palm.

"What we are made to feel we are made to remember. And there is no feeling as memorable as pain. Now *give* me your hand."

Marion reluctantly obeyed and squeezed her eyes shut in wait of another strike. But it didn't come.

"Curtsy again. More deeply this time."

Marion did as she was told, bending her knees, dropping low to the ground, taking care to keep her hand extended, palm up, just as Madame Boucherie asked her to, so that she crouched at eye level with the little woman.

When she rose again, Madame Boucherie seemed satisfied. She didn't raise the switch again. "What is your name?"

"Marion Shaw."

Madame Boucherie struck her palm for a third time. "That is no longer your name. You are Marion of the House of Hunger now, are you not?"

"Yes." She cut the word through gritted teeth. She had the sudden urge to kick the legs out from under the chair Madame Boucherie sat in.

"How old are you, Marion of the House of Hunger?"

"Twenty."

"A bloodmaid never reveals her age," she scolded, and moved to strike Marion with her crop again. But this time Marion snatched her hand away.

"I don't like this game," she said, rubbing the red welt now swelling in the center of her palm. "And I don't want to play it anymore."

"Pain is not a game," said the woman, but she lowered her crop. "My name is Madame Boucherie. I've been tasked with the grave responsibility of breaking you into the kind of bloodmaid who is worthy of this House. Shall we begin?"

What followed was a rigorous inquisition, wherein Madame Boucherie circled her making demands ("Sing me a song you learned as a child" or "Show me the steps of your favorite dance") and asking questions ("Do you know how to play the game of rummy?" or "Have you ever been touched by a man?") and inflicting the switch whenever she deemed Marion's conduct unsatisfactory . . . which was often. What this painful inquisition had to do with etiquette, Marion could not say, but she knew better than to question the woman.

Hours later, by the time the lesson was over, the swollen welt in the middle of Marion's palm was throbbing terribly. It was enough to make her hate the little pinch-faced woman, almost as much as she had Lady Gertrude.

"Enough," said Madame Boucherie, lowering her switch for a final time. "If you have the thinnest hope of becoming a bloodmaid worthy of this House, I do hope you'll perform better in the future than you have done today."

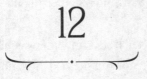

12

It's a strange thing to go from the hungry . . . to the hungered for.

—VANESSA, FIRST BLOODMAID OF THE HOUSE OF HUNGER

DINNER AT THE HOUSE of Hunger was something of a theatrical affair. Marion had to change her clothes before sitting down to dine at the bloodmaids' table with the other girls. The bloodmaids' dining room was directly below their private apartments. It was a red-walled, octagonal room, with a wide, circular table at its center. Across from the entryway was a hearth—fed with logs and burning bright—with a glass-eyed stag head hanging above its mantel.

The table was set for eight, and each place setting included an extensive array of strange cutlery—two-tined forks, a pair of scissors, stubby spoons that rather looked like seashells, long silver picks, daggerlike knives, and other odd utensils that Marion didn't know what to do with. Madame Boucherie was right. If she was to become a proper bloodmaid—of the variety that mastered the northern art of etiquette and poise—she would require rigorous tutelage.

Marion was the first bloodmaid to arrive, promptly at seven o'clock as instructed by the House Mother, and the others trickled in after her. First Mae, accompanied by her governess, then Evie—who entered reading a book—with Irene trailing after her, looking a little sallow, as if her morning bloodletting had taken more than she had to give.

Elize followed after Irene, and she was taller than Marion expected when standing up, and she had Theodore with her. The poor cat looked so limp and dead-eyed that for a moment, Marion thought he *was* dead. Upon sitting down, Elize released the poor creature and he scuttled to the far corner of the dining room, into the shadows beneath the china cabinet, where he remained for the duration of their meal.

The House Mother soon followed, and Marion was surprised to see her, for she hadn't known that she would take dinner with them. She would've expected that, given the House Mother's emphasis on the importance of observing protocol, she would've been the first to enter the room. Still, she made no pardons for or mentions of her lateness. Instead, she settled herself at the largest chair at the table, then smiled at those assembled there. "Shall we?"

At that, four footmen entered the dining room, each of them balancing a large pewter tray on his shoulder, weighted with all manner of plates and dishes, which they carefully arranged on the table.

In Prane, fine meals were taken in courses, one after the other. First there was wine and drink, then soup, followed by bread, the main course, and then perhaps dessert after that. But in the House of Hunger things were different. All courses were presented at once, every dish displayed on the table at the onset of the meal, with no detectable order on how they should be consumed.

Some of the bloodmaids began their meal with bowls of chocolate mousse; others sucked meaty oysters out of their shells, or devoured the little brown mushroom caps that oozed a bloody crimson juice when pricked with a pick. Evie ate straight from a tin of caviar, scooping up the eggs with a golden spoon. Mae was in the process of dissecting a tiered slice of cake, separating fruit from cream, and cake from icing, arranging each of the layers into their respective groups on her plate.

Marion opted for the things that looked most familiar to her—which included the roasted salmon, wine, steamed clams, and rosemary rolls. She avoided the snails that Evie slurped from their shells, but helped herself to a large portion of what she took for dessert—a dense cube of vanilla cake, dusted with powdered mace and crowned with blackberries and dollops of sweet cream that melted like butter on the tongue.

As the bloodmaids dined, they gossiped between bites and sips of wine. Talking over each other, and often holding several conversations at once, they traded rumors about the different nobles and their Houses, making their predictions for the night.

"Does Lisavet ever join you for dinner?" Marion asked, struggling to spoon the last of the marrow from what she thought was a half-hollowed veal femur, though it was rather large. Her right hand stung with the effort, still sore from the bite of Madame Boucherie's leather crop and the injury that Raul had so cruelly inflicted too.

At her question, the table grew uncomfortably quiet. Irene turned her eyes down to the table, and even Evie seemed to settle some, sipping her wine without bothering to offer an answer.

"Bloodmaids are never called to Lisavet's table," said someone from the entryway, and the whole table turned to see Cecelia, the favorite, standing there. "The only exceptions are the rare bloodmaids who rise above their station and become something more."

If Cecelia could have been described as beautiful—sitting perched on Lisavet's knee the night of Marion's arrival—she was ravishing now, in a way that was almost grotesque. She wore nothing but a short velvet night robe and a pair of white stockings held in place by frilled garters. Her hair was half-pinned atop her head in a fallen nest of day-old rag curls. As she neared, Marion saw that she had wide-set eyes, one hazel, the other brown. Her lips were much fuller than Marion's, her cheekbones higher, her jaw enviably sharp. Marion noted that the girl's arms and thighs were riddled with red-crescent bite marks. She wore these with no small measure of pride, a testament to her esteemed position as Lisavet's most coveted bloodmaid.

As Cecelia settled into the empty seat across the table, Marion scented what smelled like brandy on the air. With no deference for etiquette, the girl began to sort through the contents of the table, muttering as she helped herself to bite-size servings of each of the dishes. She sucked an oyster out of its shell, wrinkled her nose, and spit a small pearl onto her plate. "Tell me, Marion, what's Prane like? I've never visited before."

Marion thought of swirling smog and maudlum smoke, of Agnes with her cigarettes and stolen matches, of Raul on the floor, bleeding and pleading for her to stay. The way she'd stepped over him as if he were nothing at all. "It was . . . terrible enough to make me want to leave without a second thought."

Her answer wasn't entirely honest—she had struggled with her decision to go, albeit briefly—but Marion figured it was true enough to get her point across. Prane, and the miserable life she'd led in it, was dead to her now. Part of a past she was more than ready to put to rest.

"But are you not afraid to bleed?" Cecelia inquired, toying with the pearl on her plate, rolling it back and forth through a bloody puddle of wine sauce. "The life of a bloodmaid isn't as easy as one might think it is. Bleeding takes its toll after a while. One could even call it terrible, at times."

"Maybe. But bleeding here is better than dying in the slums."

"How could you possibly know that when you've never died before?" Cecelia asked, and Marion wasn't sure if it was meant to be a slight or an insult.

"One doesn't have to die to know that the experience is less than ideal."

Cecelia set down her fork, braced her elbows against the table, and leaned forward, so close to the candelabra that she nearly set her curls alight. When she spoke, spitting words across the table, she blew out several of the flames. "You know, I should quite like to have a taste of you, as Lisavet did. Just to know what it is she saw in you when she partook."

"If you're so curious, I'd be happy to oblige you," Marion quipped, and she extended her arm across the table, between the burning candles, feeling the heat of their flames on her wrist. "Would you like a taste?"

"Speaking of Lisavet," said Irene, in an obvious attempt to change the subject, "who will attend her tonight?"

The House Mother delicately dabbed the edges of her mouth with her napkin. If she seemed perturbed by the heated exchange—or Marion's flagrant, if sarcastic, offer to break one of the House's most important rules—she gave no indication. If anything, she looked a little bored. "Only two of you tonight. Cecelia . . ."

The favorite flashed a knowing smile.

"And Marion."

This was as much a shock to the rest of the table as it was to Marion. While she was less than well versed in the protocols of the bloodmaids, she knew that there was supposed to be—at minimum—a few weeks' tutelage before a bloodmaid was invited to the court of her mistress in any formal capacity. Marion had only been at the House of Hunger for a single night and had not even been called to the kitchens to bleed yet. So to be thrown into Lisavet's court—still untrained and ignorant of the statutes of courtly etiquette—was not only a shock to her peers . . . but an *insult*. And they received it as such—with frowns and silence.

But Cecelia seemed to receive this news with the most contempt. Her mouth twitched and her eyes seemed touched with fire as she scowled across the table at Marion. But then the moment passed, all traces of anger left her, and she offered her a drunken smile. "So we have a little prodigy among us."

"You will take care of her?" the House Mother inquired. It was clear to Marion that her jurisdiction, if not her authority, ended with Cecelia. Lisavet's favor placed her well beyond the confines of the strict protocols the younger, less favored bloodmaids were made to observe. "Show her the ways of the court?"

Cecelia—sullen and silent—made no promises. She plucked the pearl from her plate, licked it clean, slipped it into the pocket of her robe, and left the dining room without a parting word.

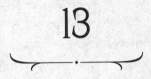

13

Favor is hard won and harder kept.

—JESSAMINE, BLOODMAID OF THE HOUSE OF FOG

SHORTLY AFTER CECELIA'S ABRUPT departure, Marion was escorted from the bloodmaids' dining room and led into the dressing chambers. The room was windowless and composed almost entirely of cedar; its walls and wardrobes were crowded to capacity. Standing among racks and mannequins were two attendants, their arms burdened with heavy gowns of velvet and brocade, all of them black, white, or red, like every other dress in the room. Such was the protocol for bloodmaids, whose attire, while diverse in style and cut, was limited to those three colors.

Neither of the women—who were both pale-skinned northerners old enough to be Marion's mother—said anything as they moved about the room, selecting different dresses from wardrobes or off their hanging racks, even stripping the mannequins bare. They were quick, and in a matter of minutes they made their final selections— a black velvet dress with a structured bodice and thick pearl choker, comprising many strands.

Another servant appeared and did what little she could to wrestle Marion's curls into something resembling submission: pinning up one strand, letting another fall loose, in a style that was fashionable in the North but in the South was typically reserved for the women who haunted street corners at night in search of fast coin. When her hair was set, they powdered her face lightly and blushed her cheeks with a lurid cream rouge that looked like something you'd expect to find on an artist's palette. She caught a glimpse of her reflection in the mirror of a nearby vanity and thought she looked like a porcelain doll that had seen better days.

Once dressed, Marion was whisked back to the bloodmaids' parlor, where she found her peers assembled around the hearth—Evie, Elize, and her faithful cat, Theodore, huddled nearby. Beside the twins, Irene cradled Mae in her lap.

"Any parting words of wisdom?" Marion asked, in a poor attempt to break the silence. She was more nervous than she had perhaps ever been. Her palms were sweaty. Her bodice was fastened far too tight. Her stomach was churning with the half-digested remnants of her dinner. She felt ready to vomit and wished she hadn't eaten so much.

"If Sir Ivor is in the galleries tonight, stay well clear of him," said Evie. "He's an ambassador from the House of Fog and he's about as charming as he is handsome. But he's got a coy and nasty way about him. Once trapped in one of his games, only Lisavet can free you from its fetters."

Irene nodded, shifting Mae in her lap. "Let no man touch you. Most wouldn't dare to lay a hand on you sober, but drink makes fools of the wisest men, Sir Ivor included, and if your honor is tarnished— even if it's against your will—you'll be immediately dismissed."

Mae leaned across Elize's lap, collected her cat, and held him against her chest even as the poor creature squirmed and struggled, even hissed once, halfheartedly. When his claws tore her arms bloody, the little girl, seemingly impervious to the pain, didn't even flinch.

"Why doesn't she speak?" Marion asked, and it was only when Mae's eyes darted toward her that she realized it was rude of her to ask the question in front of the child. Just because she could not, or did not, speak didn't mean that she couldn't understand.

Irene shifted a protective arm around the child's shoulders, as if to shield her from Marion's speculation. "They say she endured terrible things in the place—"

"The whorehouse," Evie rudely interjected.

"Where Lisavet found her," Irene finished as though the interruption hadn't happened, and drew Mae even closer. Theodore wiggled out of the child's arms and sulked beneath a nearby table. Mae stared at him, unblinking, but the faintest furrow formed between her pale brows.

"I thought she was the bastard of someone highborn?" said Marion, staring at the poor child.

"She was," said Evie. "But her mother was a bloodmaid who fell from grace and turned up in a brothel in Prane."

"Marion." The girls turned in unison to see the House Mother standing in the threshold of the parlor. Marion had no idea how she moved through the halls with such silence. It seemed impossible that her heeled boots made no echoes when they struck the marble floors. Marion wondered how long she'd been standing there, listening unnoticed. For some reason their conversation about Mae seemed private, like something she shouldn't have been privy to. "It's time."

AS IT TURNED OUT, MARION'S ARRIVAL IN THE COURT WAS NO grand event. By the time she arrived, the night was long under way, and those who did acknowledge her did so with drunken smiles and roving glances from behind fans or cupped hands, eyeing her with something close to suspicion as she shouldered her way through the thick of the crowds to an empty corner of the room.

There, she took her time to survey the scene at hand. This gathering seemed more intimate than that of the previous night. The music was softer, the chatter less lively, the mood of the night subdued. Marion caught no sign of Lisavet, or her favorite, Cecelia. In fact, she spotted not a single familiar face in the crowds. No one that she recognized from her previous venture into the court, though—upon reflection—she realized that her memory of that night was already growing blurry at the edges, taking on the way of a dream.

Her memories of Prane, too, seemed badly faded. As if that life were years behind her. She found it strange how quickly she'd relinquished the trappings of who she was before to become . . . what, exactly? A street rat disguised as a doll? A murderer feigning innocence? An impersonator of the highest degree. She wondered: How long would this little ruse of hers be allowed to continue? Surely someday they would see her for the sham that she was.

The sound of a violin dragged her from the trance of her thoughts. It was a sweet keening song that brought to mind waltzing and slow minuets. Turning, Marion followed the sound of the chords down a nearby corridor and up the stairwell it led to, climbing to the upper floors of the House. There, she entered into a wide windowed gallery, the drapes drawn away from the panes so as to give a view of the House's sprawling labyrinth and the rolling moors beyond them.

The scene before her was almost staggering in its beauty, more so than any painting she'd ever seen. The grass-furred hills rolled out to greet the ocean's ether, and the moon hung so low its edge seemed to kiss the surface of the waters. There was nothing but the horizon in the distance—no city lights or buildings lit the ragged sliver of coastline across the marsh. The stark sky was riddled with stars. In

Prane, the smog was so thick that on most nights she could barely catch a glimpse of the moon. She remembered when Raul had first told her that behind the seething pall there were countless stars, and worlds like theirs circling them, and she'd called him a liar.

If only he were alive to see this. He should've been, could've been if Marion had not killed him. The grief hit her in a great wave then. Her knees buckled and she caught herself on the windowsill a moment before she hit the floor. She mourned for Raul and who he might've been if she'd sold herself to the North only a few years earlier.

Marion might have stood there all night—moored down by guilt and grief—but a shadow moved at the edge of her eye. A man, one she'd taken as a statue upon first entering the hall, for he stood so still it seemed he was hewn from stone. As he stepped into the glow of the moonlight, she saw that he was dressed as a jester. He wore clothes of gray and silver, and stockings up to his knees that were tucked into puffy pants with frilled lace hems.

His breast coat was embroidered with silver thread that, even in the wan light of the moon, glistened brilliantly. His face was painted the same ghost white. His eyes were lined in black (but filled with red) and his lips were painted dark, too, the edges tipped up into a coy smile that his eyes didn't mirror.

Marion took a step back, and the jester faltered in his approach, raising two white-gloved hands as if in surrender. Then he bowed, snatching his cap from his head with the motion, only to plant it back on his head as he righted himself again.

"Hello to you too," said Marion, unsure whether she could trust the strange creature before her. She had never met a jester before.

The jester did not seem aware of her hesitance, or perhaps he did not care. He drew near and walked around her in a little circle, just close enough that she could catch the scent of him—fine cologne and musk in equal measure.

"Aren't you a curious creature?" said Marion.

This pleased the jester, and he did a little jig, kicking up his heels and dancing a circle, his head snapping so as to spot himself as he twirled. He was entertaining, Marion had to give him that, but there was something sinister in his manner, and his silence, that she didn't entirely like . . . or perhaps more aptly, didn't entirely *trust*.

"Don't you have lords to entertain?" she inquired. "Or are you intent upon haunting me all night?"

The jester didn't answer. He cocked his head to the side.

"Don't you speak?"

He shook his head. He smiled and his jaw broke open with an ugly *crack* that sounded much like a bone breaking. Marion stared, revolted. While his teeth were almost uncomfortably pristine, as if cut from marble or porcelain, the floor of his mouth was empty, save for a mangled nub where his tongue ought to have been.

Marion staggered back, and the jester snapped his mouth shut again. A door opened down the hall, and two drunken, hungry-looking nobles staggered into view, laughing and wild-eyed. The jester gave Marion a little shove down the hall, away from the new-comers, and then with a quick little jig he started toward the men, who laughed and pointed at his approach, too distracted to notice Marion as she slipped past another door and into the corridor that followed it.

Alone, Marion started down the corridor. Here, the halls were darker and the music quieter. The parlors there were occupied by throngs of nobles, their lips slick with blood wine, their eyes glassy. One woman snuffed powder off the back of her hand. Several others held maudlum pipes, and the air was thick and reeking with the smoke they spewed.

There were various couples of three and four, even five, en-twined together in a passionate lovers' embrace—kissing and grasping at each other with a kind of fervor typically reserved for more private settings. But these nobles had no shame. They lay—some near naked—in various stages of undress, uninhibited by the conventions of modesty, or the burden of shame.

And Marion could not help but envy them all. For in the heat of their lust and yearning they seemed to possess a freedom, or perhaps more aptly an innocence she did not. In fact, as she moved through the room, *she* felt strange for being the only one fully clothed, with her stockings held in place by garters under the weight of her skirts, her hair only half unbound. She did her best to move through the crowd as quickly as she could, dodging gazes and outstretched hands and the attention of the lords who were just sober enough to register her arrival.

But when she was halfway across the parlor, someone called out to her. "Well, if it isn't the angel from Prane."

Marion turned to see Thiago sitting in a secluded alcove, nursing a glass of what appeared to be brandy. He motioned Marion closer, shifting to make room for her on the chaise where he sat.

"I thought you'd already left," said Marion, sitting down beside him.

Thiago shook his head. "I like to make the most of my time here. There is so much to see and eat and drink." He took a pointed swallow of his brandy, then passed the cup to Marion.

She took an obligatory sip, more to appease him than for the taste of it. To her relief, the brandy didn't taste of blood, but it was cold and bitter and it burned the back of her throat when she swallowed.

Marion turned her gaze to the salon. Most of the nobles seemed pleasantly and thoroughly drunk. The women gossiped in loud whispers behind the cover of their fans. At little card tables at the corners of the room, stoic noblemen casually gambled away sums that equated to what would have been a lifetime of Marion's previous earnings in Prane.

"Is it everything you dreamed it would be?" Thiago asked, studying her above the rim of his glass. "The life of a bloodmaid?"

"It's more," said Marion. "So much more."

Thiago raised his glass to her, a wide smile on his face. "To bleeding well."

Marion raised an imaginary glass of her own. "Hear, hear."

There was silence between them then, and Marion let her gaze drift about the room. She could barely believe what was before her eyes now. How had she, a girl born in the gutters of Prane, ascended into this? She felt as though she'd stolen the life of someone else.

"When do you travel south again?" Marion asked, turning back to Thiago. He had a wistful, distant look in his eyes . . . one that made it seem as though his soul had come half-untethered from his bones.

When he spoke, there was several moments' delay. "Tomorrow, I take the night train to Brackton. From there I'll find my way through the wilds until I find something worth hauling north."

"Something like a bloodmaid of exceptional taste?"

"Yes," said Thiago. "Something like that."

The Taster stood then, stretching his limbs, his breast coat pulling tight across his shoulders. Marion had always thought him tall, but with the other nobles of the court lurking about, he seemed small . . . frail even. "Do mind yourself in these halls, Marion. In some ways, this world is just as cruel as the one you left behind."

It was an odd thing to say, given the place whence she came. She couldn't think of a place more brutal, more ugly, than Prane. But Thiago lurked there, seemingly in wait of an answer, some confirmation that she would heed his warning.

And she gave him that, with a small nod.

Thiago offered her a wavering smile, and she swore she read guilt in his eyes, though it was hard to parse the truth of his expression. He gave her a small bow, folding at the waist, and departed without saying goodbye.

After her encounter with Thiago, Marion watched the nobles of the court glut themselves on each other in the throes of their passion in a grotesque amalgamation of tangled limbs, wet mouths, and grasping fingers. In the midst of this . . . *display*, no one belonged to anyone. Even as a simple onlooker, Marion began to feel like she didn't belong to herself. Amid this feast of flesh, there was no singularity or distinction between bodies or the spirits they harbored. They were all made one by . . . hunger. That was the word for it.

By the time the parlor had emptied of lovers, Marion felt drunk to the point of dizziness, though she'd only had a glass or two of wine. Her vision—fuzzy at the edges—seemed to double and triple. And everything before her eyes took on the warm overtones of nostalgia, as though she were reliving a memory, or wading through the tepid murk of a dream. She began to wonder if that brandy had been blood-laced after all.

"Well, well."

Marion raised her gaze to see a tall, thin man standing before her. He was young and handsome, almost excessively so. His eyes were the blue of deep water, and they held a kind of boyish malice in them. He was finely dressed, in polished riding boots and a gray brocade vest, unbuttoned, to reveal his pale, bare chest, moist with sweat. His pants were only half-buttoned, and Marion recalled that he'd been one of the enthusiastic participants in the tryst that had occurred just after Thiago's departure. At the time, it had been hard to distinguish one body from the next, but she thought she remembered seeing the auburn head of a lady bobbing between his thighs. "You must be the new blood. Remind me, what's your name?"

"Marion," she said, and then, remembering her earlier lesson with Madame Boucherie, she hastily added, "of the House of Hunger."

He bowed deeply. "I'm Sir Ivor of the House of Fog, here as an ambassador."

Sir Ivor. She remembered that name. He was the man the other bloodmaids had warned her about. "It's a pleasure to make your acquaintance," Marion said, though it was the opposite of what she felt. But given Irene's warning about Ivor, she thought it better to tread carefully.

Sir Ivor peeled his gaze away from her and half turned to face the rest of the court, stragglers from the orgy and other nobles who'd gathered there. "How shall we entertain ourselves in the absence of our beloved Countess?"

"Will she not appear in court tonight?" a woman inquired, seeming anxious at the thought.

"I'm afraid she's taken ill . . . *again*," said Ivor, with no small amount of relish.

"We could drink to her good health," slurred a man, and he raised a teacup filled with rum, the drink sloshing over the edges and spattering the carpet. He drained it in a single swallow.

"We've done that already," said Ivor.

"We could gamble?" said the woman.

"I'm in no mood for cards," said Ivor, waving her off, a maestro conducting the symphony of the court. "Perhaps . . . a game of fox and hound to pass the remnants of the night?"

At his suggestion, a chorus of agreement. Noblewomen clapped their hands and lords exchanged knowing grins, rousing themselves from the stupor of their drunkenness in anticipation of the game.

"But who shall be our little fox?" said Sir Ivor, with theatrical puzzlement. He turned to Marion and feigned surprise as if in the span of a few moments he'd forgotten she was there. "Perhaps our newcomer to the court?"

Marion felt eyes, many eyes, on her. She squirmed uncomfortably beneath the weight of her skirts. Her palms went sweaty, her mouth dry. "I-I could hardly—"

"Do you know the rules of the game? You're the little fox, running through the wilds of this House. And we"—he motioned to the rest of the court, who looked on with hunger in their eyes—"we are the hounds in pursuit of you. We'll count to twenty, give you a chance to gather your skirts and run. And when the counting is done, we'll hunt you down. Shall we begin, little fox?"

"But I . . ." She stared at the expectant gazes of those in the court. There were a good eleven of them at least, all watching in wait of her answer. Despite the warnings of the other bloodmaids, she didn't want to disappoint them all, make a poor impression on her first night at court. Besides, she had never been one to turn down a game. "Perhaps just one round."

"Lovely," said Sir Ivor, and his mouth split, gashing open into an awful, toothy grin. "Let's begin. On my count. One . . ."

Marion rose to her feet, unsteadily, still a little tipsy. With a rush of exhilaration, she gathered her skirts and staggered into a nearby deserted parlor, through a series of empty wards. She could hear Sir Ivor's count echoing behind her, "Six . . ."

Marion broke into a full run, picked a doorway at random, and ran through it, into and then down a narrow hall that might've been a servants' passage. The thrill of the chase thrummed through her, and the clouds of her drunkenness parted, and she felt quick and deliriously, *deliciously* alive. The last time she'd felt this way she'd been a child, running away from the constable with a fat coin purse clutched in her hand—the spoils of a hard day of thieving—eager to show Raul. But Raul was not waiting for her here, and those who pursued her were far more light-footed than any constable she had ever encountered.

As Marion crossed into what she thought was an empty parlor, a woman in a heavy gown the bloody color of crushed mulberries lunged at her from behind a half-closed door. Marion managed to avoid her clawing grasp by mere inches and tripped over her own dress—ripping its hem—in her haste to escape.

The woman who pursued her was perhaps forty, with blond hair laced with gray hanging in limp curls about her bony shoulders. The woman staggered toward Marion, pins dropping from her half-fallen hair and skittering across the floor. She was smiling, rouge smeared across her mouth, melting down her chin. Her breasts threatened to spill from her bodice as she lurched after Marion, crying all the while, "I've found her! I've found the little fox! She's in the Sunset Salon."

There was a chorus of shouts and howls, barking, and the clamor of footsteps. The sound of her name began to echo through the House, seemingly from all directions. *"Marion! Marion! Come out wherever you are! The hounds would like to play . . ."*

Marion gathered fresh fistfuls of her skirts, hoisting them high above her calves, and began to run again, faster this time, though she was beginning to pant from the labor of her efforts. The years breathing the thick and noxious smog of Prane's slums had taken their toll; just a brief sprint was enough to leave her breathless and gasping for air.

Her pace slackened, and she could hear the yelling of the hounds in hot pursuit behind her. The evening took on the feel of a nightmare as she raced alone through the halls, pursued by the hounds who seemed to be gaining on her rapidly no matter how fast she ran. She stopped to catch her breath in the gallery, ducking behind the statue of what appeared to be a bloodmaid with her wrist upturned, ready to bleed.

Suddenly, Ivor burst toward her from his hiding place behind a statue, caught her by the arm, and wrenched her. "I've snared the fox." His grip tightened and he leered at her, as if to steal a kiss.

"Let me *go!*" Marion directed a sharp kick to Ivor's knee and felt her heel connect with cartilage with a soft and nasty *crunch*. With a cry, Ivor shoved her, and Marion crashed into a nearby vase, which careened from its pedestal and shattered on the tile floor.

Sir Ivor, grasping at his injured knee, cut a laugh that rang down the corridor. "You little . . . *bitch*."

Marion began to run again, feeling close to tears as she listened to the jeering and the nasty shouts of her name, the sound of Sir Ivor's lurching footsteps as he half loped, half limped behind her in dogged pursuit. As Marion ran, she looked for familiar faces among the nobles in the parlors she passed—hoping to see Thiago, or perhaps one of the other bloodmaids, or the House Mother. Even a glimpse of Cecelia would've been a welcome sight—but she saw no one she recognized. Those who did spot her laughed or pointed or called for the hounds to come find her.

"Better run, little one," said an old man sitting by a dying fire. He was smiling and he had a thin cane in one hand, a pipe in the other that spit a dark smoke that smelled almost toxic. "Don't let the hounds sink their teeth into you."

Marion kept running, pausing only to take off her shoes, which had pinched her heels raw and bloody. She sprinted through galleries and salons, the narrow, winding labyrinths of servants' passages, and up several flights of stairs—until, breathless and panting, she reached a wing of the House that was near deserted. Here, she could hear no calls for her name, no wolf howls or the harsh cacophony of footsteps echoing behind her.

Unlike the ballrooms and crowded galleries she'd traversed before, these halls were entirely silent, save for the echo of her own footsteps. The doors were shut. Curtains were drawn over the windows and no fires burned in the hearths she passed. It was so cold her breath took shape on the air. She looked for an open window but saw none. Marion stopped running and tilted her head and looked up, stunned to see that the ceiling was nearly as high as that of a cathedral. The walls stretched up, into the dark, until they met a glass dome that offered a beautiful glimpse of the night sky, spangled with burning stars.

Down the long corridor ahead of her were two of the largest doors she had ever seen. They were beautiful, carved into the shape of two naked figures—one man and one woman. But they were hanging upside-down, their heads where their feet should be, their bodies suspended. The woman's hair seemed to defy gravity itself, flowing around her shoulders in loose tendrils.

Just then, on the other side of the door came the sound of glass breaking, followed by a sharp cry: "You would use me up and replace me. Is that it? A new girl comes and suddenly you have no taste for my blood?"

Someone said something sharp and low in quick retort. Then there was silence.

Marion retreated down the hall and into an adjacent chamber where she hoped she would not be seen. A moment later, the double doors heaved open with a bellowing groan and Cecelia, the favorite and First Bloodmaid, slipped out of the crack between them.

She was beautiful as ever, but disheveled. Her hair fell limp around her shoulders. She wore a nightdress that was so sheer you could see every detail and contour beneath its folds. The top was unlaced, as if to expose her even more, and she wore no robe so that her thin shoulders were bare to the biting cold. Around her neck, a thick black-ribbon choker was held shut with a silver clasp.

She was crying with a violence, snatching breaths in ragged

gasps, as she staggered barefoot into the hall. She barely made it more than two steps before she struck the floor and pressed a bloody hand to her mouth in a vain attempt to smother a scream.

Before Marion had the chance to decide whether she ought to reveal herself and help her or cower in the shadows in the hope of remaining unseen, Cecelia tossed her head back at an angle that looked nearly neck-snapping and laughed at the ceiling of glass. Laughed until she began to gag, retching up a mouthful of what might have been wine . . . or blood. At a distance, Marion couldn't tell. But the motion was so violent that the clasp on her velvet choker broke, and the ribbon fluttered to the floor. Down the hall, the double doors swung slowly shut.

Cecelia stopped dead and peered over her shoulder, and when she saw that no one was there, she pressed herself to her feet, sprang forward, and broke into a full run, dashing down the same hall whence Marion had come. She heard the howling of the hounds, then cries of disappointment when they realized it was Cecelia running toward them, not Marion.

Breathless and badly shaken, Marion slipped out of the shadows and picked up Cecelia's fallen choker. It was silken, and there were two words embroidered with crimson thread into the underside of the ribbon: *Wretched One.*

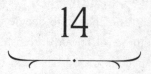

14

Of this I am utterly certain: I will never again know peace.

—VANESSA, FIRST BLOODMAID OF THE HOUSE OF HUNGER

THERE WAS THAT STRANGE word again: *wretched*. Marion didn't like the sound or feel of it in her mouth. She hated the way the brittle *tch* cracked harshly against the backs of the teeth: *wretch*.

It was a nasty little slur and Marion wondered at its origins. Was Cecelia the girl who'd carved it into the underside of her bed frame? And if so, did the word have some greater significance to her, beyond its usual definition? Was it meant to be some strange term of endearment? Or perhaps a warning? Even a threat?

Just then she heard a bout of howls, and footsteps that sounded dangerously close. Marion slipped the choker into the pocket of her skirt and dashed down the hall, through the doors Cecelia had fled through just moments before. Better to take her chances with Lisavet than remain there, in the shadows. As the doors groaned shut behind her, sickness formed in the pit of her belly, and she felt herself begin to shake. It was her first night at court and she'd already broken one of the House's most important protocols: Never go to Lisavet's chambers unsummoned. But with the hounds still hunting for her, she had no choice but to hide there until they went away. She could still hear them, see their shadows sliding along the floor on the other side of the door.

Marion held her breath, praying they'd leave the hall quickly. As she waited for them to disperse, she examined the room. Lisavet's private quarters looked like a cross between a parlor and a throne room. The ceilings vaulted high overhead, and there was an arrangement of tables and chairs gathered around a vast and roaring hearth that somehow, despite the violence of the flames, did little to light or warm the room.

The walls were hung with strange taxidermies: elk heads crowned with helms of antlers that were as large and sprawling as the branches of an oak tree, panther cats, wild boar, and peacocks with ample plumage. There were even a few insects and spiders hanging from the walls, pinned and framed in their glass displays. The corpses had been taxidermied so expertly that they were made to look alive again, as if any one of the poor creatures might stir from its slumber and attempt to move, only to discover that its feet had been tacked in place, nails pierced through the paws, hooves firmly affixed with resin. Marion had always found it odd that someone would go through the trouble of killing a creature only to make it look alive again. It seemed somehow perverse.

On the opposing wall was a carved door smaller than the two she'd just entered through. It was slightly ajar, offering a slivered glimpse of the bedroom beyond it. From those doors, a voice:

"Do come in."

Stunned, Marion stepped forward, nudged the door open with her foot, and entered the largest bedroom she'd ever seen. A chandelier that was taller than Marion hung from its vaulted ceilings on a long iron chain. The far wall of the room was composed entirely of stained-glass windows that overlooked the great sprawl of the ocean beyond them.

To the left was a bed big enough to accommodate at least half a dozen grown men comfortably. Its drapes were as dark as liquid onyx, and they hung from the ceiling and pooled around the mattress. Marion noted that the bed was in a state of total disarray. The sheets were tangled and bloodstained, the pillows gashed open as if attacked with a dagger. Feathers swirled through the air. One of the two nightstands that flanked the bed was overturned, the lamp that had been presumably standing on it shattered . . . leaking kerosene across the floor. A few paces away stood a vanity with a broken mirror, its table covered in a scattering of shattered glass.

A chill breeze swept in through one of the open windows, stirring the candles so that shadows flickered about the room. Here, it was nearly as cold as it was outside, and Marion's dress did little to warm her. There was no sign of the Countess, and apart from the black cat sleeping at the foot of the bed, nestled deep in the folds of a thick bearskin, there wasn't a single soul in that room. And yet . . . Marion had heard a voice. "Forgive the mess."

Unsure of what to do, Marion stood frozen at the threshold, and then a door opposite the bed groaned open, and in a cloud of steam, Lisavet emerged. She wore a long black robe, fur-lined at the collar, and her cropped hair was wet and raked back out of her eyes.

The Countess walked, barefoot and fresh from the baths, to the chair at Marion's side and stopped just short of her. "What brings you to my quarters unsummoned?"

"I-I was playing fox and hound and . . . I got lost. I didn't mean to come here, it's just that I didn't want the others to find me and I—"

"What others?"

"Sir Ivor . . . and his companions."

A dark look passed over Lisavet's face. While Marion was much

taller than most of the girls in Prane, Lisavet still towered a full head
and a half above her. And while Marion was no coward and had
never been one to back down out of fear or shame, there was something about Lisavet that immediately made her want to shrink into
the shadows, make herself small.

"I'm sorry. I didn't mean to come here."

Lisavet didn't scold her. She simply nodded toward the tea tray
sitting on a table by the bedroom door. On it were a small ruby-red
teacup, a steaming black-iron kettle, and a plate piled with fruit tarts
and frosted cakes. Half-folded in a pale cloth napkin was a long,
cruel-looking needle like the ones that the servants pierced girls with
in the bleeding room.

"Eat," said Lisavet, motioning to the cakes. "You're shaking."

Marion faltered, but Lisavet's gaze hung with her until she
leaned over, lifted one of the frosted cakes from the tray, and took a
bite. Then another. The cake was rich and thick and bitter, so delicious it didn't take Marion more than a few moments to finish it off.

Seemingly satisfied, the young Countess leaned over Marion to
pour herself a cup of tea. Then, with measured steps, she crossed the
room to the large desk beneath the open window. Among the rest of
the furnishings—which seemed overly ornate, almost frivolous in
their luxury—the sturdy oak desk, which was clearly built for practi-
cality, not for show, looked sorely out of place. Lisavet settled herself
on the stool in front of it and set her teacup on the edge of an open
map, next to a letter that began with the words . . . *It is my honor to
offer my hand in marriage.* The envelope beside it bore the wax seal
of the House of Umber. A few inches away, on a pewter tray, were a
razor and the skin of what appeared to be a small, brown field mouse,
a slit cut into its little belly, tufts of raw cotton bursting out of it.

Lisavet frowned at the proposal letter and drained her teacup
down to the dregs. She looked weary. Her eyes were shadowed with

bruiselike bags, and her shoulders—so thin they were gaunt—protruded through the velvet folds of her robe. She looked about as frail and fatigued as the starved factory girls Marion saw trudging home through the slums after their twelve-hour shifts. Marion wondered then about the true nature of her illness. It had to be quite grave, if she needed a constant supply of blood to keep her condition from worsening.

"I can bleed if you need me to," said Marion, turning back to the tea tray. She took the needle from the napkin it was sheathed in. "My blood may not be as sweet as that of the others, but . . ."

Lisavet stared at her, expressionless. But then something soft came to her eyes and Marion realized that the Countess was touched by her proposition. As if Marion were there, in the North, in her House for anything other than her blood. Lisavet faltered, then nodded.

Marion crossed the room, stopping just short of Lisavet, and extended her arm. She'd expected the Countess to bleed her into the empty teacup, but instead she lowered the needle to the fat vein in the crook of her elbow and pierced it quickly, driving the needle deep. The pain was sharp but short-lasting.

Lisavet leaned forward, holding Marion's arm with two hands: one at her wrist, the other at the elbow. Her lips hovered inches above the bleeding needle wound. "Do you mind?"

Marion, breathless, shook her head. "Not at all."

Lisavet opened her mouth, exposing her gold-capped canines. She arched over Marion's arm, covered the bleeding wound with her mouth, and began to lap up the blood. Her lips were warm and hot against Marion's skin; the tip of her tongue gently tested the wound, licking, then prodding just hard enough to cause a little pain. This time the Countess didn't bite her and, strangely, Marion wished she would've.

Watching Lisavet drink—her mouth crushed against the crook of her arm, her throat contracting as she swallowed, her face limned in flickering candlelight—Marion felt so entranced that neither pain nor fear had any hold on her. Lisavet's was a beauty so ruthless it almost hurt to behold it. Looking at her, she was compelled to think of nothing else.

"You have a sharp gaze," the young Countess murmured against her arm. Then she drew away and licked the last of Marion's blood from her lips. "Has anyone ever told you that before?"

Marion flushed, embarrassed to be caught staring. It was just so hard *not* to look at her. For all the splendor of the room, Lisavet seemed to single-handedly command attention. And she didn't need fine dresses or a throne to do it either. There was just something in the way of her that demanded to be admired. And Marion found it difficult, no, impossible to look away. "My father used to tell me I had eyes for the things I shouldn't see."

Lisavet appraised her in silence for a moment, produced a handkerchief from the pocket of her robe, pressed it to the crook of Marion's arm until the bleeding stopped, then tied it up like a bandage. "Tell me, do you miss your home in Prane?"

"A bit," she whispered, half-ashamed to admit it. "I had no real fondness for the city . . . at least not the parts of it I was reared in. But I suppose nostalgia gilds everything, even the worst places."

"And what of your family? Don't you miss them?"

Marion thought of Raul on the floor, bleeding at her feet, his skull caved in. She shut her eyes against the memory. "No. Not really. The ones that were worth missing are long dead."

"And the ones that weren't?"

"There's only one. And he's dead too."

"Your brother. His name was . . . Raul, wasn't it? Tell me, was it the grippe that took him in the end or was it something else?"

Marion's blood ran cold at the shock of the question. How did Lisavet know *anything* about Raul? She'd mentioned in passing that she'd had a brother but had never said his name. And it was impossible for Lisavet to know about Raul's sickness. He hadn't even received a formal diagnosis from a physician. "How do you know about my brother?"

"Your blood," said Lisavet senselessly, and with no emotion at all. "I can taste the memory of him in it. And your grief adds something of a bitter tang."

The anger hit Marion then, in a great burning wave. She had endured so many small humiliations throughout the course of her life in Prane. But she had always maintained some semblance of sanctity, privacy, within the confines of her own mind. But this . . . this was a violation of the worst degree. What memories had surfaced in her blood? Did she know what Marion did to Raul the night she fled Prane? Would her tenure end if she did? "You've tasted my *memories*?"

"As I have those of every bloodmaid who serves me. Though I must say, yours are particularly potent."

"You went through my mind uninvited?" Marion demanded, affronted, no, *revolted* by the very idea. Of all the many indignities she'd endured, this was by far the worst.

"Come now, don't be cross with me. Death, memory, grief, none of it belongs to any one person. It's all a collective. A kind of living legion."

"My memories are my own," Marion snapped in bitter retort. "It's unwarranted and unfair of you to . . . *rifle* through them."

"I've always found the southern preoccupation with fairness rather odd, given that a small selection of southerners inherit more wealth than seven generations could ever spend and the rest waste their lives sweating and slaving on the factory line."

"The mind is a different matter than the body. It's meant to be sacred, private."

"I don't agree," said Lisavet, with a kind of coldness that passed over her face so quickly Marion wasn't sure she saw it at all. "But I see that you're upset, and I apologize for my intrusion. I assure you I can't help it. I attribute emotions to colors, colors to sounds, sounds to feelings, and the taste of blood . . . to memory. It's compulsive."

Marion startled at the sound of something shattering down the hall, followed by an awful, rataplan chorus of footsteps.

Lisavet appeared unmoved. "If you want to leave, you're free to."

"I-I'm afraid to walk back to my room on my own," Marion admitted, staring down at her hands, feeling rather pitiful. "The game took a nasty turn."

Lisavet's eyes narrowed, but she stood up and offered Marion her arm. "I'll walk you back to your room. It's late and I fear the House Mother will have stern opinions about your spending the night here so early into the start of your tenure."

They walked back to the bloodmaids' chambers through a winding maze of hallways, a different route than the one Marion had traversed. She recognized not a single corridor or parlor that they passed along the way. They ventured through a large drawing room, strewn with limp and drunken nobles who were cast over swooning couches, bent over ottomans, even stretched across the floor. There was a thin pall of maudlum smoke on the air—it was strong, better than the cheap stuff Raul smoked—and the pungent aroma was not unlike the reeking ammonia solution Marion had once used to clean Lady Gertrude's floor. Among those who lay dreaming, Marion recognized Sir Ivor and a few of the other hounds that had formerly been hunting her. They must've grown impatient, lost interest in the game, preferring pipe dreams to their pursuit of her.

"You know, I do loathe parties," said Lisavet. "If they're to be endured at all, better to observe them from a distance."

"Then why host them at all?"

"I suppose I like the din . . . and the debauchery too." Lisavet offered Marion a smile more wicked than sheepish. "It makes the nights pass faster. They're so long in the wintertime."

From there, it was a short walk back to the bloodmaids' chambers. Upon their arrival, Marion was surprised to see that the parlor was occupied, both the twins and Irene wide awake despite the late hour. The girls gaped at Marion on Lisavet's arm, thoroughly stunned.

Lisavet raised an eyebrow. "What have we here?"

The reality of Lisavet's presence seemed to hit the girls all at once. Hastily, all three scrambled to their feet and dropped—in perfect tandem—into graceful curtsies. The girls remained crouched, their heads bowed, knees bent, until Lisavet bade them rise.

The Countess examined their downturned heads. "Shouldn't you all be in bed?"

The twins' gazes darted to Irene, who said in a whisper, "We heard the shouts and howls for Marion's name and we were worried about her, so we stayed up to make sure she returned to her chamber safely."

Marion's eyes went wide with the shock of this kindness. These girls were little more than strangers, and yet they were already looking after her. Perhaps Irene wasn't lying when she said she regarded her fellow bloodmaids as family.

"And what would you have done if she hadn't returned tonight?" Lisavet inquired. "Would you leave your chambers and break House protocol to search for her?"

Irene seemed to struggle with an answer; her gaze went to Marion as if to ask for help. "Yes. If it meant seeing her home safely."

Lisavet's eyes softened, if only for a moment. "To bed. All of you."

The girls quickly dispersed themselves, retreating to their respective rooms, casting lingering glances over their shoulders as they went. Even Theodore skulked from the shadows of his hiding place and slithered into the twins' room a moment before Elize shut the door.

Lisavet and Marion were left alone in the quiet of the parlor.

"They're quite fond of you," said Lisavet.

"They're good girls. So much kindness in them."

"And is there no kindness in you?"

Marion stiffened. "I'm afraid there's very little left, my lady. Sometimes I fear that whatever natural virtue I once possessed has been drained down to the dregs."

Lisavet considered this for a beat, then turned and strode to the door. But she stopped at the threshold and half turned to look at Marion over her shoulder. "I know what became of your brother. I saw him, skull buckled, ears bleeding, twitching on the floor at your feet. I saw you back away from him. I saw you turn to leave him to the dogs."

Marion's breath hitched. Tears came to her eyes but she blinked them back, refused to let them fall.

"No need to cry," said the Countess, stepping out into the corridor. "He wasn't worth mourning anyway."

15

I knew this was my calling the moment the needle bit my skin.

—ANNALISE, BLOODMAID OF THE HOUSE OF FOG

THE FOLLOWING MORNING, AT dawn's cusp, when the first day's bells began ringing, Marion was summoned to the kitchen for a bloodletting. Too groggy from the previous night's ventures to be properly nervous, she reclined into one of the armchairs by the far wall. She felt drunk, and far too weak to be bled again, but she didn't dare reveal her unsanctioned encounter with Lisavet the night prior, for fear that the House Mother would punish her.

But even apart from the House protocols, there was something grave and secret about what she'd shared with Lisavet last night. It was as though the world had emptied of everyone but the two of them. As if the confines of reality had contracted such that nothing of consequence existed beyond the walls of that bedchamber, beyond them.

Two servants appeared just after Marion took a seat in the bleeding parlor. One held a bowl and needle kit. The other bore a breakfast tray, loaded with tea cakes and cold meats, pitted cherries, fresh oranges peeled and quartered, coffee pale with cream, and two soft-boiled eggs with their tops sliced off and buttered toast points to pierce into the yolks.

"Eat and bleed," said the servant cheerily, placing the tray down on the table beside her. And Marion, obedient as a lamb, pushed up the sleeve of her gown and extended her arm. She'd never been particularly afraid of pain, and it had always seemed foolish to fear blood given that she let so much of it every month, but she didn't like the look of that needle as the servant lowered it to her arm. Strange that she hadn't felt the same squeamishness when Lisavet drank her due straight from the source.

There was a sharp, pinching pain, and the moment when it edged close to unbearable, she ceased to feel the point of the needle at all. With a kind of morbid fascination, she watched as her blood spilled into the bowl. She wondered what memories would surface in her blood. What Lisavet would see when she tasted it.

"They're starting you early," said Evie from the doorway. Marion hadn't seen the girl appear; it seemed like the little blonde was even more light-footed than Marion was. The girl bounded across the room and claimed the armchair beside Marion, poked the cake that the servant had provided her, and licked the buttercream off her fingertip. "Lisavet must be eager for another taste of you. You must've performed well for her last night."

"Don't tease her, Evie," said the elder twin, Elize. She entered the room cradling Theodore to her chest. She was still dressed in the same wine-red robe she'd been wearing the night before. Its train slithered after her as she claimed the chair at the far edge of the room, away from Marion and her sister. As soon as she was settled in her seat, a servant appeared to bleed her. Elize didn't so much as flinch when the needle pierced her skin. The cat in her lap sniffed the edge of the bleeding bowl, licking his chops, but flinched away when Elize frowned down at him. "This is Lisavet's breakfast, *not* yours."

At the mention of the Countess, Marion's memories dragged her back to the previous night, their tense discussion, Lisavet's open mouth at her wrist. And then, from the murk of reverie—and in the way of a nightmare—came the image of Cecelia on the floor of the corridor, laughing shoulders bent inward as if they'd been broken that way, her collarbones snapped in half, then retching up what appeared to be wine . . . or blood. Marion's stomach twisted at the memory, and she felt ready to choke up every bite of the tea cake she'd managed to force down. "Have you seen Cecelia this morning?"

"No," said Elize, frowning slightly. "Why do you ask?"

Marion considered telling them the full truth of what she'd seen in the hall but thought better of it. She'd only known the girls for a few days and wasn't sure where their loyalties lay, or how much she should trust them. "I saw her only briefly last night, and she seemed rather . . . indisposed."

Evie took a large bite of Marion's cake (despite the fact that a servant had already supplied her with her own) and spoke thickly through the mouthful. "She was probably just drunk."

"Yes . . ." said Elize, looking rather troubled. "Cecelia does have a taste for brandy."

"Which is to say she's an incorrigible drunk."

"*Evie!*" Irene shrieked as she entered the room. Unlike the other bloodmaids, she was already dressed and ready for the day. She settled herself in the chair beside Marion, who caught a whiff of her perfume—all amber and balsam.

"Well, she *is*. Did you know that on more than three occasions I've seen Cecelia so thoroughly soused that she couldn't even recall my name? I do think that the drink is taking its toll on her. She can barely remember anything anymore. I'm convinced she couldn't even find her way down here to the bleeding room if she didn't have a servant to escort her."

"Cecelia's nerves are strained," said Irene, and at once Marion pegged this as the sort of airy excuse that wasp-waisted noblewomen offered when they'd had too much to eat and needed a discreet place to empty their stomachs. "It's a difficult thing, wearing the title of First Bloodmaid around one's neck like a millstone. I can't imagine it."

"The only millstone around Cecelia's neck is that diamond necklace Lisavet procured her for her birthday," Evie quipped back, and then she said to Marion, "If you unseat Cecelia and become First Bloodmaid, you must promise to lend your jewels to us. It's only fair."

"I have no intention of becoming First Bloodmaid." But even as Marion said it, she wasn't sure it was true. There was some part of her—small, but hungry with ambition—that wanted to be the favorite. Perhaps that was only natural, but the more she considered the possibility the greater her desire became.

"Don't pretend to be humble," said Elize, watching her blood flow into the bowl. "We all saw Lisavet escort you back last night."

"A game of fox and hound became rather rowdy, and Lisavet walked me back to my chambers. It was nothing more than that."

"Lisavet's attention is not nothing," said Irene as a servant slipped a needle deep into the vein on the top of her hand. Strange, Marion thought, that the servant hadn't pierced her at the inner elbow, as she had the rest of them. "Her time is a rare gift. You'd have to be a fool to mistake it for anything less."

Later that day, after her lesson with Tutor Geoffrey adjourned, Marion abandoned the dense novel she'd been attempting to read (it was far too dull, the language too flowery to parse) and started down the narrow corridor that led to Cecelia's chambers. At its end were a pair of carved double doors that looked like the ones she'd fled through the night before, though they were far smaller. Both were carved with the images of two young girls, one with hair that flowed down to her ankles, the other with her hair shorn as short as a boy's.

Marion knocked twice, as a precaution, and when there was no answer, she let herself in. Cecelia's bedroom was far larger than hers, which Marion assumed was one of the many privileges of being First Bloodmaid. Like Lisavet's chamber, the room was octagonal; at its center was a bed in the same shape, set into an indentation in the floor and draped with curtains that hung from the domed skylight ceiling. On the opposite end of the room, a pair of glass doors opened out onto a grand balcony with a sweeping view of the ocean.

Shelves were fitted into the walls, though there were no books on them. Instead, there were a number of strange trinkets . . . and oddities. A marble globe, burnished to a vicious sheen; a taxidermied kitten (Marion wondered if it was more of Lisavet's work); a glass eye on a velvet pillow. There was even a small stuffed parrot mounted on a perch in a gilded cage that appeared so alive Marion half expected it to sing.

But among these treasures the most intriguing was one that Marion couldn't entirely distinguish. It was . . . some sort of *organ* suspended in liquid, displayed in a crystal jar. Upon closer inspection, she realized it might have been a kidney. Though she wasn't sure what animal it belonged to. Something large, though; a deer or an elk perhaps.

"Looking for something?"

Marion wheeled at the question and saw Cecelia standing just across the room. There was a curtain billowing behind her, and behind *that* what appeared to be a small private parlor that Marion had not seen from her vantage point at the door.

As always, Cecelia was a vision. But on that grim evening, she wore a thick black choker that was almost large enough to conceal her bandaged throat. Almost, but not quite. Marion could see the raw and ragged edges of what looked like a shallow bite mark. As she studied Marion, a range of expressions flashed across her face, beginning with anger and ending with a kind of poorly concealed annoyance. "Why are you in my room?"

"You dropped this in the hall last night," said Marion, and she slipped a hand into the pocket of her skirts, withdrawing the choker that she'd abandoned in the hall. The ribbon delicately embroidered with the words *Wretched One.*

Cecelia's faint brows drew together. She stared down her nose at the choker, as if Marion were offering her a dead snake. "No, I didn't."

"I saw you in the hall last night," said Marion. "You were crying, bleeding from the mouth."

Cecelia startled, as though she'd heard something, and prowled around the perimeter of her bed to the birdcage and stuck her finger between the bars, like she expected the stuffed parrot to stir alive and nibble at her nail. "We all bleed here."

"Some of us more than others."

It wasn't really meant to be a question, but Cecelia turned on Marion with an answer just the same. "Only if we're highly favored."

With that, Cecelia swept across the room in a flourish of silks and satins, and as she passed, Marion caught the reek of wine. After years spent in Raul's shadow, she knew the stench of a drunk anywhere. And watching Cecelia, she saw there was something tragic and hateful about her that reminded her of her brother. A little pang cut through her chest as she thought of him, and her, and all of the other people who lost themselves to the cheap comfort of a strong drink.

"You must remember that the only thing they want of you is your blood. Meat and blood. At first, they fatten you up, make you feel so full you think you'll never want for anything again." Cecelia sidled up to her, closing the distance between them so that their chests pressed flush together. "Then they'll put the needle to your arm and drain you dry, and you will know an emptiness like that which you have never felt before."

"My lady?"

Both girls turned to the servant standing in the threshold. The woman appeared startled at the sight of the two bloodmaids in such intimate proximity. She held a small, pewter tray balanced between both of her upturned palms. On it lay a crisp white envelope. Cecelia moved to take it, but the servant extended the tray to Marion instead. "From the Countess."

Cecelia flinched back as if struck, and Marion watched as the color leached from her cheeks.

Without a word she wheeled away, stalking out onto the balcony, kicking its glass doors shut behind her so hard Marion for a moment feared that all the glass panes would shatter.

Unfazed, the servant extended the tray again. "If you will."

Marion reached for the letter with shaking hands, slit the seal open with the nail on her pinky finger. Within was a short letter that read as follows:

Marion,

I'm hosting a small fox hunt tomorrow. I'd like you to attend. Your new mount will be waiting for you in the stables come morning. I look forward to seeing you on the moors.

As ever,
Lisavet

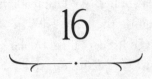

16

I am a fox caught in the maw of the hound, but I know no fear.

—CONSTANCE, BLOODMAID OF THE HOUSE OF MIRRORS

THE MARSH WAS VEILED in fog the morning of the hunt. Marion woke well before dawn, dressed in riding leathers—comprising a blood-red hunting jacket, a black equestrian gown, and a pair of stiff leather boots—that had been gifted to her by Lisavet, and ventured down to the stables. The Countess had spared no expense. Marion's new mount was a grand, hot-blooded stallion by the name of Bishop. He was tall with thin limbs and a coat the color of dense smoke.

Lisavet, in her abundant generosity, had supplied Marion with new leather tack and her own horseman—a gruff, bearded man with gentle hands—who would assist and accompany her on the hunt, following behind on a mount of his own. In addition to these provisions, Marion was supplied with a hunting rifle (carved with her new initials, *M.H.*), a brass scope, a leather crop that looked strikingly similar to the one Madame Boucherie wielded during her lessons, and a fox-hunting hound of her own—a hulking, wolflike creature who answered to the name Arrow.

Marion was a poor equestrian. Given her upbringing, she could count on one hand the times she'd ridden a horse, and she dreaded the hunt that lay ahead of her. As Marion attempted to make friends with her mount—baiting the horse with sugar cubes and bites of plum—Lisavet emerged from a stall at the far end of the stable. She was dressed in black as was her custom and was grasping the reins of a large, dark stallion. But instead of the customary riding skirts, she wore breeches, like a man, tucked into polished, calf-high boots. "Good morning, Marion."

"Good morning m'lady."

"Call me Lisavet," she said, stopping just short of her. Her complexion was much improved from the last time Marion had seen her. Some color had returned to her cheeks, and the bags beneath her eyes had faded considerably. "Have you hunted before?"

Marion shook her head. "I was raised in the city. I've never even seen a hunt."

"Well, we'll have to make your first one worth remembering."

Just then, a few nobles emerged from the House. Among them were Madame Boucherie with her crop in hand, as well as Sir Ivor, who limped toward his horse with the aid of a cane, casting Marion nasty, sidelong glances here and there. Apart from him, the court seemed in high spirits that morning, the thrill of the coming hunt enough to enliven them despite the early hour, and Marion couldn't help but notice that—in Lisavet's presence—they seemed to regard her as less an outsider than a peer. It was clear that the Countess' affections had elevated her to a new station, far beyond that which she'd occupied before.

The hunting party set out just before daybreak, traveling together along the marshes on the eastern coast of the island. But Lisavet soon peeled away from the rest of her court, motioning for Marion to follow her. Marion, struggling with her strong-willed steed, urged him to obey, kicking and pulling at the reins but refusing to use her crop.

"You know, horses can scent your fear," said Lisavet, without looking back at her. They were alone on their journey into the marshes, Lisavet having forbidden their accompanying groomsmen from following them, assuring both of the begrudging men that they would need no chaperones. "And they don't respect cowardice in a rider."

"I'm no coward," said Marion through clenched teeth. "He won't listen to me."

Lisavet tugged at the reins, and her horse turned into a tight circle. She ordered her mount back to Marion. "Then prove to him that you're worth listening to."

"I don't want to use the crop."

Lisavet half turned to her, twisting in her saddle. "I didn't say anything about a crop. One shouldn't need to inflict pain to be listened to and regarded with some measure of respect."

"Why, then, does Madame Boucherie inflict her crop with such abandon?"

"Madame Boucherie doesn't inflict her crop to win your respect. As your tutor, she has that already. She inflicts her crop to teach you the art of pain. It was the same with me when I endured her tutelage as a child. She used to beat my palms raw and bloody. The wounds would scab up overnight, only to be split open by the lash of her crop come morning."

"I-I didn't know you were one of her students."

Lisavet merely nodded. "I endured Madame Boucherie's tutelage for more than eleven years and I loathe that wretched woman to this day. But not because she didn't teach me well. Rather, because she did." Lisavet raised a hand to her mouth and tore off her leather glove with her teeth. She leaned out of her saddle and extended her hand for Marion to see. There was a thick scar there, silvered and knotted. "From her crop."

Marion took her hand by the fingers. "My God."

Lisavet stole her hand away and hastily slipped her glove back on, as if embarrassed. They kept riding for a while in silence, the path narrowing as they went. Every few moments, the wind swept inland off the sea, ripping viciously at their clothes and hair.

"Did you ever think of leaving?" Marion asked at last, wondering if perhaps Lisavet had, like her, dreamed of a better life, dreamed of freedom beyond the circumstances of her birth.

"Where would I go?" Lisavet inquired, and seemed in want of an earnest answer. "I have no skills to speak of. My health is at best poor and at worst grave."

"All the more reason to spend your remaining years wisely."

"You think I've been unwise with my allotted time?"

"I didn't mean to speak out of turn," said Marion, in a hasty attempt to excuse her bluntness. When would she learn to bite her tongue? "I only wondered why you don't see the world with the time you have left to live in it."

"The House of Hunger *is* my world," said Lisavet. "And it has a way of devouring all who enter it." She paused to remove a palm-size flask from her riding jacket. She unscrewed the cap and took several deep swallows, and licked the residual blood from her lips. "But I must admit . . . I envy those like you, who are healthy enough to venture where you please."

Marion wanted to correct her, let her know that freedom was a privilege exclusive to those who could afford it. But she held her tongue.

Lisavet kept riding, leading them into the marsh, though the path threading through it was barely wide enough to accommodate the horses. Marion followed, feeling rather ill at ease. All she could think of were the poor foxes, cowering in the high grass, and was reminded of how just two nights prior she'd been the one being hunted, with the noble hounds nipping at her heels. How quickly the tables turned.

Lisavet abruptly tugged on the reins and dismounted. The hunting dogs prowled at her feet, noses to the ground. Lisavet bent to one knee, studying what Marion saw was a paw print stamped into the soft loam of the marsh. "Fox tracks. They went this way." She pointed north, toward the cliffs. "Let's tie our horses here and continue on foot."

Reluctantly, Marion swung into an awkward dismount, nearly losing her balance upon impact. Lisavet tied the reins of both of their horses to the bough of a piece of driftwood, some giant, half-petrified tree belched up from the belly of the ocean, covered with barnacles and crawling with sand crabs. Even lying on its side, it stood far taller than Lisavet.

Armed with their rifles, they began to thread through the narrow paths that carved through the marsh: Lisavet stalking along in silence and Marion staggering through the muck behind her, muttering quiet curses under her breath, her trailing riding skirts soaked with salt water, mud sucking at her boots as she sloughed along. They walked until they reached the very edge of a copse, and Marion peered through the thinning trees and spotted the other part of the hunting party, traveling the path that threaded along the beach.

"Look," said Lisavet.

Marion followed Lisavet's line of vision to a bright spot of red, wending through the distant high grass. A small fox pup, traveling alone, its head hung, paws heavy. No sign of a mother or any littermates either. A pit formed in her belly at the sight. "It's all alone."

The hunting dogs prowled closer, their bellies pressing low to the forest floor. Lisavet's hunting dog, a black fanged creature by the name of Knight, slowly moved ahead.

"Hold," said Lisavet, in a hoarse whisper, and both dogs froze midstep, just a few yards away from the pup. The Countess half turned to Marion. "Do you know how to fire a gun?"

"I . . . no."

Lisavet backtracked and came alongside her, and the dogs followed suit. Gingerly, the young Countess shifted Marion's hands over the gun. "Hold your breath," she said in a hot whisper, her lips brushing Marion's earlobe, sending chills down her spine. "And track your heartbeats, there's a small death between each one. When you find it, pull the trigger."

The fox pup froze in the clearing, perhaps catching their scent for the first time.

Marion tried, and failed, to swallow down the stone in her throat. Her finger, curled and hovering over the trigger, began to shake along with the rest of her.

"But see there." Lisavet shifted the gun so that it was trained on Sir Ivor through a break in the trees. He was limping badly, leaning heavily on his cane. "The perfect pig. A bigger kill than the fox pup. Certainly a more impressive one. Don't you think?"

Marion might've believed she'd said this in jest, but when she risked a glance up at Lisavet she saw that while her face was expressionless, her eyes were tinged with contempt. "Lisavet—"

"We can't go home empty-handed," said the Countess, her eyes still fixed on Ivor. "So, what will it be, Marion? The pup or the pig?"

Marion's gaze shifted back and forth between Ivor and the fox pup frolicking in the glen. "Neither."

"You must choose," said Lisavet, with sudden severity. At her feet, the dogs bristled and snarled in anticipation of a kill. "It will always be someone."

Marion swallowed dry, but the stone in her throat remained. Her heartbeat quickened as she shifted the rifle from Ivor to the pup, the pup to Ivor, and then back again.

"Make your decision. Pull the trigger, Marion. Do it now."

The gun felt heavy in her hands. She peered down the barrel. Listened to her racing heartbeats, willed them to slow and tried to find the small deaths between them, just as Lisavet had instructed her to. She trained the gun on Ivor. Pulled the trigger.

The fox pup fled. Through the high grass, Sir Ivor, alive and uninjured, snapped to attention, trying to see where the shot had come from.

Marion half turned to Lisavet, breathless with exhilaration, expectant. "I-I did it," she said, and then again, this time smiling. She couldn't remember the last time she'd felt so . . . *alive*. "I did it. I pulled the trigger."

But the Countess was expressionless, utterly unimpressed. She took the gun from Marion's hand as she turned away, stalking through the grass. "Next time, don't hesitate."

———— ◆ ————

LISAVET SPARED THE FOX PUP BUT WENT ON TO KILL TWO BOARS, A brace of rabbits chased from their den, and a small quail that she shot midair, clean through the eye. That night, while the court gathered in the dining room for a feast of roast boar, Lisavet—drawn and weary—retired to her private quarters. She didn't bother to say goodbye to Marion; in fact, she didn't say anything to Marion at all. Lisavet had all but ignored her for the remainder of the hunt, and Marion knew with a bitter certainty that she'd somehow disappointed her.

Marion watched Ivor from down the feasting table, drunk and glistening with sweat, a servant girl perched on his knee, a two-pronged fork in his hand, its tongs speared clean through a greasy roast boar's ear. He smiled at Marion, slurred something about a fox on the run, and the girl in his lap erupted into a fit of laughter.

Ivor was pompous to be certain, but he was still a human being and Marion had very nearly killed him, would have if the bullet met its mark. Her cheeks burned with shame at the thought. What manner of depravity had overcome her during the hunt? What was she thinking? What was Lisavet thinking, that she would demand that Marion sacrifice her position—and perhaps more importantly her soul—by ending the life of another?

Shaken, Marion dismissed herself from the table, cutting through the kitchen on her way to the servants' stairs. She took them up to the third floor, found her way to Lisavet's room, and knocked on the door with a sharp rap of the knuckles. "It's Marion."

"Enter."

Marion pushed open the door and entered the parlor to find Lisavet seated at the desk in its corner—a pair of tweezers in one hand, a scalpel in the other—painstakingly disemboweling the quail she'd shot mere hours before. She worked by the flickering light of the single electric light bulb standing at the far edge of the desk. "What do you want?"

Marion nudged the door shut behind her. "Did you really want me to kill him?"

Lisavet frowned down at her work, taking care not to pierce the bird's intestines as she removed them. "If I say yes, will you kill him tonight?"

"I . . . no, of course not—"

"Then why do you ask?"

"Because I don't understand why you hate him so much," she blurted. "None of you want for *anything*. You don't know what it is to starve, or scrabble, or sleep on the streets. All of you have more than enough, and yet you still find the most inane reasons to loathe each other. What is there to fight over when you have everything already?"

Lisavet, exasperated, lowered her tools with a clatter, setting the tweezers on one side of the bird, the scalpel on the other. "If you must know, Ivor is the third son of the Lord of Fog," said Lisavet. Marion remembered that House from the first day of her studies with Tutor Geoffrey. They were one of the sacred four. "The Lord of Fog has long been attempting to win my hand, since I was eleven years old."

"Win your hand in . . . *marriage?*"

"Yes. But only because he knows he won't win it in battle," said Lisavet, first with a smirk, but then her eyes went empty. "I'd slit his belly and hang him with his own intestines first."

"I take it you refused him?"

"Naturally. I'm the last of my line and had I accepted his offer, my lands would have been forfeit. The House of Hunger would fall. The day of my father's funeral, he made his first offer of matrimony. I was a new orphan and he a grown man thrice widowed at fifty-six. I still remember him bending the knee in the shadows of my parents' tomb while the mourners were still singing their dirges. When I refused him several more times over the following years, he sent his conniving son Ivor to act as a spy in my court, spinning lies and sowing seeds of discord, doing whatever he can to prove me unfit . . . and moreover unworthy of my title, so that one day it can be stripped from me. Through marriage, or death if it comes to it. If he could have me killed without consequence, he would do it, so long as it meant he would inherit this House."

"How is that possible when he's not a blood heir?"

"But he is," said Lisavet. "He was born a bastard in the House of Fog, but his mother was the half-sister of my father. Meaning that should I die—"

"Ivor is next in line to inherit the House of Hunger," said Marion, stunned by both Ivor's parentage and the fact that he still wanted to marry Lisavet in spite of it. She knew that northern aristocrats often married their own kin, with little regard for the blood ties between cousins, but she still found the custom strange, and a little revolting.

"Precisely. He believes this House to be his birthright. His one chance at greatness. That's why he's so determined to stay here, to turn my own court against me in preparation for what he hopes, or perhaps believes, will be his own ascension. He wants, and has always wanted, a House and title of his own. I'm the only thing that stands between him and realizing that dream."

"Why don't you just banish him?"

"Because this House isn't a private residence, it's the very bastion of a dynasty that's held power in the North for more than six hundred years. The nobles that occupy it aren't guests, they're ambassadors, embassies in their own right. They're appointed by other Houses. The banishment of their presence can be interpreted one of two ways: weakness or the beginnings of a war."

"Is that what you wanted when you asked me to put a bullet in Ivor's head? War?"

Lisavet didn't answer. She picked up her tools again and went back to her work. The bird's belly had been carefully pinned back, its open wings tacked to the scarred surface of the desk. Most of its organs were arranged in neat lines on a large ceramic tray. Lisavet carefully added the intestines to the assortment. "Cecelia. Come here."

The girl emerged from Lisavet's bedroom. She wore a black robe that, judging by the wide cut of the shoulders and the fact that its hem pooled on the floor at her feet, belonged to Lisavet. It was tied only loosely shut around the waist, so as to reveal a deep slice of her pale chest and stomach. There were several bruises and bite marks along the side of her neck, one of them bleeding a bit. The girl looked from Lisavet to Marion, a slight frown creasing her brow, then back to Lisavet again.

The Countess didn't look at her. Her gaze remained with Marion. "Because of the precarity of my current position, in those closest to me—my bloodmaids, my confidants, my lovers—I demand loyalty without hesitation. You may think this expectation is severe, but I've come to realize I can tolerate nothing less. Thus, if I ask one of my bloodmaids to do something, you're to do it without faltering or pausing to question me."

Lisavet turned her attention back to the quail, her scalpel hovering above the assortment of its organs. They were surprisingly colorful—a pair of ruddy pink lungs, the snakes of mustard-yellow entrails, a purple liver, and other grisly bits that might have been the bladder, or the kidneys, or perhaps a deflated stomach. Finally, she settled on the quail's heart, pierced it with the tip of her scalpel, and raised it to Cecelia. "Eat."

Obedient as a lamb, the bloodmaid edged toward the desk. She braced a hand against the back of Lisavet's chair, parted her lips, and took the quail heart between her teeth, chewed mechanically, the sound wet and grisly, then swallowed with a smug little smile.

"You see?" said Lisavet, her eyes still on Marion. "Loyalty."

17

What is my purpose if not to bleed?

—LILA, BLOODMAID OF THE HOUSE OF DOVES

OVER THE FOLLOWING WEEKS, Marion's relations with Cecelia worsened rapidly. Seemingly sadistic by nature, the girl took every opportunity to humiliate, toy with, and torment Marion. During dinners, when Marion spoke or tried to enter an ongoing discussion, Cecelia pretended not to hear her and abruptly changed the subject, as if to ensure that Marion was ostracized. In her presence, the girl seized every opportunity to divulge, in detail, her meetings with Lisavet, recounting their long nights together, filled with wine and laughter, deep discussion and shared passions.

These insults were worsened by the fact that Marion hadn't received a single invitation from Lisavet since the hunt. All of the other bloodmaids had made regular appearances in court, spending their nights by Lisavet's side, but Marion was never invited. And apart from passing Lisavet once or twice in the hall (wherein the young Countess, walking quickly, hadn't even deigned to look at her), Marion hadn't seen her at all.

"I'm sure it's nothing," Elize assured her one sunny afternoon during their enrichment hour. It was too cold to take tea outside, so the bloodmaids had taken to dining in the greenhouse, where the furnaces kept the air warm and balmy. Elize, who was just as kind-hearted as she was thoroughly dense, had taken great pains to comfort Marion over the passing weeks, coming up with wild and often flimsy explanations as to why Lisavet—whose interest had been so piqued by Marion upon her arrival at the House—now seemed completely impervious to her. "Perhaps the Countess is merely allowing you to acclimate yourself to the House before forcing you to endure the rigors of the court. The nights are so long. They can be quite grueling."

Despite her best attempts, Elize's assurances did little to ease Marion's mounting suspicions that the Countess had, in fact, lost interest in her. These anxieties were further confounded by the fact that Marion noted she was being bled less than the other girls. While Irene and the twins were called to the bleeding parlor several times a week, and Cecelia almost every day, Marion often went more than a week without the servants leading her down to the kitchens to bleed.

It seemed to her that Lisavet had not only lost interest in her. She'd lost the taste for her blood too. These developments weren't lost on Cecelia, who seemed to relish Marion's abrupt fall from grace. Her insults grew sharper, her gloating more conspicuous, and she seemed more and more eager to rub salt in the gaping, fetid wound of Marion's misery.

"I don't know why she hates me so much," Marion confessed to Irene one evening after dinner. The twins had already been dispatched to court and Cecelia had refused to emerge from her chamber for bleeding, dinner, or anything else. Mae had been put to bed early that night, on account of her poor temper (she purposely emptied a decanter of wine on the floor during dinner), leaving Irene and Marion alone for the duration of their evening enrichment hours. "She's First Bloodmaid. I'm Fifth. She must know I'm no threat. I haven't been called to court in weeks and Lisavet hasn't even looked at me since . . ." Marion trailed off, not wanting to reveal the truth of what Lisavet had said the last time she'd attended her.

Across the room Irene sat, taciturn, at her vanity. Her chambers—in stark contrast to Cecelia's—were rather unpresuming. Her bedroom was even smaller than Marion's, but it did have the better view. Its windows, which like the ones in Lisavet's room stretched from floor to ceiling, overlooked the sweeping expanse of the ocean. Its walls were papered in faded red, and its hearth housed a roaring fire. It was sensibly furnished with little more than the bare essentials—a chair with an oil lamp on the table beside it, its light just bright enough to read by, a vanity, a wardrobe, and a bed tucked into the corner, its canopy curtains half-drawn. Apart from the carpet stretched across the floor, and the glass-eyed lynx head hanging on the wall above the bed, the room was unadorned.

Marion sat folded in the armchair, under cover of a supple elk hide. According to Irene, it, along with the lynx head, were the spoils of two of Lisavet's many successful expeditions. "Cecelia looks at me like she'd sooner slit my throat than smile at me, and it seems that Lisavet shares in her disdain. They both despise me."

Irene—sitting at her vanity, comb in hand—seemed distracted and didn't comment on this. It was as though the labor of attending to her hair demanded all of the energy she had left to spare. She seemed so weary that even the comb in her hand seemed too heavy for her to lift.

"Don't you have servants to assist you with that?" Marion inquired, puzzled.

Irene merely shook her head. Marion noted that without the bulk of chemises and petticoats to conceal her frame, she was quite thin. Frail, even—her bones painfully protruding, her knuckles bulbous and stiff. And while her skin was devoid of any wrinkles or blemishes, the shape of her body—its crude contours and stiff posture—more closely resembled that of an old woman than a girl in the prime of her youth. "The servants here hardly know what to do with our hair. That's why I do it myself. But on some nights . . . I feel so *tired*."

Marion slipped off the bed and stood. "I'll help."

Irene looked like she wanted to decline her offer. But, to Marion's surprise, she relinquished the comb. Irene's hair was down-soft, and it curled flush against her scalp in tight little ringlets that Marion found quite becoming.

Marion's mother had had hair like Irene's (though hers had been much thicker) and when she was just a child, she'd taught Marion how to tend it. Wet it first, she'd said, with a bit of warm water to loosen the curls (if there was no fire lit to warm it, cold water would do), divide the hair into small sections and work through them one by one with a wide-toothed comb, until all of the curls were free of tangles, then braid the hair into plaits (Marion's mother preferred two of them, one on either side of the head) to keep the hair from tangling again during the night. Sometimes Marion's mother would wrap her hair in a scarf. But on the balmy southern nights—when the air was thick and humid—she refused, saying she couldn't bear to have anything more than her own hair on her head for the heat.

Marion came to stand behind Irene at the vanity; she took the comb from her cold hand and began to work through her hair, wetting it with a bit of water from the pitcher and basin standing on the corner of her vanity. "I never thanked you for looking after me on my first night of court."

Irene didn't say anything; she was gazing at her own reflection in the vanity and her own reflection was gazing back at her, and in the moment, it seemed that there was some subtle dissonance or tension between the two. "You would've done the same for me."

"I'm not sure that I would have."

Irene met her gaze in the mirror. Her eyes were swollen and raw. "Well, I think you would've."

Marion didn't argue that. Better to let Irene think the best of her. She passed the comb through a small section of her hair, and several thick curls came away with it, tangled in the teeth. "I'm sorry, I don't know what happened. I just combed it the way I did my mother's—"

"It's not your fault," said Irene tonelessly, and she took the comb from Marion and pulled the curls free of its teeth. "I've been losing hair for weeks now. In the baths sometimes my curls fall out by the handful."

"Have you seen a doctor?"

"I don't need to. I know it's the bleeding." Irene lifted the sleeve of her robe to show her the great bruises blooming in the crooks of her elbow. "They started taking more when I became Second Blood-maid a few months ago."

Marion began combing again, more gingerly this time, taking care not to pull too hard for fear that Irene would lose what little hair she had left to spare. "Can you not ask them for a few days to recover? Or perhaps a week or two of rest?"

"I could if I'd like to see my rank diminished. Or if I'd like to be replaced."

"Come now, that's ridiculous. You won't be replaced. Surely Lisavet wouldn't allow it."

"Lisavet is gravely ill, and her condition demands a constant supply of blood. And not just any blood, blood from the healthy, with the healing properties she needs to keep her condition from deteriorating further. If I myself am ailing, then how can my blood be of any use to her?"

"You're more than just a vessel to be bled. You're Second Blood-maid. You're a companion."

"There's no dearth of lovely girls who'd be willing to bleed. Girls whose memories taste better." Her gaze briefly flickered to Marion's. So Irene did know about Lisavet's gift. Somehow, this came as a disappointment to Marion, who had wondered if Lisavet's confession was a secret contained to the two of them. "There will always be someone younger and more beautiful ready to take my place."

Marion couldn't imagine anyone more beautiful than Irene. Even frail with thinning hair and bags beneath her eyes, she was ravishing. As far as Marion was concerned, even Cecelia couldn't compare to her. In Marion's eyes she had only one equal: Lisavet herself.

"It's a mistake to believe that Lisavet has some special attach-ment to us. There will always be a girl whom she favors more . . . and loves better." Irene picked the last of her ringlets from the comb's teeth and handed them back to Marion. "Do go on. I'll lose it either way. Better that what I do have is free of tangles."

Marion finished the last of the combing and began to braid Irene's hair, what little of it there was to braid, that was. She took pains to drop the fallen curls and brush them beneath the vanity with her foot, to keep Irene from seeing just how many she'd lost. By the time she finished, she'd managed to collect the remnants of Irene's hair into two meager braids. But the plaits did little to cover the places where her hair was so thin you could see the bare patches of her scalp between the strands. If Irene continued to ignore her condition and bleed, would she lose the rest of her hair too? Would her health continue to deteriorate? What would she lose next?

Marion set the comb down on the vanity. "Does the word 'wretch' mean anything to you?"

Irene stiffened. "Why do you ask?"

"I found it carved into the leg of my bed. Along with this." Marion reached into the pocket of her robe to produce the small molar she'd found the night she first arrived at the House. She'd taken to carrying it with her like a kind of totem. "I think it might've belonged to the girl who carved that word. But I'm not sure."

Irene took the tooth, pinching it between index and thumb, and examined it for a moment by the spare candlelight before slipping it back into the pocket of Marion's robe. "Can I offer you a word of advice? As a friend, as family?"

Marion nodded.

Irene stood up and started for her bed. "Don't ask questions that lead to nasty answers."

The two girls slept huddled together that night. At least, Irene did. Marion tossed and turned and sank in and out of fitful dreams until—after waking with a start from her third nightmare—she got up and left Irene's room. The hearth fire in the parlor had long died, and the air held a bitter chill. Marion snatched a shawl from its heap on the floor and wrapped it around her shoulders for warmth. She peered at the clock on the mantel. The time read eleven o'clock, but she could still hear the lively voices of the nobles echoing from down the hall.

For them, the night was young. Most wouldn't retire until the wee hours of the morning.

Marion sorely envied them. The court was exactly the lively distraction she wanted to keep her from lying awake and ruminating about Lisavet through the long hours of the night. She felt pathetic, like a scorned lover. All the while, Lisavet had all but forgotten her. Had she come all the way north just to be slighted like this? All because she'd hesitated to kill a man? For shame.

A daring idea occurred to her then: Why didn't she simply go to

Lisavet and prove her fealty? Assure her that her allegiances were true? That she was no less loyal than Cecelia or any of the other bloodmaids? She'd already gone to Lisavet unsummoned once and lived to tell the tale. Besides, she had nothing left to lose. If she didn't act soon, she feared her tenure would be annulled when it had barely even started.

Marion, barefoot, in nothing but a night robe and shawl, slipped out of the bloodmaids' chamber and followed the sound of voices down the hall, trying to remember the way to Lisavet's private chambers. It didn't take her long, Marion being something of a quick study when it came to her sense of direction; she had the labyrinthine streets of Prane to thank for that.

When she reached Lisavet's private chambers, she passed through the double doors and into the dark of her parlor. The bedroom door was light-limned, and just ajar. From behind it, Marion could hear the rustling of sheets, the breathless murmurings of pleasure.

The hoarse gasp of Lisavet's name, once, twice, three times over.

"Lisavet," said Evie, with a sigh, then a laugh. *"Lisavet."*

And Marion swore she heard another voice, higher pitched, belonging to Elize, but she didn't dare to open the door and confirm this suspicion, for fear of what she might see if she did. Listening to them together, a harsh and unholy chorus of shared pleasure, Marion felt like she was falling, as though the floorboards were shattering beneath her feet. She caught herself on the wall, stunned not by the betrayal of Lisavet lavishing her affections on another (she'd expected as much) but for the simple fact that it *felt* like a betrayal at all. She barely knew Lisavet, and yet already some part of her longed for her fidelity . . . or worse than that, love.

There was laughter beyond the bedroom door. The pattering of footsteps.

Then Lisavet's muffled voice, a kind of tenderness in it.

Marion edged up to the door, dropped to a crouch before its lock, and peered, breathless, through the keyhole. The three were on the bed, and at distance, through the small opening of the keyhole, it was hard to distinguish the twins from each other. But from what little Marion could gather, they were dressed in matching nightgowns thin as spun gossamer, their pale legs tangled in their skirts. They flanked Lisavet, who took turns lavishing her affection on each of the sisters. Kissing their necks, letting her hands wander past the gaping collars of their nightgowns, grasping and reaching. Her eyes, first shut when Marion lowered herself to the keyhole, opened slowly.

And for a moment, Marion swore their gazes locked.

18

I'll never know an evil so debased as my love for her.

—CECELIA, FIRST BLOODMAID OF THE HOUSE OF HUNGER

SIX DAYS LATER, MARION was summoned to court for the first time in several weeks. She received this news in the bleeding parlor. The invitation was sheathed in a crisp, white envelope and left at the edge of her breakfast tray, handwritten by Lisavet herself.

Marion,

I'm hosting a small gathering tomorrow and I'd like you to attend. I look forward to seeing you.

Yours,
Lisavet

The twins eyed her as she read the letter and quickly sheathed it in its envelope again. Marion had made a point to distance herself from the two after what she'd seen through the keyhole that night, and they had begun to notice her new aloofness.

"Good news?" Elize inquired; she was the more sensitive of the two, so Marion's distancing seemed to affect her more. Marion had noticed how the girl seemed to hang on her every word, straining forward to listen, wide-eyed and rapt, trying to account for the new tensity between them.

But her younger counterpart, Evie, was more withdrawn. Sometimes, based on her edginess, Marion swore that she'd caught her spying that night. Or perhaps Lisavet had simply told her. There was something dark and knowing in her eye. Something that looked a lot like shame.

"It's nothing," said Marion, and she crumpled up the letter, left it to be discarded with the picked-over remnants of her breakfast. She didn't want to talk to Lisavet, or her lovers the twins.

What she had witnessed that night still haunted her. The abhorrence of it. The obscenity.

The scene had been replaying itself in her nightmares for days.

It was a great effort for Marion to pay attention in classes that afternoon. Even Tutor Geoffrey, a remarkably forbearing man, grew impatient with her. "Do you have somewhere more important to be?" he finally demanded, exasperated with her distractedness.

Marion apologized but couldn't drive the dark ruminations from her mind.

Defeated, Tutor Geoffrey ended their class early.

Marion's class with Madame Boucherie was no better. Halfway through their etiquette lesson (wherein she was asked to use the proper utensils to eat an extensive six-course meal), Marion received so many biting strikes from the crop that her palm split open, and Madame Boucherie was forced to relent and switch to striking her left hand instead of her right.

"You dense girl," she said through gritted teeth, gripping the handle of her crop in white-knuckled fury. "This is *precisely* why Lisavet doesn't call you to court anymore. I'm sure she's beginning to suspect what I already know. You were never fit to be a bloodmaid. And you never will be."

Those words haunted Marion as she readied herself for court. The House Mother had commissioned new dresses for her, and she wore one of them that night. A striking black gown with a choker to match (she checked, there were no words embroidered into its band). A servant materialized to bandage her scabbed, crop-bitten hand with gauze and matching black ribbon. In defiance of fashion, Marion opted to wear her curls down that night, flowing freely over her bare shoulders.

On that night, the court gathered in the garden, crowding within the fog-hazed walls of the hothouse. The air was heavy with humidity, so thick Marion felt like she was drinking rather than breathing it. Someone had dragged a dining room table into the aisles that cut through the orchard, half-shaded with swaying palm fronds. The food—an array of roast meats and tiered cakes, cheeses, and hollowed-out pumpkins filled to the brim with thick stews and oyster chowders—was arranged in a line down the center of the table. Riots of roses and dark fern fronds and pine branches stuffed the empty spaces between each of the dishes displayed. Other decorations included glacier ice carvings of swans and the headless busts of naked men and women that wept into the large porcelain basins where they stood.

Marion took a seat at the far end of the table, next to Irene, who had also been called to court as a replacement for Cecelia, who had allegedly fainted in the bleeding room that afternoon. She turned her attention down the table, watched the candlelight flicker over the faces of the nobles whose names she didn't know and couldn't remember. Lisavet wasn't among them. The chair she was meant to occupy at the helm of the table stood empty for the duration of the meal, until a drunken Ivor tramped through the garden to claim it. There was a girl with him bleeding gently from the neck, though as far as Marion could tell, she wasn't a bloodmaid, just a servant snatched from the kitchens if her soiled apron was any indication at all. She was far from the equal of Cecelia or Irene, but she was pretty enough.

Watching a drunken Ivor lavish his affections upon the poor girl, lapping at her bloodied neck, Marion wrinkled her nose. "He'll drain that girl dry by the time the night is done if she lets him."

"Better her than us," said Irene, which was, perhaps, less than caring, but it was also true.

Eventually, Sir Ivor lost interest with the servant girl, and she slipped out of his lap and retreated into the depths of the greenhouse orchard, disappearing into the pall of fog, returning to the House to tend her wounds. In her absence, Ivor amused himself with a maudlum pipe, freshly filled and lit by one of the House's newest guests, a Taster with greasy blond hair by the name of Leo, whose ship was docked at the harbor on the north end of the island.

His imports, bloodmaids, were a set of sisters who'd formerly been indentured at the House of Mirrors and, upon the completion of their four-year tenures, were now seeking new placement. Of the three, the youngest was the most beautiful, with a fine nose and full lips painted a vicious shade of red, her cheeks powdered ghost-pale. She was nothing short of a marvel, and the court was hers to lose. The nobles seemed raptured by her presence, and in turn she rehearsed the choreography of innocence and most importantly humility. It became clear to Marion that the girl had already learned a vital lesson: The nobles of the North were *gluttons* for gratitude, and they loved a girl who knew how to grovel.

Marion could not help but think she favored Cecelia, though she was, perhaps, a less striking version of her. In Marion's opinion, she lacked the dark thrall that made Cecelia so alluring. Still, the girl sat nearest to her Taster, leaning left every few minutes to whisper in his ear with a soft smile that—to Marion—seemed rather cunning beneath the veneer of innocence. That was to her credit. In a bloodmaid, deviousness was less a vice than a virtue. Watching her, Marion feared that she was staring into the face of her new replacement. The girl that Irene had once assured her would bleed better, *be* better, for Lisavet. A girl who could fulfill the Countess in all of the ways Marion could not.

In addition to the new bloodmaids, the Taster brought maudlum and medicinal cocaine, which he claimed was a powerful remedy for a variety of ailments and was second only to the consumption of blood. On Leo's suggestion, the nobles crushed it into powder, cut it into narrow lines, and snuffed it off pewter plates with tightly rolled banknotes.

Sir Ivor removed a slim, leather-bound checkbook from a hidden pocket in his breast coat, tore out a slip of paper, tightly rolled it, and leaned forward to snuff up several thick lines of the powder. Then he stood up, rather suddenly, pausing to wipe the white mustache from beneath his nose, and clapped his hands. "Shall we play a game of forfeits?"

The game itself was simple enough. Each person received a turn to challenge another person (chosen at random, on the whim of the chooser) to complete a task. If they failed to complete the task, whether because of refusal or lack of ability, they could forfeit and receive a punishment, chosen by the person who picked them. Marion—along with Irene and the other nobles and bloodmaids seated at the table—reluctantly agreed to play, so as not to be the odd one out.

At first, the game advanced predictably enough. Nobles were asked to do a number of harmless, if bawdy, punishments and challenges: removing one of their breasts from their bodice, swimming naked in the frigid cold of the ocean, or downing a decanter of wine within a specified window of time. Irene was asked to juggle several blood oranges; when she failed (after a valiant effort), she was ordered to swallow a small pebble whole, which she did dutifully and without complaint. But then it was Ivor's turn to level the challenges. He immediately chose Marion. "I order you to take up a needle and fill this goblet with your blood and allow me to drink it."

There was a chorus of whispers and grumblings. Everyone knew it was a breach of protocol for a bloodmaid indentured to the House of Hunger to serve her blood to anyone but Lisavet.

"I forfeit," said Marion. She was already treading on thin ice, and she suspected such an egregious compromise of House protocol would be enough to warrant her dismissal.

"Fine," said Ivor, looking a little disappointed. He gazed around the room, searching for a suitable punishment. His attention fell to the noblewoman seated to his right, to the maudlum pipe in her hand. He took it from her and extended it to Marion, staring her down through a milky pall of smoke. "Tell me, do foxes dream?"

Irene clenched Marion's knee beneath the table, hard enough to leave a bruise. "Don't."

"Come now," said Ivor, chiding her. "Don't be so chaste. Lisavet doesn't like a prude, and she likes a poor sport even less."

Marion took the pipe. It was lighter than it looked. Its stem was redwood, carved to resemble the slender silhouette of a woman's form. It had a ceramic bowl, which housed a burning black maudlum pill around the size of a small pea. Marion drew the pipe to her lips. The mouthpiece was still warm. She pretended to toke and began to pass the pipe back.

Ivor shook his head, feigning disappointment. "I do believe we have a cheat among us."

A chorus of boos erupted from the nobles seated at the table. Irene tried to comfort her over their jeering, but the noise drowned out whatever it was she was trying to say.

Ivor looked pleased. "You have one more chance, Marion. Do bear in mind that your lovely competitors"—he motioned to the new, prospective bloodmaids seated nearby—"have been enthusiastic and *honorable* participants in our little game. And there are only so many bedrooms in the bloodmaids' quarters. Surely Lisavet would prefer it if they were occupied by girls who are principled enough to observe the rules of the games they choose to play instead of—"

Marion snatched the pipe back, cheeks burning with the shame of being caught. She drew a short breath, tasting a perfume of flowers before dragging the burning smoke into the pits of her lungs, and exhaled fast and hard with a racking cough. It wasn't her first time smoking maudlum. On his more cheerful days—when he'd had luck at the gambling tables—Raul liked to share his vices and would often offer Marion a few tokes on his pipe. But Marion could immediately tell that this stuff was a lot stronger than whatever Raul smoked. It hit her fast, scattered her thoughts, and sent her reeling into the thin realm between dreams and reality.

Time slowed, and Marion felt a strange sinking sensation, as though the past were a muddy mire and she was half-sunk in it, submerged up to the chest. A pleasant heat spread through her body, like the gentle beginnings of what would become a bad fever, and with it a drowsiness she tried hard to fight. Intent on seeing Lisavet, she didn't let the dreams take her.

So the dreams of the past became the present instead.

Across the table, Ivor's face morphed into Raul's. He looked just as he had when Marion left him, his skull buckled inward, blood slicking the left half of his face. When he spoke, his jaw seemed to unhinge itself, and Marion could see that his mouth was alive with writhing worms that crawled behind his teeth and chewed at the soft, gray meat of his tongue. When he huffed a laugh, a storm of horseflies erupted from the depths of his throat and swarmed the air.

"I shouldn't have left you," she said to her brother, who was not really her brother at all. When she spoke, her tongue felt thick behind her teeth, and it was hard to talk through her tears, but she managed to do it anyway.

"Marion?"

She blinked back her tears and half turned to see Irene leaning toward her. "It's your turn."

Marion realized then that the eyes of the table were on her. Some of them looked on, confused by her tears. Others laughed and whispered behind cupped hands or the shade of their fans, mocking her.

Across the table, Ivor, who had appeared to her as Raul just moments ago, smirked at her. "I suppose the smoke doesn't agree with her."

Marion's cheeks flushed with shame; hastily she wiped away her tears. A peculiar and sobering rage came over her. The feeling was enough to drag her back down into her body and ground her there, firmly. She fixed her eyes on Ivor. "Is it true that you wish to unseat Lisavet and claim this House for your own?"

Sir Ivor grew very pale and for a moment he looked almost fragile, like a bird-boned little boy.

Marion persisted, rubbing a gritty fistful of salt into the sore of Ivor's wounded pride. He had humiliated her, and she would do the same to him. "It's almost pathetic, that you're so thoroughly lacking in charm that Lisavet could never lower herself to love you. A low-ranking castoff in the House of your birth—a bastard son, beloved by no one—and now the only way for you to realize your ambition is to pick at the leavings of another's inheritance like a vulture stripping meat from a bloated corpse. At least, that's what's rumored. Tell us, Ivor, is it true? Or would you prefer to forfeit in the interest of protecting what little remains of your dignity?"

Ivor's upper lip twitched, then curled, pulling away from his gritted teeth. He looked like he wanted to lunge across the table and strike her, and Marion almost wished he would if only so that she had reason to swing back. She should've killed him when she'd had the chance and was stunned by the vehemence of her own hatred for him.

Ivor leaned across the table. "You fork-tongued *whore—*"

"That's quite enough," said a voice from behind her. Marion wheeled to face her Countess. She wore a high-cut velvet gown, with a thick gold chain strung from shoulder to shoulder.

Ivor kicked back from the table, his chair striking the dirt behind him. He stormed through the orchard, tramping through the brush, crushing flowers underfoot. A beat later came the sound of the greenhouse door slamming shut with so much violence that Marion half expected it to shatter.

Down the table, Taster Leo stood up, rather awkwardly. There was a gossamer film of white powder below his nose, and he wiped it away. "My lady, might I present the Doyle sisters?"

He motioned to them with a flourish of his hands. The girls stood, drunk and a little shaky, simpering at Lisavet. They dropped into unsteady curtsies. The youngest nearly toppled, and caught herself on the back of a nearby chair.

To Marion's immense relief, Lisavet didn't so much as look at them. "I won't be requiring any new bloodmaids."

The youngest of the prospective bloodmaids seemed so stunned by this curt dismissal that her mouth gaped wide open. The bloody rouge on her bottom lip smeared, leaving a scarlet mark on her chin.

The Taster, perhaps eager to collect his finder's fee, rushed to intervene. "But my lady—"

"It's been a pleasure," said Lisavet in curt dismissal. Her tone made it plain there would be no further negotiation.

Thus, resigned to his startling defeat, the Taster dismissed himself and the sisters—his scorned prizes—with a curt bow and a muttered "Good night."

As the four shuffled out of the greenhouse, no doubt retiring to their boat docked in the estuary, the Countess fixed her eyes on Marion. "Might I have a word with you alone?"

Stunned, Marion nodded. When Lisavet stepped away from the table, she followed suit. The two of them threaded through the throng of nobles in unspoken tandem, one trailing after the other. Lisavet led her outside—where the air was sharp with cold and the festivities of the feast far from them—and into the overgrown labyrinth beyond the kitchen gardens.

Lisavet's pace quickened and Marion, in her heavy gown, had to hoist up her skirts and began to jog a little to keep up with her. "Wait!"

The Countess half turned to look at Marion over her shoulder. She smiled boyishly, her mouth canted, a deep dimple pressed into her cheek. Then she began to run, disappearing around the corner of an overgrown hedge.

Marion slipped on a moss-slick cobblestone and fell. "Lisavet!"

There was soft laughter.

Marion scrambled to her feet and kicked off her slippers. They were pinching her heels anyway. "I don't like this game."

"And yet I insist that you play it." Lisavet's disembodied voice seemed to seethe through the hedges and brambles.

Marion rounded the same corner Lisavet had, only to discover that the path had forked. And she saw no sign of Lisavet and had no idea where she'd gone. She went left, down the narrower of the two paths, her skirts ripping on brambles as she squeezed through. As she rounded yet another corner, one of the thorns slit her cheek and she began to bleed.

But she kept going through the winding passages of the labyrinth until she reached the great stone mausoleum that stood at its center. Lisavet was waiting for her there, her back to Marion.

"When my father died, my mother, his bloodmaid, insisted upon being entombed with him. So, on the day of his funeral, they bricked her in alive with his corpse."

Marion's blood ran cold at the thought.

"A week after her funeral, I summoned the courage to venture here. I swore I could hear her nails scrabbling on the other side of the bricks. Sometimes, even now, I can hear it. If I'm quiet enough. Listen. Do you hear it?"

Marion listened. Heard nothing but waves breaking against the cliffs, the distant din of the party. She stepped out into the courtyard, stopping just short of the Countess. "Lisavet, what am I doing here?"

Lisavet turned to Marion then, saw the bleeding scratch on her cheek. She smeared the blood away with her thumb and, with her eyes on Marion, licked it clean. "I've been cruel to you."

"Yes, you have been, and I'd like to know why. Because as far as I can tell, I've done nothing to warrant this . . . *coldness*."

"I was afraid. Your blood is the most potent I've ever tasted. My father told me that every Count or Countess who sits at the mantle of the House of Hunger will find a bloodmaid that is their equal in every way. A muse, a kindred companion that supersedes all of the others that have come before her. My father found that in my mother. But I never believed I would find my own match . . . until the night I met you. From the moment I first sampled your blood, I knew you were different. And that frightened me." Lisavet stared down at her, searching, her eyes touched by the wan moonlight. "If you'll forgive me for my coldness and give me the opportunity to overcome my cowardice, I would have you completely. I would make you First Bloodmaid."

Marion's eyes widened. She waited for Lisavet to laugh, or smile, or give any indication that this abrupt proposition was a cruel joke. But the Countess just continued looking at her, wide-eyed and expectant, as if she was waiting for Marion to break her with a single word. "What about Cecelia?"

"I've informed her of my decision," said Lisavet. "She's aware."

Marion stared at her, stunned. "But I haven't even agreed to accept."

"Cecelia is sick; either way she would've been replaced," said Lisavet. "Besides, she doesn't fulfill me the way that you do. None of the others do."

"I saw you with the twins," said Marion, rather sharply. It was too hard to continue containing her hurt. "Did you ask one of them to be First Bloodmaid too?"

"The twins were a distraction," said Lisavet. "I needed them to keep my mind off you. Because I was . . . intimidated by my desire for you. That's why I stayed away. I thought the distance would help, but it only made me want you more. I can't continue to fight my hunger for you, Marion. I want you near me. I would give you everything. All of me, if you'll only let me have you."

Marion stared at her for a long time in silence, trying to parse truth from mere presumption. She didn't know whether what Lisavet was saying was true, or if she merely wanted it to be. She was happy to be rid of the burden of her doubt, of the memory of Lisavet with the twins, of Cecelia's stinging slights, of her own humiliation. It was easy, then, to digest all that Lisavet had said, take it as truth, and let her words ease that gnawing lust for significance, for *power*, that Marion had nursed within her since she was just a little girl, hoisted up on her mother's hip, gazing into the frosted windows of the night train, eagerly awaiting the day that she would sit among its passengers as a bloodmaid of the North.

This was the validation she'd been yearning for. She had waited years for this moment.

She decided, then, to seize it. "I'm already yours."

The Countess took her roughly by the chin and dragged her into a vicious, bruising kiss. The force was such that Marion staggered back, the jagged stones of the mausoleum crushing into her back. When they finally parted, both were gasping for breath. Marion tasted blood and had the strange and uncanny suspicion that it was Irene's.

Lisavet tipped her forehead to Marion's. She was breathing hard and shallow. In her eyes were the same desperation and want that Marion often saw in the glazed eyes of the children who haunted the street corners of Prane in the wintertime, frostbitten fingers out-stretched to the passersby, begging for coin. Marion, once one of those children herself, knew the magnitude of that hunger. A depri-vation so complete it became almost punitive. A want that made the knees go weak.

Marion raised a shaking hand to Lisavet's pale cheek and angled close enough to feel the heat of her mouth. "Kiss me again," she said, and as the young Countess drew Marion into her arms, she swore she heard the sound of nails on stone, scratching.

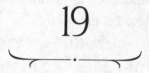

19

As I sit with the needle buried deep in my arm
I wonder, do I empty myself in vain?

—AURIEL, BLOODMAID OF THE HOUSE OF MIRRORS

IN THE DARK HOURS before dawn, Marion retired to the blood-maids' quarters, her cheeks flushed with cold, her lips swollen and bruised, her head still a little light from all the maudlum . . . and the passions that Lisavet stirred in her. She stole across the parlor as quietly as she could and had nearly reached her bedroom when she heard a strange sound coming from behind the shut door of Cece-lia's room—glass breaking.

She faltered. A part of her wanted to pretend she hadn't heard the sound, but pity kept her feet pinned firmly in place. Cecelia had fallen from grace, and Marion had risen to replace her. And while she knew that guilt was not her burden to bear—Cecelia certainly didn't deserve it—she couldn't help but feel a little sorry for the girl. It couldn't be an easy thing, to be bested and shunned so suddenly.

Marion approached Cecelia's door cautiously and knocked, but there was no answer. Just the rustling of fabric. The sound of bare feet slapping the floor. Marion leaned her forehead against the door. "Cecelia, are you awake?"

A long pause. Then a soft voice that seemed to come from the keyhole. "Yes."

"What was that sound?"

"It was nothing."

Odd. Very odd. "Could you open the door?"

"No," said the girl, whispering through the keyhole. "I don't think that's wise."

Silence, apart from the sound of labored breathing. And then, in a ragged whisper: "Remind me . . . what's your name?"

Marion's blood ran cold. Had she . . . *forgotten*? "It's Marion."

"Marion . . ." Cecelia said, first testing her name. Then said it again, this time as a question. "Marion?"

"Yes, Cecelia?"

"I've thought about it . . . and I think I would like you to come in after all."

Marion froze. There was the sound of a key fitting into the lock, the soft *click* of the bolt sliding out of place. Cecelia opened the door by no more than a crack, and Marion slid sideways into the dark of the room.

"It was kind of you to come," said Cecelia, and she locked the door behind them, slipped the key into the pocket of her silken robe. "You know, I think you *are* kind. Maybe that's why Lisavet took such a liking to you. She likes kind little things."

Marion stepped forward, felt something cold seeping through her stockings. She peered down and saw that they were stained dark with what appeared to be . . . blood. "Are you hurt?"

Cecelia gave a strained little laugh, seeming sheepish. It was then that Marion saw the wound at her neck, and her wrists, poorly bandaged with what appeared to be torn bedsheets. "I keep filling bowls for her, but the servants won't take them. They tell me Lisavet doesn't crave my blood any longer. Apparently, she's turned off by the taste." When she spoke, blood collected in the corners of her lips and dribbled down her chin.

"Cecelia—"

"I even thought to give her these." She fished through the contents of her pockets and produced a few teeth, still slick with blood and spit, red at the roots. "Pried them out myself this evening. But she didn't want them."

"You're bleeding," said Marion, and when she reached for Cecelia's open wrist the girl raised her hand and slapped Marion across the face with so much force she staggered back and crashed into a nearby bookshelf.

One of Cecelia's oddities—a kidney housed in a large jar, suspended in a greenish brine—fell off its perch at the edge of the shelf and shattered, the organ hitting the floor with a wet *smack*, glass shards skittering everywhere. The reeking brine spilled across the tiles, seeping through Marion's stockings, mixing with Cecelia's blood.

Stunned, Marion raised a hand to her bleeding nose. She saw stars, and in the thick of her shock all she could think to say was: "Why?"

Cecelia didn't answer. She had no expression on her face as she reached into her pocket and withdrew what appeared to be a wickedly sharp, long bleeding needle affixed to an ornate hilt.

"I'm not like you, Marion. I don't have any kindness in me. I'm just . . . well, I'm rather wretched, aren't I?"

Marion threw out a hand. "Wait—"

Cecelia stepped forward—barefoot—walking through the puddles of her blood, through the brine and glass, the shards carving deep into the soles of her feet as she staggered forward. She paused to nudge at the kidney on the floor with her bare toe. "It was my gift from Lisavet. From an elk she killed just after she made me First Bloodmaid." She dropped to a crouch beside it, speared the organ with the tip of her needle, but it was too heavy, and it tore, and slid to the floor again. "I suppose I won't be receiving gifts like this anymore. Now that you've replaced me."

Marion's gaze shifted from Cecelia to the bedroom door. "I'm not your enemy."

The former favorite didn't listen. Slowly, she rose from the floor and held the point of the needle to the hollow crook between Marion's collarbones. "Lisavet no longer has a taste for my blood. But she can't get enough of yours. So perhaps I ought to give her that instead."

Marion raised her leg and kneed Cecelia in the soft of her belly. Before the girl had the chance to recover, she drew back her fist and punched her, hard, the way that Agnes had taught her to, years ago. Her reflexes might've been a bit slowed by the maudlum, but she was still sober enough to put up a fight.

Cecelia staggered back, bent double, both hands cupped over her face. Then, to Marion's horror, the girl erupted into a fit of giggles, throwing back her head, as she succumbed to the throes of her own hysteria. Her racking laughter. Her mouth was open so wide that Marion could see the red gaps at the back where she'd pried her molars free of her gums.

Marion elbowed past her, rushed to the locked door, and began to beat on it, toggling the knob and screaming for help. She could hear servants on the other side, people—or perhaps the other bloodmaids—crying her name, but they couldn't enter without a key.

Watching Marion struggle, Cecelia began to laugh even harder, this time with the same unbridled derangement that she had that night in the hall, the first time Marion was summoned to court. "Are you calling for our beloved Lisavet?" she asked, edging closer. "You want her to lick your open wounds and whisper sweet nothings in your ear?"

Marion wheeled to face her. Stooped to snatch a vicious shard of the shattered jar—slick with blood and brine—from the floor. She raised it between them. "Not a step closer."

Cecelia didn't listen, but kept advancing so that Marion, afraid of being cornered, was forced to abandon her position by the door, sliding along the wall, following the perimeter of the room until her back faced the balcony. She stumbled backward, trying not to trip on the hem of her dress as Cecelia brandished her needle.

The girl wasn't laughing anymore; in fact, she looked like she was on the verge of tears.

Marion backed onto the balcony, peered over her shoulder, and risked a glance at the fall below. The bloodmaids' quarters were on the fourth floor of the House, she knew that, and Cecelia's room overlooked the rock-studded estuary, where marsh and ocean met. It would be a long fall from the balcony's edge to the frigid water and jutting boulders below. Marion gathered her skirts, preparing to jump, when the bedroom door swung slowly open.

Lisavet entered the room. "On your knees."

Cecelia crumpled, a puppet with her strings cut. The needle flew from her hand and slid across the floor, beneath her bed.

Lisavet's eyes shifted to Marion. "You too."

Marion did as she was told, lowering herself to the floor in a puddle of Cecelia's blood, feeling it soak—cold and sticky—through the fibers of her stockings.

Lisavet examined the both of them, crouched at her feet. Behind her were all of the bloodmaids—Irene, Evie, Elize, even Mae—crowding in the doorway behind the House Mother, who looked on in stony silence. And just behind all of them, servants and nobles gathered to see the spectacle.

Lisavet dropped to the floor in front of Cecelia, took her by the chin, and raised her head so that the girl was forced to look at her. "What is the meaning of this?"

"I-I bled . . . but you didn't come. So I—"

Lisavet kissed Cecelia then, with tenderness that fast became passion, and passion that grew into a kind of violence—lips and teeth gnashing together, all open mouths and blood and hunger. And Cecelia, timid and shaking at first, began to kiss Lisavet the same way, straining toward her as though she couldn't get enough. Their display was so passionate that Marion's cheeks began to warm, and she felt she should look away but couldn't bring herself to.

After a few long moments, and with sudden roughness, Lisavet ripped away. There was blood on her mouth and Marion wasn't sure if it was hers or Cecelia's.

"I'm sorry," said the fallen bloodmaid. "Forgive me. Please."

The Countess kept hold of her, fingers crushing into the soft of the girl's cheeks as she squeezed. "Cecelia of the House of Hunger, your tenure has come to an end."

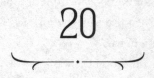

20

*It is only natural that bloodmaids form certain affinities
for their peers. However, favor is a fickle thing and
rivalry makes enemies of the kindest souls.*

—NONA, BLOODMAID OF THE HOUSE OF LOCUSTS

CECELIA LEFT BEFORE SUNRISE. The bloodmaids weren't allowed
to say goodbye to her before she departed. In the wake of her at-
tack on Marion, all of them were ushered to their respective bedrooms, where they were told to remain until morning, under penalty
of severe punishment. Marion stayed up until daybreak, sitting on
the floor of her chamber by the door, listening to the commotion on
the other side of it. There were footsteps and half-hushed murmurings, hissing whispers and the sound of furniture scraping across the
floor, candlelight and shifting shadows that leaked through the crack
beneath Marion's bedroom door.

When the bloodmaids were finally allowed to emerge later that
morning, it was to the discovery that the servants had emptied Cecelia's bedroom of all personal belongings, so that there were no
traces of her left. It was as though she had never been indentured to
the House. As though she had never known Lisavet or any of her
affections. In a way, it seemed as if she had never existed at all.

Instead of going down to the kitchens to bleed, all of the blood-maids were escorted into the House Mother's private parlor, where a small breakfast had been assembled for them.

"Do make yourselves comfortable," said the House Mother, motioning for them to seat themselves around the large hearth fire. The twins—silent and skittish—sat hip-to-hip on a chaise at the far corner of the room. Irene claimed a small armchair, and Mae sat on her lap. Marion, unsure of what she was meant to do, sat alone on a small ottoman, well apart from the twins, who took turns casting her sharp glances across the parlor, and Irene, who barely seemed able to look at her, as though this dark turn of events was, somehow, her fault.

And perhaps it was.

When all of the bloodmaids were comfortably settled, the House Mother prepared each of them a cup of tea. There were a selection of scones and finger sandwiches on a small table at the heart of the parlor, but no one touched them.

"I want to apologize for Cecelia's poor conduct," said the House Mother, finally settling herself in the large wingback armchair that stood before the fire. "It was a grave embarrassment and I'm so sorry you were made to witness it. I assure you that I will *never* allow such barbarity to occur within this House again."

The girls seemed unmoved by this attempt at assurance. No one spoke.

"Marion will replace Cecelia as our new First Bloodmaid and, as such, she will move into the chambers that Cecelia left vacant."

This news was received in utter silence and Marion flushed with shame. She'd never intended to be Cecelia's rival or replacement, but she'd become exactly that. Her arrival at the House had been Cecelia's downfall, and now she'd made enemies of her peers who remained. Even Mae seemed to shun her, refusing to meet her gaze across the parlor as though she couldn't stomach looking at her.

Once again, Marion had found herself resigned to the fringes, with no friends or allies to speak of . . . except for perhaps Lisavet.

Marion knew she ought to feel triumphant now that her dream had finally come to fruition. But gazing at the other bloodmaids, she didn't feel even remotely victorious. In fact, she didn't feel much of anything at all except, perhaps, a peculiar hollowness. As though she'd lost something and couldn't remember what.

The House Mother frowned at the girls, her graying brows knitting together. She set her teacup down on a nearby table. "Girls, we should offer Marion our warmest congratulations and well-wishes as she embarks upon this new journey. Jealousy is far from becoming."

There was a beat of silence. Then, as if startled from a trance, Irene began to clap and the twins followed suit, offering a brief round of obligatory applause that seemed, to Marion, more like mockery.

"Irene, your rank remains unchanged," said the House Mother, sipping from her little cup of tea. The bone-pale porcelain was painted with a watery rendering of a fox hunt. "Evie and Elize, you will also remain at the levels of Third and Fourth Bloodmaid, accordingly."

"May I ask what will happen to Cecelia?" Evie inquired lightly, the only one among them who was brave or perhaps stupid enough to broach the topic.

"Cecelia has departed for a period of respite at a sanatorium in the North, where she will receive the help and care she so desperately needs. But her tenure here has ended, and she won't be allowed to return."

"Can we write letters to Cecelia?" Irene inquired.

The House Mother offered a terse little smile. "What a kind gesture. I'm sure Cecelia would love to hear from you. Please direct all of your letters to me, and I'll make sure she receives them."

Their meeting ended with that. Irene, Mae, and the twins left the House Mother's parlor talking softly among themselves, their backs to Marion, exchanging whispers behind cupped hands. They made it clear that Marion wasn't welcome to follow them, so she didn't try.

Alone, and unsure of how to spend her day without classes or bleeding to distract her, Marion found her way into Cecelia's newly vacated room, the chambers that she would now occupy as First Bloodmaid of the House. All of Cecelia's belongings were gone—the clothes, the books, the oddities, the jewelry and powders that had cluttered her vanity—and the floors had been wiped clean of blood and brine, all of the glass shards swept away.

The bed had been stripped, dressed with crisp, white sheets. The balcony doors were thrown open, and a harsh and brackish wind swept in off the marshes. In the distance, beyond the estuary's end, lay the vast expanse of the open ocean.

Marion went first to the balcony to look at the view and watch the white-capped waves roar and wreck themselves against the cliff below. Then she explored the room, examining what few items had been left behind, running her fingers over the furniture as the servants came in and out, moving her belongings in.

Marion pulled open the drawer of Cecelia's former vanity and faltered. There was a small word carved into its bottom, the same one that Marion had discovered etched into the leg of her old bed: *wretch*. In the hours that followed, Marion found that word in more than a dozen other places. It had been carved into one of her bedposts, and on the headboard, hidden just behind the mattress. With what appeared to be the tip of a needle, she had etched it into the underside of the painted pedestal table that stood beside the reading chair in her sitting room. It had even been cut in tiny letters into the ceiling above the bed, as if to ensure it was the last thing one saw before falling asleep.

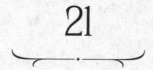

21

*It is imperative that a bloodmaid learn to set the burden
of morality aside. The North has no place for it.*

—NORA, FIRST BLOODMAID OF THE HOUSE OF RAVENS

THAT EVENING, WHEN THE rest of the bloodmaids gathered for
supper in the dining room, Marion, to her immense relief, was
summoned down to the baths to attend to Lisavet. The servants had
prepared a light meal for them, consisting of a cheese board covered
in a variety of selections: cold meats—ham sliced thinner than paper, hard rolls of spiced blood sausage, and raw-smoked trout—as
well as a limited selection of breads and fruit. By the time Marion
entered the baths, Lisavet had already started eating and was sipping
on a glass of wine, which she extended when Marion entered. "I've
been waiting."

Marion accepted the offering and took a chaste sip, only to discover from the metallic flavor that it was blood wine, and she
promptly spat it back into its cup.

"Not to your taste?" Lisavet inquired innocently, and Marion
realized it was meant to be a prank.

"You're entertaining, if a little unkind," said Marion, and she wiped her mouth on the sleeve of her dress, staining the fabric with a rusty smear. "Is it mine?"

"The last of Cecelia's," said Lisavet, and she opened her robe. Her body was beautiful enough to be the envy of any bloodmaid. Her chest was fairly ample, the hard buds of her nipples a dark blush, in sharp contrast to her skin. She had a nipped waist and broad, well-cut shoulders. Her skin—milk pale—was spangled with bluish bruises (a symptom of her blood disorder, no doubt) but also silvery scars and the crescent moon marks of bite wounds and pinprick needle marks long healed. "My father."

"What?" said Marion, snapping to attention and dropping her gaze to the floor. How long had she been staring?

"The scars," said Lisavet lightly, walking toward the hot spring of her choice, a dark burbling pool cast in a blanket of steam. "I got them from my father. He claimed that the blood of the young was sweeter and more powerful."

Marion's stomach turned. "I thought it was a crime for children to be bloodmaids."

"The scars are from bloodlettings," said Lisavet, and she ran her finger along one of them, a silvery mark that traced the path of a large, bluish artery, "but I was no bloodmaid."

"I didn't know the northern nobles partook from each other."

"They don't. My father was plagued with a . . . formidable hunger. Nothing—not sex or blood, riches or violence—was enough to sate his appetite. He was always in want of more." Lisavet trailed into silence, her eyes emptying of all emotion. "Men like him don't care about taboo. Their desires are paramount and everything else comes second to them."

"How much blood did your father take from you?" Marion asked, though she knew she had no right to. It was a dangerous game that the two of them were playing, edging tenderfooted through a minefield riddled with vile secrets, each of them threatening to implode beneath their feet should someone ask the wrong question . . . or say the wrong thing.

"More than I had to give," said Lisavet, wading waist-deep into the steaming waters of the bath. When she turned to face her again, peering at her through the thick of the steam, Marion immediately dropped her gaze to the floor, a violent blush burning her cheeks. But if the Countess noticed her staring, she paid her no mind. "Frankly, I'm surprised he didn't extract my bones and crack them open to feast on the marrow."

"Did your mother ever intervene?" Marion inquired.

"My mother was a bloodmaid and she stood by and watched. I think she was more concerned with her indentureship than she was her daughter. It wasn't in her best interest to protest my mistreatment. Sometimes I suspected she was . . . jealous that my father preferred my blood to hers."

"That's horrible."

"She was wretched," said Lisavet, her eyes going glassy. It took her a long moment to recover herself, but eventually she did. "At some point I realized that it would have to be me or my father. I knew that if I kept bleeding for him, he'd drain me dry, so I devised a little scheme. One day, I must've been around eleven or twelve at the time, I walked down into the marshes in search of crimson caps. Have you heard of them?"

Marion shook her head.

"They're white with black gills and they grow rather low to the ground; makes them difficult to spot amid the sea of the marsh grass. Sauteed, with a bit of thyme and butter, a splash of white wine, and they make a most delicious dish. If you cut them raw, they'll bleed just like us. And that's where the poison is, in their blood. A thimbleful of theirs is enough to turn ours toxic. But you have to consume them raw."

"I think I've seen them," said Marion, thinking back on one of her first meals at the House of Hunger. The House chef had served them, stewed in a bloody sauce of wine and their own juice. They'd been delicious . . . but she had no idea they could be so lethal. "You ate these mushrooms?"

Lisavet nodded, wading deeper into the bath so that the water stopped just short of her collarbones. "I found a ring of them near the marshes, plucked them from the ground, and ate every single one. Then I went into the House kitchen to bleed for my father, as I did almost every night and morning. I served him the bowl myself, watched the apple of his throat bob up and down as he drank his fill of my poisoned blood. He was dead before dinner. And I very nearly followed him."

"You poisoned yourself to poison him?" Marion asked, disbelieving, a chill skating down her spine at the thought. It was hard to imagine Lisavet, a little girl of no more than eleven, having the resolve, and the means, to successfully poison and *kill* her own father, knowing that there was a good chance she would poison and kill herself in the process. What could drive a young girl to the depths of such darkness? What kind of monster had been made of her at such a young age?

"Don't look at me like that," said Lisavet, staring at her. "We're not so different. I killed my father. You killed your brother. We're both sticky with their blood. The day I poisoned my father, I scrubbed my hands until the flesh peeled away from my palms in sheets. I felt so . . . *dirty.*"

Marion knew that feeling. The stickiness of guilt. Like honey on the skin.

Once again, Lisavet's eyes took on the glazed and faraway look of someone dragged back to a memory they'd sooner forget. But the moment passed quickly, and she focused on Marion again. "Are you coming in or not? The water's quite warm."

Marion swallowed dry. "I . . . of course."

Hastily, she undressed, fumbling with the buttons and laces, wishing that Lisavet would avert her gaze and in doing so spare her from the humiliation of being examined. In the wake of Lisavet's striking beauty, Marion felt hideous, with her shapeless figure and large feet, her skinny, freckled legs that bowed outward at the knee. But despite her many flaws, there was something in Lisavet's gaze as she peered up at Marion through the shifting steam that made her feel . . . desired. Lisavet looked at her as if she was something worth looking at, which was more than Marion could say for the lovers she'd shared beds with in Prane, women who could barely bring themselves to look her in the eye or admit that what they felt for her was far more than the fondness between friends. Those girls had always averted their gazes, even when Marion made love to them. They didn't feel, or perhaps didn't *allow* themselves to feel anything remotely close to tenderness. And they had certainly never bothered to regard her as Lisavet did now.

"There," said the Countess, still staring at her through the rolling steam. Her eyes were narrowed, and there was hunger in them. "Now we're equals."

Marion tested the water with one toe and recoiled with a hiss. "It's almost boiling."

"Don't be weak."

Gritting her teeth, Marion forced herself to take a step deeper; the stinging water licked at her calves. She peered down, the fog parting as she waded, and to her surprise she saw that the water was as red as blood.

"It's the minerals," Lisavet said, splashing the water across her neck and shoulders, eyes closed. "Red salts, they call them."

Marion gritted her teeth as the water reached high enough to lick her belly button. The salt stung her skin until it felt like her whole body was burning. "This is meant to be relaxing?"

"Not exactly. But the pain is part of cleansing. It seeps into your wounds. Makes them heal faster. There were rumors that springs like these once held so much power that a corpse bathed in them would come to life again."

"Is there some kind of magic in it?"

Lisavet nodded. "Apparently, these springs ran with the blood of the slain gods who fell to their deaths on the northern mountains. It was said that their blood ran down the slopes and flooded the ocean. That's why the water turned brackish."

"I've never heard that story before."

"I don't think they tell it in the South," said Lisavet. "Probably because it's a foolish rumor. If these springs held any such power, I would've been healed long ago."

Silence fell again, save for the gentle lapping of the water. It was the kind of quiet that wasn't meant to be broken, so Marion was almost surprised by the sound of her own voice when she opened her mouth and said, "Does your sickness have a name?"

"Not a proper one. My father, and all of my ancestors who came before him, simply called it the hunger. The sickness is this House's namesake. It's been with us for generations. Since the very beginning of our bloodline."

"What does it feel like?" Marion asked. It was, perhaps, a forward question. But there was something about the quiet between them and the way Lisavet looked at her that made her feel like they were no longer Countess and bloodmaid. They were less . . . or perhaps more.

The Countess eyed her carefully, her gaze so sharp it seemed to slit Marion down the middle, cut her open, exposing her innards for Lisavet to see and scrutinize. She didn't answer the question and was quiet for some time. "When I was younger, my hunger was all nose-bleeds and stupor. Bruises stamped across my skin and a chill that never left me. But now, when I'm laid low, it feels like starving. It's as if I'm housing a storm of locusts in my belly, and they're hungry for all of the things I'll never get to do or see. The people I'll never meet. The mountains I'll never climb. The oceans I'll never sail across. The lives I'll never lead."

Marion very nearly reached for Lisavet's hand but stopped short.

"On the worst days—when I'm at my weakest and I swear I can feel the cold shadow of death cast over me—it feels like the locusts are chewing through the walls of my stomach to be free of me." Lisavet studied her through the rolling steam, and Marion could see it in her plainly then: a small starvation growing bigger the longer that she looked at her. "Just when I feel like the creatures are going to gnaw their way out of me, or devour me down to my very bones, a cup of tea laced with your blood arrives at my bedside, delivered by a servant. I drink it and buy myself a few more hours . . . or days. So I've learned to live moment to moment. I never imagine a future beyond the next cup of blood. The next girl who bleeds to fill it."

Lisavet looked at Marion for a moment longer before she managed to peel her gaze away. She was quiet for a while after that, began to bathe herself in silence, her fingers shifting across countless bite marks, the dark stains of the bruises. Watching her, Marion could not help but feel they were beautiful. *She* was beautiful, maybe more beautiful than she ever had been, with hair hanging limp and her bare shoulders flecked with silvery droplets of water. "Tell me, Marion, do you hunger for me?"

Marion was glad her cheeks were already flushed from the heat so Lisavet couldn't see her blushing. "You're not my bloodmaid. I have no right to."

"You can hunger for things that don't belong to you."

Marion made herself meet Lisavet's lingering gaze. "Why would I let myself want what I can never have?"

The Countess waded forward, closing the distance between them. She cupped Marion's face with a trembling hand, sliding her thumb across her open mouth. Her other hand disappeared beneath the surface of the water and traced along the inside of Marion's leg, her fingers finding their way to the slit space between her thighs, then moving higher still. Marion's breath hitched as Lisavet's fingers entered her.

The Countess smiled. "The hunger will come. Whether or not you let it."

Marion braced a hand on the edge of the bath to steady herself as Lisavet's fingers plunged deeper.

"Do you want this, Marion? Are you hungry?"

Marion—heart racing, heat seething between her thighs—nodded.

And with that, they were upon each other.

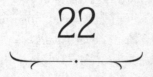

22

Upon the beginning of her tenure, a bloodmaid
will soon discover that the terrain of her
master's heart is often wild and uncharted.

—AUGUSTINA, BLOODMAID OF THE HOUSE OF ORCHIDS

AFTER THEIR FIRST TRYST, Marion was summoned to Lisavet every night. They would spend their passions in the waters of the bathing room, or in the privacy of Lisavet's chambers. Marion gave herself over to Lisavet—again and again—in the throes of a hunger the likes of which she had never known before. The nights would have been perfect, if not for the fact that Lisavet made certain the two of them separated before dawn.

Most of the time, Lisavet would send Marion back to the bloodmaids' quarters shortly after their passions were spent. On the rare occasion that she let her stay, Marion would always wake to discover an empty room, Lisavet's side of the bed long gone cold, her whereabouts unknown. Marion began to suspect, with a nasty pang of jealousy, that she had another, secret lover. But she happened upon no evidence to that end.

One night, when the snow was coming down thick, Marion woke in the darkness and discovered, yet again, that the Countess was missing. This time her curiosity got the better of her and she got up and tried to look for her in the salons, among the members of court. But she wasn't in any of the parlors, or the ballrooms, or with another bloodmaid. It seemed no one had an explanation as to where Lisavet was then, or how she spent her nights.

Weeks passed into months. The House of Hunger grew to become a home to Marion, the only one she'd ever had. In Prane, she'd never felt such a strong sense of belonging, even when her parents were still alive. She'd always felt like an outsider, as if she'd been born into a life that was never meant to belong to her. But in the House of Hunger, Marion lived as the person she was born to be.

Most mornings, she bled dutifully, often to the point of feeling faint. With Cecelia gone, and Lisavet's health declining, more blood was required from the remaining maids, and they all struggled to meet the demand. After bleeding, she attended her classes with Tutor Geoffrey and Madame Boucherie, who had softened toward her considerably after her promotion to First Bloodmaid. The woman almost never used her crop on Marion anymore, and instead of exercises in humiliation, their daily etiquette lessons had expanded into the more extensive studies required to, in Madame Boucherie's words, make a bloodmaid deserving of the title *genteel*.

On one morning in particular, the woman had held the handle of her crop in a white-knuckled vise grip, looking on with tears in her eyes as Marion played the harpsichord in the corner of the ballroom, her fingers crawling across the keys like the legs of a spider. She hadn't believed herself to be playing particularly well; she struggled with a few chords, struck the wrong note with her thumb several times, and squinted at the sheet music trying to distinguish Ds from Gs and make sense of the hatchings of the measures and the black dots of the notes that seemed to swim before her eyes like gnats as she attempted to interpret them into a song. But Madame Boucherie seemed to hear something Marion didn't. She closed her eyes, a few tears leaking down her hollow cheeks, and even began to sway as she listened to Marion labor through the last of the melody.

In the early evenings, before she was summoned to Lisavet, Marion dined with her fellow bloodmaids, who, with time, had come to reluctantly accept her new role as First Bloodmaid, though Marion could tell they still held her at an arm's length, not entirely trusting her intentions. But Marion had also noticed, over dinner and during afternoon tea in the greenhouse garden, that the girls had begun to regard each other with suspicion.

Marion noticed that Irene had grown reclusive, spending more time alone in her room or apart from the other girls, as if intentionally avoiding them. Relations between the twins seemed similarly strained. They were always attached at the hip—as if fused together—but she'd sensed some budding rivalry between them. Once, while Marion was penning a letter to Agnes in the parlor (one of several she'd sent over the passing months), she heard them feuding in their bedroom, in a rapid-fire volley of hushed whispers. Their argument culminated with Elize fleeing the bedroom in tears, Evie slamming the door shut behind her.

After dinner with the bloodmaids, which was always tense and rather quiet, Marion spent most of her nights in court. She'd become quite good at playing cards and had picked up dancing too. On more nights than one, she'd waltzed until her heels chafed raw on the backs of her slippers, and the open sores began to bleed. When her time in court was finished, she would be summoned to Lisavet and spend the last of the night indulging in pleasures the likes of which she had never known before.

All was well and right with Marion's little world in the House of Hunger.

She wanted for nothing except, during the day and in the latter half of the night, Lisavet.

"When you leave me, where do you go?" Marion asked one evening while braiding Lisavet's hair. In comparison to Marion's dense curls, her hair was slack and thin, and it didn't hold a plait half as well. But Marion liked the way it moved—slick and cool—like oil between her fingers when she combed it.

"Why do you want to know?" Lisavet inquired, picking at a mote of dirt beneath her fingernail.

"Because it's time I'd like to spend with you."

"Don't you have enough of me?" Lisavet asked, looking up at her. "Are you not content?"

"I'll be content when we can see the dawn together. Like proper lovers do."

"You wound me," said Lisavet. "I thought we were lovers in every sense of the word."

"Lovers lie entwined until night dies into morning. They spend their days together. They make promises to each other that they know they can't keep."

"Did you read that in a book?"

"I hate reading and you know it."

Lisavet paused, her pen stalling at the edge of the letter. "If I were to make you a promise like that, what would you want it to be?"

Marion thought on the question for a long time, turning it over in her head. "I'd want you to say that you belong to me as much as I belong to you."

"I do."

"You don't mean that," said Marion, turning away as her mood soured. Most nights with Lisavet felt . . . suspended, as if they existed within a reality of their own, where nothing beyond the limits of their bodies mattered much, and everything between them felt sacred. But this was no such night.

Lisavet took her by the hand, studied her fingertips. "You're cross with me. Why?"

Marion didn't know how to answer . . . except to say that sometimes, when she lay with Lisavet, she felt like Cecelia and all the others who came before her—bloodmaids whose names Marion didn't know—were dwelling there with them. And their spectral presence was enough to make Marion feel like whatever she believed to be true about Lisavet—and the passions the two of them shared—was somehow less sacred.

"Why did things end with Cecelia?" Marion asked at last. "What went wrong between you two? You never told me the story."

Lisavet brushed the blankets away, exposed Marion's bare legs to the cold. The Countess then leaned over her lap and began to trace her lips along her inner thigh. "There's no story to tell," said Lisavet between kisses. "When she first arrived, years ago, I thought that she and I were kindred because like me, Cecelia had a palate for the more . . . demanding delights of the flesh." Marion felt a sharp pang of jealousy. "I believed that our shared interests made us compatible, and perhaps they did for a time. But in the end, Cecelia was very sick."

"Sick with what?"

Lisavet didn't answer. She continued trailing her lips along Marion's inner thigh, then bit her there, her canines cutting so deep she drew a little blood, and hastily licked it away.

Marion, who had become accustomed to Lisavet's playful love bites and nipping, didn't mind the pain. She cupped the Countess' face, tilted her chin so she was forced to look up at her. "What was Cecelia sick with?" she asked again.

The Countess licked her gold-capped canines clean of Marion's blood. "She loved me and was afraid of me in equal measure. That mixture turned to madness, I think."

"Did Cecelia have reason to be afraid?"

"Yes," said Lisavet, after a long beat of silence. "Hunger makes monsters of the kindest souls. And to be quite honest . . . I've never been particularly kind."

Marion went very still and quiet at this.

Watching her, Lisavet seemed to shrink, her eyes wide with a vulnerability that made it easy for Marion to see the child within her. The little girl who'd been bled and bitten, terribly abused. "Are you afraid of me too?"

"No," said Marion, and she caught the Countess by the hand and studied it. Her fingernails—square and pale, cut down to the quick. On her left hand, around her index finger, her signet ring set with a misshapen ruby so large and bloody on first glance it appeared to be some type of small organ, like a rat's heart cut fresh from its chest.

"Do you like it?" Lisavet inquired. "The stone alone is worth more than this House and everything in it. Here, try it on." Lisavet slipped the signet ring off her index finger and, taking Marion gingerly by the hand, slid it onto her thumb. It was heavy, so heavy she had a hard time holding her hand up. "It's been in my family for generations."

Marion stared at the ring, studying the face carved, crudely, into the hard ruby. "Who is he?"

"They say he came from the sea—a creature less than man, though not by much. His belly burned with a hunger that couldn't be satisfied with the cold fish and the slithering eel and the brittle crustaceans that crawled at the bottom of the sea. He craved something more, something warm and bloody, so he followed his hunger up from the depths, into the shallows, to the surface of the water, where he discovered an island through the fog that blanketed the surface of the ocean."

Marion slid the ring off her finger and slipped it back onto Lisavet's.

The Countess frowned down at it, as though she didn't want it returned to her. "For months, maybe years, he wandered the island in solitude. Hunting the warm-blooded creatures—badgers and elk, foxes and cranes—that called the island home, trying to quell the hunger in his belly. One day, on the same beach where he first surfaced, he found a girl, lying wounded in the wreckage of a ship, rent by the winds of a terrible storm. The man carried the girl back to the cliffs by the seaside, where he had made his home in the caverns beyond the reach of the ocean tide. There, he nursed the girl back to health. In return for his kindness, he asked only for one thing. That the girl slake his hunger . . . with her body and her blood and the stuff of the spirit. The girl's name was Enna, and she was the first bloodmaid. The man from the sea was the first Count of the House of Hunger and father of all of the many Houses that came after it. Every noble in the North drinks blood, as is custom, because of his formidable hunger and the girl, Enna, who slaked it."

———— ◆ ————

THAT NIGHT, MARION PRETENDED TO SLEEP UNTIL LISAVET SLIPPED out of the room. When she heard the door close, she climbed out of bed and followed the sound of her footsteps, tiptoeing barefoot through Lisavet's private parlor and into the public halls of the House.

She spotted the tail end of Lisavet's robe flicking around the corner and followed suit, trying to keep her footsteps light and remain unnoticed. Lisavet took a strange path through the House, sometimes venturing through servant passages or taking shortcuts

Marion had no former knowledge of. At one point, Marion was certain she knew she was being followed, but as she froze in the hall—waiting for Lisavet to turn her head—the Countess kept walking.

Finally, Marion followed Lisavet around a corner only to discover that the hallway dead-ended just a few feet from where she stood. There were no doors or windows on either side of it. And Lisavet, like a specter, was gone.

23

Love is an act of sacrifice.

—NOEL, BLOODMAID OF THE HOUSE OF STORMS

TWO WEEKS LATER, MARION found herself in the bleeding parlor with Mae perched on her knee. The girl had been pestering Marion to play fox and hound all morning, tugging at her sleeve and trying her best to draw her into the empty ballrooms where she liked to begin her games. She'd grown clingier in the weeks after Cecelia's abrupt annulment, and Marion suspected this was the result of some latent fear that the remaining bloodmaids, too, would disappear. She did what she could to appease the child, but Mae's demands for her attention grew more insistent as time passed, not less. Sometimes she felt like she had a second shadow as the girl followed her through the halls of the House.

"We'll play after I'm done bleeding," said Marion, taking a small sip of tea.

Mae watched Marion's blood pool at the bottom of the bowl. It was already half-full, and she knew the bleeding servant was taking more than she usually did, both on account of Cecelia's absence and because Lisavet's sickness had worsened considerably over the past few days. There had been several nights when she was so ill, she hadn't had the strength to raise her head from the pillow when Marion entered the chamber, and they had slept huddled together through half the night, Marion counting each of her breaths, until Lisavet stirred and dismissed her.

"I feel like an overworked dairy cow," said Evie, drawn and pale, her head tipped back, her eyes on the ceiling. "I fainted in the hall after yesterday's bleed and very nearly bruised my face. Likely would have if a footman hadn't caught my arm midfall. They're working us too hard. We need a replacement for Cecelia or else we'll all be drained dry by springtime."

Marion was about as tired of being bled as Evie was. She had permanent bruises in the crooks of her elbows, and she often felt faint. The servants had begun to take blood from the artery at the base of her thumb, and on several occasions her inner thigh, because the vein in the crook of her elbow had been punctured far too many times, and was in jeopardy of collapsing.

Despite this, Marion loathed the very idea of Lisavet taking on a new bloodmaid, a new potential favorite, some fresh young girl—perhaps yet unbled—to lavish with her sparing affections. What would happen then? Would she unseat Marion as First Bloodmaid, the way that Marion had unseated Cecelia? The thought alone filled her with spite.

"We don't need more girls," she said firmly. "Lisavet is feeling ill, but when she recovers, her hunger will lessen. I'm sure of it."

When the bleeding bowl was filled to the rim, Mae slipped out of her lap. The attending servant stanched her bleeding with the firm application of a cloth compress. Marion stood up moments later and her knees buckled beneath her. Her vision went, and her hearing a split second after. If not for Mae, who encircled Marion's waist with her tiny arms, intent to keep her aloft, she was certain she would've collapsed, there on the floor of the bleeding room.

"Are you certain we don't need more girls?" Evie inquired, with a smirk. "I daresay you look a little green."

Marion chose to ignore that comment and left for the bloodmaids' quarters hand-in-hand with Mae. She'd promised the girl a game of fox and hound and had been putting her off for days, having felt too tired from bleeding, or her rough nights with Lisavet, to muster the energy she needed to play.

"I only have time for one round," Marion said, which wasn't true. She had several hours open to her, until her classes with Tutor Geoffrey around three. But the truth was—given her current state—she feared she didn't have the strength to play more than one round. Climbing up a flight of stairs had been something of an effort as of late, so running from Mae for anything more than a few minutes was entirely out of the question.

Undeterred, Mae tugged her hand and motioned for her to go and hide. Mae was always the hound when they played together. She liked the chase so much that, on occasion, Lisavet would take her out on fox-hunting expeditions. On her sixth birthday a few weeks prior, her party had been themed around fox hunting and, as a gift, Lisavet bestowed her with an air pistol and a real stuffed fox she'd killed on a hunt for the little girl to cling to at night. Lisavet had come to the bloodmaids' quarters to hand-deliver the gift, the red fox with a crimson bow tied around its neck, nestled in a wicker basket. Marion had wondered at the time if it was the same fox pup she'd first spotted in the woods during the hunt all those months ago, and was troubled by the thought.

Mae began to count, silently, and Marion ran to go hide. The rules of the game (as created by Irene) were this: Mae was to count for three minutes, and the game was to be limited to the western wing of the House, fourth floor only, to make it easier for the hound as well as to keep the game from dragging on too long.

Marion scrambled to find a hiding place that she hadn't used already. It was only a few moments into the game, and she was already out of breath. "Just one round," she muttered to herself, stepping into an empty parlor off the same hall where Lisavet had disappeared weeks prior. Panting, and a little dizzy from the bloodletting that morning, she resolved herself to hide behind the curtains, knowing that Mae would find her within minutes. But then she crossed through to another room—this one an empty bedchamber for the bloodmaids of guests—and decided to take cover in the armoire pushed against its far wall.

Marion climbed inside and drew the door shut behind her. The dark was thick, and the place reeked of mold and other wet, fetid things, and she began to cough a little. She tried to open the door, just a crack, to let some fresh air in but it was jammed shut.

"*Fuck*," Marion muttered, after kneeing the door several times, scrabbling at its edges until her fingernails went ragged. She called for Mae, but there was no answer.

Frustrated, Marion slumped with her back against the armoire and felt the paneling . . . give a little. With some effort, she managed to turn around, and she pressed both palms to the back panel and pushed once, twice, and then, the third time, the panel fell backward, and Marion fell with it, landing on her belly so hard that the wind was knocked out of her. She gasped for breath, seeing stars and feeling close to fainting. Finally, she managed to recover herself and stand up. By the spare light that leaked in through the cracks of the wardrobe, she turned to peer down what seemed to be some sort of servants' passage, albeit one that was rarely traversed.

Marion stepped forward, raising a hand to the wall, but she drew it back with a small shriek as soon as her fingertips brushed it. The wall was moist to the touch, fuzzy with blooming fungi. Tentatively, with a single finger skimming along the mold-furred wall, Marion ventured into the dark. She could feel the brush of cobwebs against her cheeks, the soft *pitter-patter* of dripping water, though she never found its source. Then a horrible rattling groan carried down the hall. It sounded just short of human. Something in the way of the cry, the accent of it (if a scream like that could have an accent), made Marion believe she'd heard it before. Was there some kind of animal—a starving cat or bats perhaps—trapped within the walls?

Terrified, Marion stood frozen in the hall—waiting, listening. There was another sound: the faint scraping of metal on stone. Then a whimper so soft Marion wasn't sure she'd heard it at all. Then, once again, silence, save for the soft rhythm of the falling water.

Shaken, but spurred onward by a dark curiosity strong enough to overcome her fear, Marion attempted to follow the sound. The corridors led to something, she was sure of it. Perhaps she'd find an answer at the end of the winding halls, the secret place that kept Lisavet away night after night.

Each cautious step brought her deeper into the darkness, but closer to answers, too, and she felt along the walls trying to find another panel or door by which to exit, but the hallways just wended into bricked-off archways and dead ends. There was even a short and twisted staircase, which Marion took down to a lower level of the House, only to discover a new labyrinth of halls at its end.

In a panicked moment, she wondered if she could even find her way back to the wardrobe where she'd first entered, as she hadn't been memorizing every turn she took. But then she felt the mold-furred plaster give way to splintered wood paneling: a *door*. She heaved on it with her shoulder a few times before it gave way.

There was a blinding light, a rush of fresh air, motes and swirling yellow mold spores flying through it, and Marion stumbled forward and hit the ground, coughing. She managed to right herself and stand up, picking the pale, soft threads of cobwebs from her curls and squinting into the light as she struggled to determine where, exactly, she'd ended up.

"I see you've found a passage," said Tutor Geoffrey, looking up from his book on the histories of the North that Marion was meant to read before their lesson that day. "They run throughout the House. Though most are sealed off."

"What were they used for?" Marion asked, stepping into the library, turning to see the half-ajar bookshelf that was the hidden door she'd entered through.

"Well . . ." said Tutor Geoffrey rather slowly, and with apparent reluctance. "There are rumors that there were once secret chambers— red churches, some in the South called them. It was said that many years ago, back in the days when the consumption of blood was still largely illicit and illegal, nobles of this House would . . . *partake* there, in secret."

Marion recalled the story Lisavet had told her. The one about the founder of the House of Hunger, who'd lived in the caves it was built on. She remembered the girl he'd fallen in love with, who'd satisfied his lust with her blood. Enna, the first bloodmaid to ever live.

The hairs on the back of Marion's neck bristled, stood on end. She recalled that strange gargling cry she'd thought she'd heard in the passage. She remembered what Lisavet had told her about her father . . . and his cruelty. The way that he preferred the blood of children, his own daughter, to that of bloodmaids like herself. "I heard something back there," said Marion, in soft confession. "When I was in the passage."

Tutor Geoffrey went very pale and Marion read something on his face, a passing shadow, the ghost of what might have been suspicion. "Voices do tend to carry through these halls."

"This was different," she said, with new conviction, as though the retelling of the story assured her of its validity. "I don't know how to describe the sound. It was more than animal and less than human."

"I'm sure it was nothing," said Tutor Geoffrey, but even as he said it . . . Marion didn't believe him. He gave himself away with his trembling hands, the beads of perspiration collecting above his thin upper lip.

"It didn't sound like nothing," Marion said.

She watched him break then, something giving way within him, like one of the cornerstones upon which his pretense was built had cracked. "Marion, there's something you need to know about—"

Just then, a high clear voice rang through the library. "I daresay that's enough chatter for today. Your lessons should've already begun."

Marion turned to see the House Mother, standing hand-in-hand with Mae, whose eyes were red and raw from crying. The House Mother glowered at Geoffrey, and her gaze was still rather hard when it shifted to Marion. "Mae came to find me. She said you disappeared."

"We were playing fox and hound. I hid in the wrong place and found my way to some sort of hidden passage." She motioned to the bookshelf behind her, but the House Mother didn't look where she pointed. "I'm sorry, Mae. I didn't mean to frighten you or abandon our game."

The House Mother appeared unimpressed. Angry even, but it

seemed her quarrel was not with Marion because her gaze cut sharply to Tutor Geoffrey again. "A word?"

Tutor Geoffrey swallowed hard, collected his papers hastily. "It's been an honor," he said to Marion, and that was to be the last she ever saw of him.

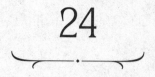

24

*It is wise to retire facets of oneself before taking up the title of
bloodmaid. Rebirth depends upon these small acts of suicide.*

—DELPHINE, MOTHER OF THE HOUSE OF MIRRORS

THE FOLLOWING MORNING, MARION was forbidden from bleeding. A nasty bruise had formed in the crook of her elbow, where
the servants drew her blood, and the skin around it was hot and swollen, taut with the beginnings of what the House Mother believed to
be an infection of the blood. In lieu of her usual breakfast of tea
cakes, hard blood sausages, toast points, and poached eggs, Marion
was made to down a nasty draught of medicine that she gagged up
several times before successfully swallowing it down.

Fearing sepsis, the House Mother insisted that Marion was to
remain confined to the bloodmaids' quarters through the duration
of the day. The fever set in just before afternoon tea, a flush that
burned red circles into the apples of her cheeks and chilled her to
the bone. Her heart beat a frantic and irregular rhythm against the
backs of her ribs, and she was so exhausted she slept through the
twins' daily opera practice without so much as stirring.

When Marion finally woke, the sun was setting, and the girls were dressed in their formal attire, but she couldn't tell whether they were going to or coming from dinner. She squinted at the clock that stood on the mantel, but its face blurred and doubled, and try as she might she couldn't focus her eyes enough to tell the time.

"You look like death," said Irene from above the pages of her book. She sat close by, in an armchair facing Marion. Marion wondered how long the girl had been sitting there, watching. For a fleeting moment, Marion forgot the new animosity between them, and wondered if she'd been keeping vigil at her bedside while she slept.

"I feel like it," said Marion, hoarsely. Her tongue felt swollen and dry. She wanted water but didn't dare ask for it. The other girls resented her enough already, and she was certain any request she made would be interpreted as further evidence of her conceitedness. She propped herself up on her elbow and the room spun.

Across the parlor, Marion saw the smeared image of the twins standing by the door of their bedroom. But her vision was too blurry to assess their expressions.

Irene, for her part, seemed genuinely concerned. She closed her novel and sat down beside Marion. She felt her cheek and winced. "You're burning."

"You don't have to be kind to me out of pity."

"I'm not . . ." The girl trailed off, shook her head. "I have no particular contempt for you."

"That's not true," said Marion. "Ever since I became First Blood-maid you act like I wedged a dagger between Cecelia's shoulders when her back was turned."

"Didn't you?" said Evie from across the parlor. "You seemed eager enough to take her place."

"Someone had to," said Marion, and it came out harsher than she meant it. "I know that any one of you would've taken the role, had it been offered. None of you would've refused Lisavet. So don't blame me for what you yourselves would've done. Jealousy is one thing, but hypocrisy is another."

Marion's voice broke on those final words, and she could feel the tears collecting, a hot pressure, at the back of her throat. To her surprise, the girls received this rebuke in silence. What she had thought would be the beginning of a nasty argument seemed to defuse the discussion entirely.

On the chaise beside her, Irene seemed to deflate, her frail shoulders bowing inward. "You're right," she said. "I'm sorry. You didn't deserve our ire. You're our friend, and you never deserved to be treated as less than that. It's just that this place, this House, it has a way of turning people against each other. Sometimes I feel that despite my best efforts, the kindest of my affections sour and become something—"

"Hideous," said Elize softly, finishing for her. "At least, that's how I feel."

"I feel it too," said Evie, and this was as close to an apology as she seemed willing or able to offer. "It's like there's something in the air here and it's sickening me."

Marion, too weak to sit up, reclined into the soft pillows of the chaise. Irene leaned closer, reached for her hand, and Marion smiled at her touch.

"You're my friends," she said, and there was meant to be something more after that, but before she could wrestle feelings into thoughts, thoughts into words, she succumbed, once again, to a thick and febrile sleep.

———— ♦ ————

HOURS LATER, THE PRESIDING HOUSE PHYSICIAN, A WIZENED BUT surprisingly cheery old man who dressed like a mortician, was called to Marion's bedside. After inspecting her swollen arm, he pulled her eyelids apart to examine the whites, prying them open wide until they burned and watered, checking for signs of jaundice. He pressed a hard wooden stethoscope against her chest—its mouth biting a soft circle above her breast—and listened to the quick rhythm of her heart. When these examinations were complete, he let her blood— not for consumption (it was deemed unfit for that), but to drain the infection out of her body. The bowls of blood were soaked up with rags and burned in the parlor hearth.

The doctor departed. Despite Marion's fevered protests, Evie was called to Lisavet's quarters in her stead. Left alone, Marion spent the long hours of the night imagining Evie encircled in Lisavet's arms, drawn tight to her chest, their legs tangled in the sheets, each lavishing their passions on the other. It was perhaps because of this distraction that Lisavet did not deign to visit her sickbed, though the House Mother relayed her well-wishes and empty assurances that Lisavet had not forgotten or grown tired of her, that she was still beloved.

"If she hasn't forgotten me, then why won't she come?" Marion asked, murkily, drifting in and out of sleep. "What keeps her away?"

The House Mother didn't answer. She pressed a hand to Marion's brow.

Her palm, dry as paper, felt very cold.

———— • ————

HAVING SLEPT THROUGH THE DAY, MARION LAY WIDE AWAKE through the duration of the night, her eyes fixed on the ceiling, reading the word that Cecelia had carved there over and over again:

Wretch. Wretch. Wretch. Wretch . . .

The word replayed itself in her mind until it lost all meaning and became like the grating chorus of nails scratching, as if there were someone—perhaps many someones—trapped behind the walls of her chamber, trying desperately to dig their way out. Was that what

Tutor Geoffrey had wanted to tell her? That this House had souls trapped within its walls? Specters lurking in the narrow hollows between rooms and hallways, their ragged nails rasping along the plaster.

Marion shifted, restless and half-maddened from the incessant sound of the scratching. A shapeless pressure tamped down on her chest, making it hard to raise her head or even draw a deep breath. Despite the thick covering of her blankets, she began to shiver. Her arm, red and swollen fat at the elbow, throbbed incessantly. She began to suspect she was dying.

Horribly dizzy and far too weak to stand, or even sit upright, Marion tossed out a hand, reaching for the bell on her nightstand as a sharp and horrible pain clenched through her belly. She gasped, groaned, folding into herself, writhing. Her fingertips brushed the side of the bell and it toppled, striking the floor with an ugly clatter and rolling beneath the shadow of her bed. Marion split her chapped lips apart, tried and failed to will her tongue to form words, summoned what little breath she had left in her lungs to cry for help, but her voice was a faint whimper too soft to reach beyond the confines of her chamber.

A beat of silence. Then, as if in answer to her pitiful cry, the door opened. Lisavet stepped into the room, crossed it, and set a teacup— filled to the brim with blood—on the nightstand, in the empty place where the bell had been. She sat at the edge of the bed. With one hand she cradled Marion's head, pulling her up from the pillows. With the other she raised the teacup and placed its rim to Marion's mouth. Blood pooled, warm and viscous, against her sealed lips.

"Compliments of Evie," said the Countess. "Drink."

Evie's blood was thick. It seeped through the cracks of Marion's teeth and coated her tongue, gagging her when it reached the back of her throat. It tasted of wine and metal, and other flavors that Marion couldn't put words to. She choked on the first swallow, and the next four after that, but Lisavet was slow and patient, tipping the cup ever so slightly, pausing to let her choke and breathe, wiping her mouth clean on her sleeve when she retched, only to raise the cup again.

When Marion tried to push it away, Lisavet collected her by the back of the neck and made her keep drinking, draining the cup down to the dregs. When the gory deed was finally done, the Countess pulled back from the bedside and stood.

"Wait," said Marion, the word scraping along the sides of her throat. "Stay with me."

Lisavet faltered, her gaze shifting between Marion and the door.

"Please. Just for a little while. I don't want to be alone."

Lisavet, relenting, settled herself beside Marion once more, but this time she kicked off her slippers, drew her knees up into the mattress so as to lay folded into her side.

They lay like that for a long time in silence: Marion nursing the pain in her belly, folded against Lisavet, their legs tangling as she writhed. Lisavet with an arm snaked around Marion's waist, chin tucked above her head.

"Marion?"

"Yes?"

"If I asked you to leave this House would you do it?"

The words might have just as well been a bleeding needle, stuck between the ribs, piercing deep into the soft meat of her heart. "You . . . want me to leave you?"

Lisavet kept talking, rapidly, as if she was trying to convince herself. "I'll procure you a ticket south. You can have your pension. You can go home to Prane as soon as you're better. You just have to go as soon as you're able—"

"This is because I'm sick, isn't it? You don't want me anymore.

You don't want me," she said again, once, twice, three times over in slurred repetition as the reality dawned on her. "My blood goes sour and you're ready to cast me aside. You want to discard me. Send me to the sanatorium where you put Cecelia."

"That couldn't be further from the truth."

"Then what is it?" Marion demanded, crying now. "What else would make you want to drive me from your side?"

Lisavet, watching her break, leaned forward, crushing her mouth to Marion's. Their shared kiss tasted of Evie's blood. "Forgive me," said Lisavet, murmuring into her mouth. "Forgive me for all of it. I'm sorry. I love you. I won't make you go."

They remained like that for some time before the clock in the parlor tolled twelve. Lisavet, stirring at the sound, as though roused from a trance, stood up.

"Where are you going?" Marion asked, squinting up at Lisavet, her vision cloudy with the lingering miasma of sleep. "Can't you tell me? Just this once?"

Lisavet leaned forward, pressed a kiss to Marion's brow. And then she was gone, and Marion—half lost to her dreams, her aching belly full of blood—was left alone.

———— ♦ ————

IN HER NIGHTMARES, MARION FOUND HERSELF WANDERING THE halls of the House. She heard distant laughter and the murmurings of conversation. The tinny clatter of cutlery on porcelain. Marion followed the sounds until she reached a room she'd never before seen: a banquet hall.

There, Lisavet and the rest of her court were seated around a large feasting table. There was Ivor, Madame Boucherie, Tutor Geoffrey, the House Mother, Mae, and even the bloodmaids all assembled for the meal. Thiago was there, too, as was Agnes, gazing down the table at Lisavet, and even Raul, gray and decaying, half-slumped against the back of his seat.

There was only one dish on the table: a large suckling hog, with a greasy plum clenched between its jaws. It was half-carved, Lisavet cutting slices from its side, serving them up, the plates passed, person to person, down the long stretch of the banquet table until they reached its opposing end. But as Marion drew nearer, she saw that it wasn't a suckling hog at all.

It was a human body. Her body.

Marion's corpse lay prone and naked on a large silver platter, nestled among an ample garnish of pine branches and salt grass. Her skin burnt and buckling and sloughing away from the bone, roasted almost beyond recognition. The open eyes poached soft in their gaunt sockets. The charred fingers, flesh shriveling away from the nails.

It was a strange thing, to examine one's own body not as a body but as an object. But she felt no horror as she watched the others partake of her, chewing on gnarly mouthfuls of meat. Mae devoured fatty pieces cut from her thigh—which her nursemaid had deftly sliced into neat little cubes. She speared them with the prongs of her fork and ushered them into her mouth, one by one, chewing with her eyes on Marion. The others ate their fill as well. For Agnes, rib meat, falling from the bone. Beside her, Raul held his fork in a white-knuckle vise grip and swallowed down a thick mouthful of grisly meat.

The bloodmaids helped themselves to her corpse; too impatient to wait for it to be carved for them, they began to serve themselves. The other nobles followed suit, leaning forward with their forks and knives, plates at the ready, eager to dismember and dine.

But Lisavet did not eat. She carved. Serving slices of her. One for Irene, one for Madame Boucherie, another for Tutor Geoffrey.

Marion edged up the table. She leaned over Lisavet's shoulder and pried the plum free of her own burnt mouth. She turned it over in her hand, examining the bruised flesh and puncture wounds where her canines had pierced the skin, which was lard-slick and gleaming in the candlelight. Turning to lock eyes with Lisavet, she raised the plum in toast and took a bite—her front teeth sinking so deep they struck the stone at its heart. She chewed slowly—bloody plum juice dribbling down her chin—and swallowed hard.

Lisavet raised a hand to Marion's lips. Smeared the plum juice and grease away with the pad of her thumb, then licked it clean. "Sit," she said, motioning to the empty chair at her side. "Eat."

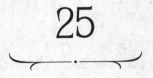

25

It is not uncommon for a bloodmaid to adopt the dark inclinations
of her patron, though this is an outcome best avoided, for a
bloodmaid scorned is a frightening prospect indeed.

—DINAH, MOTHER OF THE HOUSE OF NOON

TWO DAYS LATER MARION'S fever broke. She woke to weak sunlight seeping through her bedroom window, chapped lips crusted with blood (she wasn't sure whose), and a throat so dry and sore she could scarcely speak. The swelling in her arm was down, and she found she could move it without any pain. Her stomach pains were gone.

News of her miraculous recovery spread quickly through the House. Marion's fellow bloodmaids rushed to her room. Irene was the first to arrive, throwing open the door and shouldering past the crowd of nurses. She tossed herself onto the bed and gathered Marion into a fierce embrace, burying her face deep into the crook of her shoulder. Evie arrived minutes later, panting from what Marion suspected was a sprint across the House. A governess was ushered in with Mae, who seemed pleased to see her. Elize came, too, with her cat, Theodore, whom she promptly dropped in Marion's lap. The sullen creature nuzzled Marion's hand a few times and purred, as if to assure her that he, like the bloodmaids, was relieved to see her awake and alive.

Lisavet was notably absent. But the House Mother relayed her regards.

As the bloodmaids piled themselves onto Marion's bed—preening her matted curls and chatting incessantly about the latest gossip of the court—a servant girl entered with a breakfast tray. On it were a large cup of tea, a small plate of sliced cold meats and sausages, a bowl of pitted cherries, buttered rolls with an accompanying pot of blackberry jam, two fried eggs (the yolks staring up at her like open eyes), and in a shallow soup bowl, a pinkish porridge thin enough to drink.

"It's laced with my blood," said Irene, looking rather shy, as though she feared Marion would turn up her nose to it. "The House Physician says you'll need a steady intake to make a full recovery. So down the bowl to the dregs."

Marion's stomach clenched at the thought. "Doesn't House protocol mandate that we only bleed for Lisavet?"

"The Countess has made an exception for you," said the House Mother, looking on. "She wants you well. So, drink up."

Marion took up her spoon. The porridge was laced with veins of red, but when she took a whiff of the steam, she smelled nothing but vanilla and nutmeg. She ushered a single, dripping spoonful into her mouth. It was sweet and rich at first, but when she swallowed, she tasted the tang of blood.

———— ◆ ————

EAGER TO RETURN TO HER CLASSES, MARION—AGAINST THE REC-ommendation of the House Physician—dressed and headed to the library. But upon arriving, she was stunned to discover that the library—like Cecelia's room—had been emptied of all of Tutor Geoffrey's personal belongings. There was no trace of him left.

"He was fired," said the servant girl, dusting the bookshelf in the corner. Marion wondered if it was she who'd stripped the library of Tutor Geoffrey's belongings, or if he'd been allowed the small dignity of packing himself. "He left the day after you took ill. I've heard it rumored that Madame Boucherie will take on his role."

"Why was he fired?" Marion asked, a pit in her stomach, but she already knew the answer. She went to the hidden door she'd stumbled through that day—now it felt like long ago—when she and Mae had played fox and hound. She gave it a shove and discovered that it had been replastered, bolted, and sealed tightly shut.

Furious, Marion stormed to the House Mother's study, shouldering past the footman posted at her door. She let herself in, only to discover that the room was empty.

"The House Mother is out on business," said the footman.

"Then I'll await her return here," said Marion, resolute. When the man began to protest, Marion simply refused to listen to him. She half expected him to drag her from the study, cast her out into the hall.

But the man, pale and drawn, perspiration collecting on his upper lip simply . . . . stood down. "As you wish, my lady. I'll inform her of your presence immediately and tell her you're waiting."

This was an unexpected change. Marion, who had spent so much of her life being scolded or worse ignored, now found herself in a position of power. She was First Bloodmaid of the House of Hunger, and that title lent her a certain gravitas to which she was still unaccustomed.

Marion nodded primly, trying to contain her surprise, and sat down at the House Mother's desk, the same place she'd signed her contract all those many months ago. Things had changed since the last time she'd sat at that desk. *She* had changed.

The footman shut the door, leaving her alone.

Marion spent a few moments in silence, letting her gaze flicker about the room. When she grew tired of waiting, she got up, examining the contents of the House Mother's bookshelves (there was nothing of particular interest, and many of the books seemed more ornamental than anything else). Eventually, Marion found her way back to the House Mother's desk. Her gaze shifted back and forth between the letter opener and the lock on the drawer, and an unpleasant thought came to her head. She recalled the House Mother mentioning the records she kept on previously indentured bloodmaids. She'd always wondered about the contents of her own file . . . but also the files of the bloodmaids who'd come before her. Those phantom girls that Lisavet could scarcely bring herself to mention, and never by name.

Marion picked up the letter opener, which was brass and much heavier than it looked. Risking a glance at the door, listening for footsteps, Marion lowered it to the lock and began to pick it. She only struggled for a few moments before it gave with a soft *click*.

Marion drew the drawer open and whistled softly. Within were files, long accounts of all of the bloodmaids that had come before her. There were at least two dozen. The girls were young (fifteen to twenty-two), and most had not remained at the House for more than a year before their indentures came to an end, a far cry from the seven years of service that the House Mother had assured Marion was average.

She even found the file of the girl who occupied her chamber before her. The girl was called Cora Taylor; she was indentured at the age of nineteen and was the last bloodmaid tenured to the House before Cecelia had arrived, and their indentures had very nearly overlapped. In fact, her tenure abruptly ended a mere four days before Cecelia's began. It must have been her tooth beneath the bed; there was no other explanation. With a pit in her stomach, Marion wondered if she'd pried it from her own gums as a present for Lisavet, the way that Cecelia had at the height of her madness.

None of the files included information on why the bloodmaids' contracts were terminated so early into their indenture. But Marion noticed a pattern. Most of the girls came in batches of three or four overlapping tenures, with monthlong breaks between the beginning of each new batch. By this logic, it seemed that Cecelia had never known any of the girls who were tenured before her. It also explained why Irene had no knowledge of any other bloodmaid, except those indentured currently.

Strangely, despite the detailed accounts included in each of these files, none of them referred to the pensions that were supposed to be paid when a bloodmaid's indenture ended. It would have been unheard of for all of their indentures to be annulled, so Marion was left wondering why the accounting files and receipts of their pensions were absent. Surely there had to be some ledger that outlined these things. How else would the House Mother know who was owed what and when?

Perplexed, Marion withdrew her own file. Predictably, her signed contract was sheathed within it. As was what appeared to be a receipt, or ledger, detailing how the House of Hunger had paid a vast sum of five thousand pounds to cover the cost of Thiago's staggering finder's fee. More than double the two thousand pounds he'd claimed he'd receive.

"That rake," Marion muttered, both stunned by the figure and sorely wishing she hadn't underestimated her worth. Had she known, perhaps she could've negotiated with Thiago to receive a cut of his fee.

Marion selected Cecelia's file next. There were the usual details—contracts, notes, receipts (as it turned out, Lisavet paid almost twice as much for Cecelia as she had for Marion)—but then something unusual caught her eye. Within Cecelia's files were unaddressed letters that weren't penned in the House Mother's hand. Upon shuffling through the letters, skimming their contents, Marion discovered that their seals had been broken. She gasped as she began to read them. All of the letters were addressed to Cecelia, and they'd been written by the other bloodmaids. There were several from Evie, four from Elize, and five from Irene. The House Mother had opened them, broken their seals, and likely read them, but she'd never sent them like she'd promised to.

A dark and terrible thought surfaced at the back of her mind: What if the letters had never been sent because Cecelia had never left?

Marion swallowed dry. She folded the letters hastily and slipped them back into Cecelia's file. She was about to reach for Mae's when she heard the sound of footsteps and quickly shoved Cecelia's file back in place, shut the drawer, and rounded the desk to sit on its opposite side.

"Marion, to what do I owe the pleasure?"

Palms slick with sweat, Marion stammered. "Tutor Geoffrey . . . where is he?"

"He was called to the bedside of an ailing family member. I'm afraid he won't be returning. I instructed Madame Boucherie to inform you that she would be taking on all of your studies."

"I heard as much. I just wondered if our previous discussion about the back halls of the House may have resulted in the termination of his position here." Marion was surprised by her own bluntness.

The House Mother merely blinked. "Why would a folktale result in his firing?"

"I don't—"

"Marion, tell me, who is the sitting Lord of Doves?"

"I-I'm not sure."

"All right. Who was the second Countess of the House of Hunger and how did she die?"

"I don't know."

"Fair enough. Can you name the three Houses that established themselves through the mining of diamonds?"

"No."

"I see." The House Mother slowly rounded the desk. Her gaze immediately snared on the letter opener, and then shifted up to Marion . . . searching. "I didn't ask those questions to humiliate you, only to make it clear that Tutor Geoffrey's tutelage was . . . lacking, to say the least. As First Bloodmaid, you deserve better instruction than what he was capable of providing. Madame Boucherie will give that to you. You can trust her with the last of your education."

26

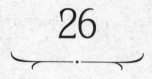

My sins are too many to count . . . but I feel
I've bled enough to absolve them all.

—ARACELI, BLOODMAID OF THE HOUSE OF DOVES

LISAVET WAS IN A dark mood that night. She scarcely spoke to Marion as she sat at her desk, frowning over her letters, scribbling things with her quill pen only to crumple her writings and toss them on the floor. Watching her, Marion wondered why she was there at all.

Finally, she got up, crossed the bedroom, and stood behind Lisavet's chair. She put her hands on her shoulders and began to work the muscles, squeezing through the soft velvet of her robe, the way that Madame Boucherie had instructed her to in an early lesson of hers, months ago.

"A bloodmaid must know how to put her mistress at ease," the woman had said, between strikes of her crop when Marion squeezed too hard or pinched at the wrong muscle.

Lisavet, however, seemed to enjoy Marion's efforts. She could feel her mistress' muscles slackening beneath her hands, and her posture—rigid when Marion first entered the room—softened considerably at Marion's touch. Still, she didn't look up from her work.

"I was wondering . . . if you'd had any word from Cecelia?"

Lisavet faltered, her shoulders going stiff beneath Marion's hands. Her pen went still at the edge of the letter she was writing. A fat ink splotch stained the paper. "No, why do you ask?"

Marion wanted to bring up what she'd discovered in the House Mother's desk but thought better of it. She was First Bloodmaid, and the favorite, yes, but she wasn't sure that Lisavet's sympathies toward her would extend far enough to forgive her snooping. "Some of the other bloodmaids mentioned that they hadn't heard back from her, even weeks after sending their letters."

"Cecelia held a dagger to your throat and very nearly killed you, just hours before her departure." Lisavet snatched her half-written letter from the desk, crumpled it, and tossed it to the floor. "What care do you have for her well-being?"

"I simply wondered if she was . . . alive. Given her state."

"I can assure you, she's alive and well." Lisavet slipped a fresh sheet of paper from the drawer of her desk and began writing again. She appeared to be refusing yet another marriage proposal from some lord in the west.

But what piqued Marion's interest was not what Lisavet was writing, but rather the small palm-size oil portraits weighting a stack of letters at the corner of her desk. Narrowing her eyes to study them further, she realized that they were advertisements for girls, potential bloodmaids, that detailed intricacies like height, age, estimated weight, and hair and eye color, as well as a list of qualifications and talents that ranged from singing and needlepoint to hunting and acrobatics.

"You're looking for new bloodmaids?" Marion demanded, with a sudden pang of jealousy. She couldn't help but receive this unwanted news as anything other than an example of her failure to slake Lisavet's hunger, meet her needs. If she was truly happy with Marion, why would she need to seek new bloodmaids? Was what they had not enough?

Lisavet didn't look up from her paper, but her shoulders tensed beneath Marion's hands. "It's rude to snoop."

"I don't think it's snooping to inquire about new bloodmaids," said Marion, removing herself from Lisavet entirely, as the sting of the betrayal grew sharper.

"It's a violation of my privacy . . . and my independence."

"Your privacy? *Your* independence?" Marion demanded. "I'm the one who will have to share living quarters with them, make small talk in the bleeding room, take my meals with them."

"Would you like to select them, then?" Lisavet inquired, raising a dark eyebrow. "Would that make you feel better about who I choose to spend my time with? Whose blood I choose to consume?"

"Just how many bloodmaids do you intend to employ?"

"Indenture," said Lisavet, correcting her in an infuriatingly flat tone, as if she was too bored to continue conversing. "I employ servants. Bloodmaids are indentured. There is a difference, and it should be distinguished as such."

Marion bowed her head with mock respect. "Yes, milady."

Lisavet eyed her for a beat longer, then returned to her work, pouring wax over an envelope to seal it shut, pressing the House emblem into the puddle with the thick signet ring she wore on her middle finger. "If you must know, I'd like to acquire no less than four additional bloodmaids over the coming months. I find that my hunger has been . . . rather demanding as of late."

"Which is to say I don't meet your need?"

"Precisely, and you would be dead if you tried to," said Lisavet, and she set the letter aside. "I'm doing what little I can to protect you. I've noticed that you've appeared rather fatigued. Your complexion has changed. You've fallen ill once before—"

"I'm fine," said Marion, sharply. "I can meet your need. I'm not sick like Cecelia was. If you're hungry, I can bleed more."

"You bleed enough already. And I fear for you when you say things like that."

"Why?"

"Because I will kill you if you let me," said Lisavet, and she looked anguished and terribly ashamed. "My hunger will kill you. Your blood is the only thing that can cure me, and even if I drained you dry it wouldn't be enough to save me. I would still need more. Do you understand my meaning?"

"Yes."

"But?"

Marion hung her head. She didn't know how to tell her that the very idea of her taking another girl into her arms, loving her, made her feel like someone was sawing into her heart with a dull butter knife. It was pathetic, but she would almost rather be dead than watch Lisavet come to love another. She wasn't even certain she'd survive it. "But . . . I don't want you to indenture more bloodmaids. Our time together is already limited enough."

Lisavet grasped her hand then, ran her thumb back and forth over her knuckles. "This will be better for us. My needs are too great to be met by the four of you alone. If anything, the addition of new bloodmaids will strengthen our bond, not weaken it."

"And if you're wrong?"

"I'm never wrong," said Lisavet, and she pressed a kiss to her knuckle and stood again, with some effort, closing her eyes and taking a moment to steady herself. Then her nose began to bleed, and when Marion reached out for her, she slapped her hand away, produced a white handkerchief from the pocket of her breeches, and pressed it to her nostrils to stanch the flow. The blood soaked through within seconds.

Marion stood up. "I'll fetch the physician—"

"Don't," said Lisavet, catching her by the wrist. "There's no help to be had for it."

"But Lis—"

"Sit *down*," the Countess ordered, and Marion, knowing that she had no choice but to obey her, returned to her seat. She watched as Lisavet's blood soaked the handkerchief, forcing her to replace it with a cloth napkin from a nearby tea tray. "The House Mother mentioned you were asking after Geoffrey."

"Yes . . ." said Marion, helplessly watching Lisavet bleed. "He left before I had the chance to say goodbye. I wanted to wish him well."

Lisavet studied her in cold evaluation, as if she were little more than a stranger. "Do you have feelings for him?"

Marion stared at her, stunned. She felt nothing, less than nothing, for Tutor Geoffrey. The thought of him being anything more than her instructor was absurd. The only person in the House of Hunger that she'd ever had feelings for was Lisavet. "Th-that's not it at all."

"Then what is it?" Lisavet demanded, and she lowered the red-stained napkin. Her nosebleed had slowed to a dribble, and she wiped the last of it away on the sleeve of her robe. "You come to me in my weakness, complaining about my medical need for more bloodmaids out of nothing more than petty jealousy. And now you demand to know the whereabouts of a former employee of this House that you're clearly besotted with—"

"I'm not," said Marion in sharp refute. "I just wanted the chance to say goodbye to him."

Lisavet didn't heed her. It was as though she hadn't heard Marion's defense at all. She'd already decided who she believed Marion to be: a traitor. Never mind the fact that Marion's heart was so full with Lisavet, she scarcely had room to love anyone else. Lisavet—or perhaps more aptly Marion's own obsession with her—had so thoroughly consumed her that the prospect of loving anyone else was beyond farcical, it was a complete impossibility. "You liked the attention he lavished you with on all those mornings you spent with him, maybe a few nights too."

"I didn't. I *never*—"

"And now you want to run away with him. Is that it?"

"No," said Marion, shaking her head, "and I'm sorry if anything I did made you think that my intention was different. I don't want to be with Geoffrey. I never even considered it. My place is with you. If I could stay here all my life, I would. This House has become my home. The only home I've ever had, and I don't want to leave it . . . or you." Marion felt her eyes fill with tears at the thought. How could Lisavet ever believe that she wanted to leave the House of Hunger? After all they'd shared? After all she'd bled for her? Marion would've been quite content to sacrifice the last years of her youth—and with them, any chance she had at marriage, or children, or noble love— just to remain by Lisavet's side. If it came to it, she would willingly endure sharing her with another, even being replaced, if it meant that she could remain with Lisavet only a little longer.

Sometimes, she thought that if Lisavet's House were to fall, if she'd lost all of her money and had nothing more than the clothes on her back, Marion would remain with her in squalor and be happy to do so, even if Lisavet could never love her the same. Even if they never saw the sunrise together, or spent an entire night entwined in the same bed. Even if Lisavet made her bleed until Marion teetered on the very brink of death. She would've done it gladly, and it would have been enough.

"I don't know how you could mistake me for anything more than entirely loyal to you and you only," said Marion, in a shaking voice, and the tears she'd been fighting back spilled down her cheeks. "Sometimes I feel like I've been building you a House out of my own bones. And still, you look at me with so much contempt and mistrust. You complain because there are gaps in the roof of my ribs, and you ask me to give more of myself to fill them. You want my hips to be the bowl you drink from. My shoulders, your bed. My arms, your walls. My legs, the very ground you stand on. You want your fill of my blood whenever you crave it. What more do you want from me?"

"Your teeth," said Lisavet.

"My . . . what?"

Lisavet withdrew a small dagger from the inner pocket of her robe, its blade only a bit wider than that of a bleeding needle. She extended it to Marion. "I want your teeth. I want you to open your mouth and cut one out for me. Pry it free of the gums."

Marion's eyes went from the dagger to the Countess. "You can't be serious."

"Go on. Prove your loyalty."

Marion took the blade, her hand shaking, parted her lips, and pried her jaw open even as every instinct within her screamed at her to stop. But the desire to prove her fidelity superseded impulse or nature, morality or common sense. She raised the dagger to her chin, then a little higher until its tip touched her bottom lip. She opened her mouth wider, so as not to cut herself, felt the cold steel of the blade kiss the back of her tongue and gagged. She tasted metal. Began to shift the point of the blade toward her molars—

The Countess caught her by the wrist. "*Enough.*"

Marion slid the blade free of her mouth so quickly she accidentally nicked the corner of her lip and began to bleed. She dropped the dagger and it clattered to the floor at their feet.

The Countess appeared as shaken as Marion. Marion could see her heart beating a brutal rhythm, her pale chest heaving.

Marion wiped her bleeding mouth on her wrist. "Have you had your fill? Or should I cut out my tongue and offer it up on a platter in order to appease you fully?"

Lisavet stooped to lift the dagger from the floor, then stood, looming over Marion. She placed the cold blade of the dagger beneath her chin, forcing her to look up.

Unflinching, Marion met her gaze. "Well? What are you waiting for?"

Lisavet drove the blade, upright, into the surface of the desk with so much force the ink pot jumped and toppled; black spattered across the portrait of the bloodmaid and seeped across the letter she'd been writing. Her mouth crushed against Marion's with a violence, and the two of them began to claw at each other, as animals might, tearing at their clothes until seams ripped and buttons popped, skittering across the floor of the bedroom.

Lisavet slipped the signet ring off her middle finger and set it on the desk. Then she drew Marion's skirts up to her hip bones. By the time they reached the bed, her hand was moving up between her thighs, to the soft, wet gap between them, then pressing deeper still, burying her fingers inside her. Marion arched her back—her head slamming painfully against the headboard—and gasped.

When Lisavet ducked and disappeared under the tent of her skirts, Marion bucked her hips against her mouth that she might better satisfy her yearning, a yearning that Lisavet fed with hungry kisses, eager strokes of her tongue. As Lisavet emerged from the covers of her skirts, Marion caught her around the back of the neck and dragged her close for another kiss. They managed to tear away the last of each other's clothes and entangled themselves naked on the bed, appeasing each other with sweet nothings and empty promises murmured against the skin, interrupted by bites so vicious they drew blood. When they kissed, Marion tasted metal.

Lisavet slipped into her again, her fingers a steady pulse within her.

Marion came with a racking shudder, her legs straining, seized by what felt like the stiff rigor of death. For a moment she thought she was dying, but then the violent waves of pleasure subsided, and spent, Marion collapsed limp into the bed. "I do loathe you sometimes," she murmured into a pillow.

"And I you," said Lisavet, tracing a finger down the hard plane of her sternum. "You wretched girl."

27

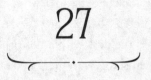

To love is to devour.

—HELENA, BLOODMAID OF THE HOUSE OF ROSES

THAT NIGHT, WHEN LISAVET slipped silently out of bed, Marion cracked one eye open. She watched as the Countess snatched her robe from the floor and slipped into it, tying the velvet sash tight around her waist. She paused to put on not her house slippers, but a pair of stiff leather riding boots. Then she seized one of the heavy, four-pronged candlesticks and lit every wick. From a small drawer in her desk she removed a pair of black leather gloves and tugged them on with her teeth.

By the fluttering candlelight, Lisavet walked to the far wall of the room. She stopped short of a bare stretch of paneling, half-concealed behind a curtain that she gingerly dragged away. Marion watched, frozen, as the Countess leaned toward the wall—the candlelight burning so close to the plaster that it charred it. She pressed her hand flat against it.

From down the hall: a howl and crash. Someone crying Lisavet's name in a peal of drunken laughter. Lisavet drew her hand away from the wall, sharply, as though it had burned her. She cursed under her breath and hastily dragged the curtain back into place. But not before turning to look at Marion, who managed to squeeze her eyes shut a moment before the Countess' gaze fell to her.

Lisavet cut back to the desk with a flourish, the light of the candles extinguishing themselves with the speed of her movements. She set the candelabra down on the desk with a firm thud and peeled her gloves off.

Someone else cried her name. This time Lisavet answered and left the room.

When her footsteps faded to a dull echo, Marion sat up, hastily snatched her chemise from its place crumpled on the floor, took a lone candlestick from the nightstand, lit it, and started toward the wall Lisavet had left abandoned. She brushed past the heavy curtain, registering the faint smell of dust, and pressed her palm flat against the paneling, as Lisavet had done. It shifted an inch or so. Marion, straining, braced her shoulder against it and the panel dropped away completely, swinging back to strike the wall of a narrow hallway. Marion pitched forward, very nearly dropping her candle, but managed to recover herself a moment before she fell. She stared into the dark of the passage; it was nearly identical to the one she'd discovered days ago just before Tutor Geoffrey was fired. Where did this one lead? And why was Lisavet hiding it?

Hastily Marion turned back, drew the velvet curtain back over the door, and closed it behind her. She stepped forward. The plaster floor was cold beneath her bare feet. At the hall's end, barely within reach of the flickering candlelight: a staircase twisting down into the darkness.

Marion took it, moving slowly, her footsteps ringing on the iron stairs. As she descended, a wet breeze cycled up from the depths of the House and extinguished her candle. Blind in the darkness, she picked her way down the stairs, one guiding hand along the wall, the other gripping the iron rail.

Halfway through her long descent, she saw light below her. As she climbed down the final steps, she entered what appeared to be a cavern, lit with oil-lamp sconces. Its walls were furred with a strange, black fungus that was soft and moist to the touch. All around her hung pillars of jagged stalactites, and the distant caverns echoed with the sound of dripping water.

What she found at the mouth of the cavern, in the wan halo of the oil lamps that lined its walls, were not the dungeons she'd expected to discover in the bowels of an age-old manor like the House of Hunger. The room, at first glance, struck her as a kind of study. There was a work desk at the center of the space—nearly identical to the one in Lisavet's bedroom in make and style—although this one stood on tall legs and its surface was wide enough to accommodate two women lying shoulder to shoulder. The air there was thin and wet, difficult to breathe, and it was heavy with the saccharine stench of formaldehyde and, below that, raw sewage.

The walls of the room were lined with shelves that, upon closer inspection, she realized were cut directly into the stone. On them, spaced apart at regular intervals, were jarred viscera. There were stomachs, hearts, and kidneys, all of them big enough to belong to large animals. In addition to the jarred specimens were organs and other body parts set behind panes of glass that were so thoroughly dehydrated Marion couldn't possibly identify them, and a glass crock filled with animal teeth.

At first she took these strange specimens to be nothing more than an extension of Lisavet's taxidermy collection. But then, among the dozens of jars, she spotted something horrifying. Fingers, *human* fingers, floating suspended in dark pickling juice. Stunned, Marion staggered back, crashing into a shelf. One of the jars pitched

forward—brine sloshing against its glass walls—and plummeted to
the ground. Marion caught it a moment before it struck the floor and
shattered. To her horror, it contained a small human fetus, its um-
bilical cord wrapped, serpentine, like a noose around its neck.

In the far corner of the room, between jagged stakes of stalagmite, was an iron rack with an assortment of tools hanging from its
hooks. There were scalpels and razors, pairs of handcuffs and small
bridles, forceps and a branding iron with Lisavet's initials, bone saws
in varying sizes, and barbed riding crops that looked like crueler it-
erations of the one Madame Boucherie wielded. The instruments
were fit only for the dual tasks of torture and dissection.

Horrified, Marion realized this wasn't a taxidermy studio at all.
It was a den of torment.

Marion wanted to flee then, but some dark compulsion to un-
cover the truth drove her onward against her better instinct, leading
her down an adjacent hallway where she discovered twelve empty
cells cut straight into the thick stone walls of the cavern, their doors
barred shut with cruel iron rungs. The room opened out onto what
appeared to be another network of caverns, and as Marion edged
closer, she thought she saw an iron spiral staircase carving up
through the bedrock, almost identical to the one she'd just descended. An exit, an escape.

She started toward it—relieved she wouldn't have to risk retrac-
ing her steps and returning to Lisavet's bedroom—when she saw
something stir in the cell closest to her. A figure moving from beneath a heap of soiled rags. As she sat up, Marion saw that it was a
person, so starved and gaunt that she could see the shadow of a
skeleton beneath her paper-thin skin.

The poor creature reached out, forcing a mangled hand through
the bars of her cage. Her fingers were warped with age, and badly
broken. There were age spots and needle marks dotting her wrinkled

forearms. When the woman pressed to her feet, her bulging knees creaking, Marion saw that they were roughly the same height. She gazed at Marion, dead-eyed but smiling, and Marion gazed back, too terrified to utter a single word for fear of breaking the silence. There was something in the woman's gaze that was decidedly . . . *familiar.* But Marion couldn't place her.

"I . . . know your face," said the old woman, and she seemed to struggle with the words a bit, as if it was hard for her to remember their proper order.

Marion froze. "What's your name?"

The creature stirred and shifted, her shackles rattling across the wet stone floors. When she turned her head to look at Marion, she could see the sharp protrusion of her cheekbone pressing through the skin at a crude angle that made it look almost broken.

And perhaps it was.

"I am called the Wretch," she said, and Marion stopped dead.

"Are you . . . a *bloodmaid*?"

The Wretch laughed, a nasty bark that rattled the congestion in her chest. She spat something rusty green onto the cobbles between her feet. "No, not a bloodmaid. A Wretch's blood is not fit for drinking. It's barely fit for bathing."

"But you have needle marks on your arms."

The Wretch gazed down at her ragged nails, chewed on one of them. "Not a bloodmaid . . . *now.* But that does not mean I was *never* a bloodmaid."

And then it hit her. The truth of the creature, the woman, crouched before her. "Oh my God. *Cecelia*—"

Before the woman, the creature, that had once been Cecelia could respond, a door groaned open. Marion saw a shadow trace along the walls, and the woman before her shrank back against the far wall of her cell, cowering and shaking so violently her chains rattled across the cobbles. In turn, Marion fell back into the shadows, stumbling over the uneven floor in her haste to stay hidden. Panicked, she lunged behind a thick stake of stalagmite, a few feet from where she stood.

There were footsteps. After them, a voice: "I'm home."

Marion froze. She would have known that voice anywhere; it belonged to Lisavet. Cringing behind the stone, Marion listened. She heard the grating groan of a cell door swinging open, a muffled plea, the seething hiss of chains slithering across the stones.

"A Wretch has nothing left to give," said the one who was once Cecelia. "Please. Show mercy."

Marion carefully peered from behind the rock to watch from the shadows. Lisavet appeared unmoved. Stoic, she strode to the cell, her robe trailing along the wet floor behind her, her hands gloved in leather.

"Mercy," said the Wretch, and she shrank into the corner of her cell. Her gaze darted left, toward the place where Marion crouched—wrapped in shadow—and for a moment she feared she'd betray her in order to save herself. "Please."

To this request Lisavet gave no answer. In fact, she did not seem to regard the Wretch as truly human at all. It was as if her pleas were nothing more than the squealing of a pig in a slaughterhouse.

Lisavet's boots struck a sharp rhythm across the floor as she crossed the cell, unlocked its door, seized the woman by her chains, and—with a single, vicious yank—dragged her from her cage. The old woman scrabbled at Lisavet's boots, without the slightest attempt to protect herself or flee. It was clear to Marion that the will had long been beaten out of her.

"What's your name?" Lisavet asked, gently, and with that crisp aristocratic accent. Even now, amid this depravity, she was no less the Countess.

"The Wretch," the woman whispered, with her lips pressed to the toe of Lisavet's boot. "I am called the Wretch."

"And what will the Wretch do at the behest of her mistress?"

The woman pressed a final kiss to Lisavet's boot, her chapped lips crushing painfully against the leather. "She will bleed."

"And does it honor her to do so?"

"Yes. Yes, it does."

"Then rise . . . and bleed."

The Wretch extended her arm. Lisavet took it, and her mouth closed around her wrist, and her gold-capped canines pierced the skin and muscle, sinking bone-deep. Lisavet's throat contracted, violently, like she was gagging almost. And Marion watched in horror as what little youth was left in Cecelia drained from her. Crow's feet etched themselves into the corners of her eyes, and her skin—once milk pale—became mottled with purple age spots. The flesh at her jowls slackened and hung loose. Her mouth wrenched open in a silent cry of pain, and Marion watched as her teeth yellowed and rotted before her eyes.

Lisavet kept feeding, eyes touched with a terrible light, nothing in them but hunger. This, Marion realized then, was the magic of her ancestors. The sickness, the depravity, that had dragged the House founder from his dwelling place in the depths of the sea. The urge, no, the compulsion, to drain and devour and feed. To take a barely living thing and bleed it of what little life it had left to spare. Lisavet wasn't just draining Cecelia of her blood, she was draining her body of its very soul.

Marion looked on in silent horror as the Countess continued to devour her, Cecelia's flesh withering away from shrunken muscle, her skin wrinkled and puckering, hanging loose from jutting bone. Her eyes seemed to recede, deeper and deeper, into the caverns of her sockets—the whites shot through with red blood vessels swollen to the point of bursting. Then one of them did burst, and Marion watched as her left eye filled with blood. She was dying. She was wasting. Urine streamed down her legs. And Marion, too cowardly to do anything more than watch, backed silently into the shadows, turned toward the stairway, and fled.

The dead answer to no one.

—DOREN, BLOODMAID OF THE HOUSE OF FERNS

"WAKE UP," MARION HISSED, snatching the blankets off Irene. "We need to go."

The girl rolled over groggily, scrubbed at her eyes with the heel of her hand. "What?"

"You have to get up," said Marion, pacing the room in a panic. She threw open the doors of Irene's wardrobe, began to rifle through her clothes. Selecting stockings and scarves and other items they'd need on the icy trek to the night train's station. "We've got to leave. Tonight. There's no time."

Irene stood up. "What's the meaning of this?"

Marion paused to catch her breath, bracing herself against the dresser. She was winded from fleeing up from the caverns. After scaling the stairway, it had taken her more than thirty minutes to navigate the labyrinth of passages that ran behind the walls of the House. Finally, she'd found an entrance that led to a servants' passage, not far from the bloodmaids' quarters, and had been able to find her way back from there. "I can't explain now; we just have to go. You have to trust me."

Irene plucked a tattered cobweb from Marion's curls. "You look . . . *awful*. Where have you been—"

Marion wheeled to face her, tears in her eyes. She caught Irene by the wrist, dragged her across the parlor and into the twins' shared suite on its other side. Their room was almost perfectly symmetrical, as if it was designed that way just for the twins. There were two beds, one set into the left wall, the other into the right. In them, the twins were sleeping soundly: Evie with her head at the foot of the bed, Elize contorted, her left leg dangling limp off the side of the mattress, snoring into the thick of her pillow. Theodore slept soundly at the foot of her bed, one paw covering his eyes, folded into a shape that made him look not unlike a very furry, very round loaf of bread.

Irene reluctantly woke Elize, and Marion shook Evie awake. The two girls bolted upright, bleary-eyed, their hair knotted into tight pin curls. Marion turned and locked the door before facing the girls.

Studying them by the wan light of the hearth, she noticed little things she had missed before. The crow's feet etched around the edges of Evie's eyes. The faint age spots that spangled the backs of Irene's hands, and her hair, which had thinned even more over the past few weeks. And then there was Elize, gaunt, her eyes watery and vacant. Even now, they were aging beyond their years. Lisavet was *draining* them, of their health, their youth and time.

"I need to tell you something," said Marion, her voice thin and ragged. "And when I tell you, I need you to swear that you won't breathe a word of this to anyone. Your lives and mine depend on that."

"You have our word," said Irene, without a beat.

"There's something horrible beneath this House. I saw it tonight. Lisavet almost entered this secret passage, like the one I found that day playing fox and hound with Mae. I walked through it and it led me to this staircase and at the end of it there was . . . the unspeakable." Marion's voice cracked. She began to cry, spitting words out between sobs. "A glimpse of hell itself. Cecelia was down there . . . and . . . and—"

"I don't understand," said Irene, in a trembling whisper. "Help us understand."

"I think the fever might've gotten to her," Evie grumbled, but she looked afraid. Perhaps she suspected she was going mad, just like Cecelia had.

Elize seemed to share in her suspicion, because she slipped out of bed, began to back away toward the locked door. "Perhaps we should fetch the House Mother—"

"Will you just *listen* to me?" Marion demanded, tears in her eyes, her voice breaking on the words. Elize froze, one hand extended to the doorknob, and Marion had the sudden urge to seize her by the shoulders and shake her. "Please?"

The twins looked toward Irene, who stood with her arms folded tight over her chest, like she was trying to hold herself together. "Let her finish," she said.

So, in a choked whisper, Marion disclosed all of the horrors she had witnessed that night. The jarred specimens, the scalpels, the bone saws, the crops and shackles and all of the other devices of torment hanging from the walls of that vile chamber. She told them about the cells and the starved and aged woman who was once Cecelia, now called the Wretch. She told them that she saw Lisavet there, in the dungeons, draining her of what little life and blood she had left in her. She even told them, in brief terms, about the founder of the House of Hunger, Lisavet's ancestor who had once devoured his lover in the same way Lisavet was devouring them, centuries later.

After Marion finished her dark confession, Elize began to cry. Even Evie cracked, her chin wrinkling with the effort of fighting back tears. "But . . . but that's impossible. Cecelia is at the sanatorium. We've been sending her letters—"

"And have you ever received a response?" Marion demanded. "Have any of you?"

Silence. Evie and Irene shook their heads. Elize spoke then, in the tentative and testing way that people do when they're deciding whether they believe what they're saying: "Well, the House Mother says Cecelia won't be able to respond until her health improves—"

"The House Mother is a liar. She hasn't been sending your letters to Cecelia," said Marion, speaking in a whisper. "I know because I found them, the seals broken, unaddressed and unsent in her desk."

Irene's eyes went wide. "You broke into the House Mother's *desk*?"

"Let me finish," said Marion, sharply. "The reason your letters were never sent is that Cecelia's never left the House. She's been here all this time. Beneath the House. They've all been lying to us. Lisavet, the House Mother, maybe even the servants."

When Marion's grim confession was finally finished, there was silence. The twins, holding hands, peered at Irene again, searching for guidance. But she said nothing, did nothing. Her eyes glazed over, and for a moment she seemed close to tears, though her expression betrayed no emotion.

"Do you think I'm lying?" Marion asked, her gaze shifting to Irene. Of all of the bloodmaids in the House, it was Irene that she looked up to, Irene that she had come to consider a friend. Or if not that, a confidant, someone she could trust with the truth. Without her, Marion was truly and properly alone, with no one left to turn to. "Don't you see that we only have each other? Lisavet has tried to pit us against each other from the moment we set foot in this House. She's used us as leverage and bait. Broken our friendships, breached the trust between us all to ensure that the only person we're loyal to is her. If we don't have each other, we have no one. And that's exactly what she wants. Orphans and castoffs, victims and wretches. Girls with no one alive to mourn them. That way, when Lisavet drains us dry and discards us, it's as though we never existed at all."

"But Lisavet wouldn't do that," said Elize, crying openly now. "She loves us."

"Lisavet loves our blood, but only until our blood isn't enough for her. Then she moves on to the next girl and . . ." Marion's voice broke, and she shook her head. "Lisavet has been consuming us since the day we first arrived in this House. She's been devouring our memories, our years, our spirits, our youth. She told me herself that her hunger would kill me if I let it. No matter how much blood she takes from us, it will never be enough. She'll drain us of all life and then, when we have nothing left to give—when we're half-mad with sickness, when we've forgotten who we are—she'll cast us down into the bowels of this House. Make wretches of us all, just like she did Cecelia. And then the cycle will repeat itself again, with a new batch of bloodmaids. I've already seen portraits of new prospects on the corner of her desk. She told me that she wants to indenture four new girls."

"Our replacements," said Evie as the full and horrible truth of the matter dawned on her for the first time.

"I heard a servant say Thiago has come from the South with new girls," said Elize, anxiously and in a hissing whisper. "*Sisters*, like Evie and me. The youngest fifteen, the oldest two and twenty, and there's a third and fourth sister who—"

"*Thiago* is back?" Marion demanded, trying and failing to mask her horror. More bloodmaids at the House meant that she and the others would be sent down to the caverns to make room for them. As Ivor had cruelly pointed out months ago, there were only so many beds in the bloodmaids' chamber. For girls to come, other girls would have to go below.

"Apparently, Thiago's confidence was bolstered by Lisavet's taking to you," said Elize. "The sisters are said to be blood-related to none other than the founding Countess of the House of Day. Apparently, they descended from the bastard of her brother. I hear they speak four languages and they're all blue-eyed and—"

"Have they been formally indentured already?" Marion demanded, cutting Elize short yet again. She caught her by the arm. "Have they signed their contracts yet?"

"I don't know—*ouch*," Elize shrieked, struggling to pry her arm free of Marion's grasp. "You're holding me too roughly! That hurts. I don't know anything beyond what I said."

"We have to go," said Marion, musing more to herself than anyone. She'd known that Lisavet would eventually replace Cecelia. But she hadn't expected four new girls to arrive at the House so soon. "We should leave tomorrow when everyone's at court. The House will be full then, so we could slip into the caverns while Lisavet is distracted in the salons, rescue Cecelia—"

"And how do you propose we do that?" Evie demanded, and Marion could tell the girl was terrified. "You're recovering from sepsis. We're all weak from bleeding—"

"We'll find a way. The twins will distract Lisavet. Irene is responsible for Mae. I'll go below and free Cecelia." If Cecelia could be freed, if she wanted to be, but Marion dared not say that to the girls for fear of breaking their spirits more than she already had. Better to let them cling to what remained of their hope. "At midnight, the six of us will meet in the garden and make our escape to the night train's station. If we're stealthy, we may be able to row across the estuary, secure our tickets, and board the train before anyone even notices we're gone."

Irene seemed ill at ease. "Let's say your plan works, where will we go?"

"Anywhere. You have family in the Isles, don't you?" Marion

inquired, remembering how Irene had told her about the island in the far South where she was born. It seemed a world away from the House of Hunger, which made it as good a place to settle as any.

"I haven't heard from my family in months," said Irene, looking wounded. "And even if they were willing to take us in, it will take us weeks, if not months, to scrounge up the coin we'd need to buy six tickets to the night train. Let alone the additional money that we'd need to ferry us down to the Isles," said Irene softly. "We need more time."

"We don't have it," said Marion. "We have to leave as soon as possible. We have to find a way."

Elize piped up. "We could stow away on the baggage car."

"That's too risky," said Irene. "The clerks will discover us."

"Fine. Then we'll just . . . buy the tickets outright."

"With whose money?" Irene demanded.

"Why not our own?" said Evie. "Why can't we just take the money? By law it's ours upon the end of our indentures. It's not stealing if it's from the pensions we're owed anyway."

"We don't have pensions."

The girls all turned to look at Marion, shocked.

She realized then that amid her panic, she'd failed to disclose the rest of what she'd discovered in the House Mother's desk. The files full of ledgers, more than a dozen girls who—according to those records—had never seen a penny of their pensions. "When I broke into the House Mother's desk I found more than a dozen ledgers, tallying the finder's fees and investments made in the bloodmaids indentured to this House. But there wasn't a single mention of any girl ever receiving her pension. Because none of the girls are alive to receive them. They're all dead."

Irene and Evie digested this grim news in silence, their lips quivering with the effort of holding back tears. Elize, the most fragile of the four of them, muffled a sob in the sleeve of her nightgown.

"Then we'll . . . sell our jewels," said Evie, composing this flimsy plan as she went along. "Perhaps a pearl goes missing from a bracelet, an emerald from your favorite ring falls out during a night at court, or you lose a single earring while strolling through the labyrinth."

Irene considered this proposition for a moment, her eyebrows knitting together. "And who will take our stolen wares to the market and smuggle the money back to us? How will we both steal and pawn these items without arousing suspicion? There's not a single noble in the court who'd buy stolen jewels off a bloodmaid."

"Do you not have allies in this House?" Marion asked, lowering her voice even further. She knew that the bloodmaids were set apart from the other servants, but it was inconceivable to her that Irene and the other girls had no trusted confidant to turn to after the months they'd spent in service. She searched the faces of her peers for an answer. "Is there no one we can trust?"

Irene paused to consider this for a moment, then dropped her gaze to her hands. "No one that I know of."

"We're bloodmaids," said Evie, exasperated. "The servants around here have spent their lives on their hands and knees scrubbing our floors, squeezing our feet when they ache. They make our beds, ladle food into our mouths, keep our hearths lit, and empty our chamber pots when we fill them at night. Do you really think that any of them have any fondness for us? Any loyalty? We're on our own here."

Something dawned on Marion then, the seed of an idea. "It's true that we're alone in our plight . . . but that doesn't mean that others don't share in our disdain for Lisavet."

Irene, the quickest of the four next to Marion, whispered. "*Ivor.*"

Smiling, Marion nodded. "The enemy of our enemy may just become our ally. Lisavet told me, months ago, that he was the next heir to the House of Hunger after her. Apparently, his mother is her father's half sister, or something of the sort. If we can bait him with the promise of orchestrating Lisavet's downfall, of deposing her once and for all, then perhaps he'd be willing to help us escape."

Just then, a knock at the door. Irene and Evie recoiled, the former drawing against the wall, the latter drawing her blankets up to her chin. Evie snatched Theodore to her chest. The cat startled awake and clawed furiously at her chest. Marion edged forward and seized the poker from its holder by the hearth. She put a hand to the doorknob and half raised the poker. "Who's there?"

No answer.

"Don't open it," Evie hissed. "What if it's her?"

Marion eyed the door for a long time. Weighing her decision. Shadows shifted in the crack between door and floor. She turned the knob.

And there was Mae, standing in the parlor, bleary-eyed and inquisitive. Marion hastily lowered the poker, slipping it back into its place by the hearth, and Irene rushed forward to herd Mae inside, chiding her about the late hour and how respectable little girls aren't awake to see it. Marion locked the door again.

"We have to go," she said, watching Irene draw Mae tight into her arms. "If we don't, then one day it'll be Mae that Lisavet bleeds, when she's old enough. Mae that she drains of her youth and life. And if not her, then some other girl. I know it's frightening, and I know you're all scared. I am too. But if we don't do this, we'll die below this House just like all of the other girls who came before us."

Irene peered down at Mae, tears coming to her eyes for the first time. "Tomorrow," she said, nodding her head. "Tomorrow we go."

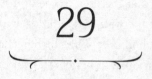

29

A bruised plum is always the last chosen.

—LUCILLE, BLOODMAID OF THE HOUSE OF HUNGER

SIR IVOR OCCUPIED THE eastern wing of the House, in a large suite that overlooked a reeking strip of marshland. His private quarters included a large salon, a room with no windows, one roaring hearth, and three circular tables around which a range of nobles sat gambling, despite the early-morning hour. Some of them appeared to have played through the night, if their bloodshot eyes and rumpled clothes were any indication at all. Marion noted that Lisavet wasn't there and felt relieved.

"Marion," Ivor cried. He was seated at a table in the far corner of the room along with several others, and webs of maudlum smoke hung on the air around their heads. "To what do we owe the pleasure?"

Marion approached the table. Ivor stared at her from behind a fan of gilded playing cards that glinted brilliantly in the candlelight. At the center of the table was a heaping stash composed of crumpled banknotes, a smattering of gems, jewelry, a few human teeth (like Cora's, which Marion had taken to carrying in the pocket of her skirts like a kind of good-luck charm), and, of course, piles upon piles of golden coins. The money on the table would be enough to afford them at least three tickets on the night train, maybe even double that. It was a horrible sight to see, enough money to afford the blood-maids their lives sitting there on the gambling table, to be squandered by nobles who would never know what it was to fight for their very survival.

Marion claimed a seat near Ivor. "Leave us."

The noblewomen seated with him seemed so stunned by this curt dismissal that their mouths gaped wide open. They looked to Ivor, awaiting directions that he didn't offer. He merely withdrew a checkbook and pen from an inner pocket of his vest. He tore out a check, scribbled a ridiculous sum, and signed it. Marion paid particular attention to his signature, memorizing each stroke of the pen, an *I* so large it spanned almost the entire height of the slip, followed by a string of letters so small they were almost indecipherable. He didn't bother to designate his last name with anything more than a large *HF*, presumably for the House of Fog.

"Your winnings," he said, rather bitterly, and passed the folded check to the noblewoman to his left, who carefully palmed it. She glanced between Ivor and Marion once more, as if confused whether to stay or go.

"I won't repeat myself," said Marion.

The women fled.

When they were well out of earshot, Marion fixed her eyes on Ivor, who was collecting the cards his companions had abandoned. "I'd like to play."

Ivor muttered something about how the game was better suited for four than two. "Besides, do you even know how to play?"

"Yes," said Marion. She'd learned as a child. Some of her friends—fellow pickpockets, all of them boys—used to gamble with hand-drawn card decks and a winning stash of stolen marbles and bottle caps and whatever baubles they'd been deft enough to pickpocket over the course of the week.

Ivor begrudgingly dealt her a hand. "Well, you'll need to scrounge up something to gamble with."

"What about the truth?" Marion said, and she helped herself to some of the wine, filling a goblet to the rim with a decanter. "Is that a currency you'd be willing to accept?"

"It depends on what you know," said Ivor, examining his cards. "Some morsels of truth are more valuable than others."

"Mine relate to Lisavet . . . and her secrets."

Ivor arched an eyebrow. "I'm intrigued. Continue."

Marion didn't know how or where to begin, and for the first time she considered the very real possibility that Ivor, like, she suspected, the House Mother and a few of the footmen that Lisavet employed, might very well know her secret. It was unfathomable to think she'd managed such an extensive endeavor alone. Others had to know. If Ivor was one of them, Marion was as sure as dead.

She decided to broach the topic gingerly, the way one traverses a pond frozen over with a thin sheet of ice, testing each step before risking their full weight. "I've seen something . . . below the House."

Marion examined Ivor's expression for any signs of suspicion, shock, the inklings of anything remotely similar to recognition. But he betrayed nothing.

"And?" he asked, looking thoroughly unimpressed. "What exactly did you see down there that has you so shaken? Did a rat cross your path?"

"I saw hell itself."

This seemed to intrigue him. He looked up from his cards, scanning the other tables in their vicinity to ensure that no one was listening in. "Do go on."

In a scraping whisper so soft she could barely hear herself above the din of the salon, Marion recounted the horrors below the House. Ivor digested all of these details—the specimens, the instruments of torture, Cecelia drained of youth and life, Lisavet's consuming power, her depravity—in utter silence. But while his expression betrayed nothing more than boredom, Marion noticed that his hands shook slightly as he shuffled. The playing cards slipped from his hands, fluttered down like gilded moths, and scattered across the table. Hastily, he collected them and reshuffled the deck.

When her story was finished, he let the silence stretch between them for a long time. Finally, he spoke. "Who else knows about this?"

"I'm the only one," Marion said, a boldfaced lie. In the event that Ivor betrayed her trust, better that the other bloodmaids maintain a veneer of innocence. Perhaps it would buy them time.

Ivor laid one of his cards facedown on the table. "You girls always think that you're so special. Lisavet expresses passing interests, provides you a contract to sign, and all at once you begin to believe that you're different, that your blood runs redder and tastes better, than all of the other girls who came before you and all of the miserable souls who will come after. Pathetic." He spat the word. "Utterly pathetic in your innocence. It would almost be amusing if it weren't so terribly sad."

Marion stared at him, stunned, her cheeks burning with both anger and embarrassment in equal part. She'd known for some time that Ivor was a selfish, insufferable, handsy fop . . . but she'd underestimated his callousness. That now, of all moments, he would seek to humiliate her, twist the knife in the wound. If he had any reaction to this revelation about Lisavet, it was not out of compassion for the girls she'd tortured. It was only in response to his own interests. It became clear to Marion, in that moment, the depth of his depravity. He would let all of them—her, Irene, the twins, and even little Mae—rot in the dungeons if it advanced his agenda.

Perhaps he'd suspected, already, that the girls Lisavet indentured met untimely ends. After all, he had been at the House of Hunger for some time. He must have seen the girls coming and going and had questions he saw fit to leave unanswered. Or perhaps he hadn't cared to answer them at all. Marion saw now that the bloodmaids meant nothing to him. In his eyes, and the eyes of the other nobles of the House, they weren't even human. Less, even, than animal. They existed only to be admired, and then devoured.

"I almost killed you," said Marion softly. "Out on the marsh during the hunt. Lisavet asked me to. She trained the rifle on your head and ordered me to put a bullet in it."

Ivor appeared unmoved by this confession. "Are you trying to imply I owe you a favor?"

"Not a favor, no. The arrangement I'm presenting is mutually beneficial. You'll front us the money for six tickets on the night train and in return, I'll testify against Lisavet. I'll confess everything— about all the missing girls, the dungeons below the House. Lisavet will be investigated, tried for her crimes, and imprisoned. Lisavet has no heir or living relatives, apart from you. She told me herself, months ago, that you longed to inherit this House. She called it your dream; said she would do anything in her power to crush it. But this is a way, perhaps the only viable way, for you to make that dream a reality."

Ivor considered this proposition for a while in silence, rifling casually through his cards. "You and I are always playing games, aren't we, Marion? Fox and hound. Forfeits. Though I dare say this simple card game is the most dangerous we've played yet. High stakes indeed." He laid down his cards faceup. Marion followed suit. She won the round: seventeen to twenty.

Ivor frowned, collected the cards with a pass of his hand. "The money is yours."

Marion could've wept with relief. She reached for the stash of coins and banknotes at the center of the table. But Ivor caught her by the wrist and she dropped a fistful of coins. A few of them rolled across the table and skittered across the salon floor.

"Are you quite daft?" Ivor hissed. "*Not* now. I'll prepare a check for you to present at the train station. It'll be enough to cover your tickets south, but not a penny more than that. I'll slip it to you tonight, while we're in court. Lest we arouse suspicion."

Marion nodded and drew her hand back. "Tonight, then? Do I have your word?"

"Of course," said Ivor. Behind a fan of gilded cards, he grinned.

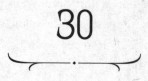

30

I belong more to her than I do myself. Is that not love?

—THE WRETCH, FORMERLY CECELIA,
FIRST BLOODMAID OF THE HOUSE OF HUNGER

THE GIRLS SPENT THE last of that day plotting in secret. Irene had taken it upon herself to pack small parcels containing necessities like soap, bleeding rags, banknotes, and, for Mae, the stuffed fox that Lisavet had given her. Evie, who was almost as good a pickpocket as Marion, had deftly assembled a secret stash of jewelry, coins, and other baubles that could be pawned when they disembarked from the night train and reached the Southern Isles. Elize, bless her, spent the bulk of her time devising ways to carry Theodore to the night train. Her most recent solution: the large decorative birdcage that had once housed Cecelia's stuffed parrot. She'd discovered it in one of the libraries, and, by a stroke of luck, it was just the right size to house her beloved Theodore, whom she ardently refused to leave behind.

Marion, trying to be the voice of reason, gently attempted to coax her otherwise. "He'll claw you bloody if you try to get him into that cage," she said. "And besides, Lisavet doesn't drink the blood of cats . . . that we know of. Perhaps he'll be fine staying behind."

"He's as much my companion as the rest of you," said Elize, utterly resolute. "And if I leave him Lisavet will have him stuffed out of spite. I just know it."

Across the parlor, Evie hiked up her skirts and forced a hand between her thighs, trying to adjust the coin purse that was dangling between them. She'd taken thorough measures to sew coins and banknotes into the folds of her dress, and she'd weighted both her shoes and corset with jewelry, so they'd have money for food and lodging when they reached the Isles. "At this rate I'll have to waddle my way to the night train . . ."

Marion and Elize began to laugh, but Irene was quiet. Unlike the rest of them, she remained reserved, less confident in the mechanics of their carefully plotted plan. Her faith in Ivor was far from absolute. "If something goes wrong . . ."

Marion squeezed her cold fingers in a futile effort to massage warmth into them, get the blood flowing again. "Ivor gave me his word. By midnight tonight we'll be on the night train headed south. You're going to see your mother again. We're going to be safe . . . maybe even happy."

The dinner bell rang. And, in a rare formality, the House Mother appeared to walk them to the dining room. "Marion?"

"Yes, m'lady?"

"Lisavet has requested your presence at her table tonight. You'll dine with her."

This came as a shock to Marion. Lisavet never invited bloodmaids to her table. Even Cecelia, in the long months of her reign as First Bloodmaid, had never received a dinner invitation. The other girls seemed to share in her alarm. The twins exchanged sidelong glances and Irene seemed quite stricken, clasping her hands so tightly that Marion heard one of her knuckles pop.

Marion quickly made her way to Lisavet's quarters, eager to get dinner behind them so that they could go to court and resume their plan to escape that night. When she arrived, she saw that there were two footmen posted at the door. Odd, given that she'd never seen them there before. Lisavet preferred to maintain a sense of privacy and almost never allowed anyone beyond bloodmaids and servants to enter the domain of her private chambers.

The footmen let her in.

Lisavet's chambers comprised three rooms. Two Marion had visited before, the parlor (where Lisavet's taxidermy collection was displayed) and the bedroom. One Marion had not: the private dining room adjoining the parlor. Marion entered the parlor and saw that the doors of the dining room were open to her. The room was as ornate as the rest of the House and larger than Marion had expected, with high vaulted ceilings and large windows that overlooked the ocean. It was a smaller version of the grand hall, where court was often hosted.

To the left of the door, a long buffet table ran along the wall. On it were a wide selection of dishes: roast pheasants, broiled eel, vats of soup and bisque, oysters on beds of ice, thick gravy, poached mushrooms that bled when you cut them, julienned vegetables, and steaming mince pies fresh from the ovens. For dessert, a four-tiered rum-soaked fruitcake, adorned with paper-thin slices of candied blood orange.

At an oval table at the center of the room, in the chair both farthest from the door and facing it, sat Lisavet. It was the first Marion had seen of her since the horrors below the House, and she was every bit as beautiful and as terrible then as she was now, sitting before her, lips slick with blood wine, eyes touched by hunger.

The Countess stared at Marion above the rim of her raised goblet and took several long swallows before speaking. "Good evening."

"To you as well," said Marion, and she seated herself at the only other place setting at the table, just to the left of Lisavet. Along with the expected cutlery, there was a bleeding kit awaiting her use, comprising a bowl, a leather tourniquet, a long needle, and a bundle of bandages.

"Bleed for me," said Lisavet.

Marion swallowed thickly. All of the girls of the House had been thoroughly instructed on how to take blood themselves, but it was the first time Marion had attempted the task alone without oversight. On account of her infection, she opted for her left arm, instead of her favored right, which was the best for taking blood. The vein in her left arm wasn't as ample as the one in her right, but she buckled the tourniquet tight around her bicep and, after a few moments, the faint artery in the crook of her arm began to swell. She picked up the needle and pursed her lips, as she always did in wait of the pain. The needle pierced clean through her vein with a sharp pinch, and when she slipped it out again the blood began to flow. She tilted her arm so that the dark rivulet slipped down the crook of her elbow and spilled into the bowl below.

Lisavet watched her bleed, her eyes alight with the hearth fire, lips slightly parted as if primed to take her first sip. Marion could see the hunger in her.

"Is that enough?" she asked, when the little bowl was nearly half-full. Her heart was racing. She felt the sudden urge to be sick.

Lisavet nodded and Marion slipped the tourniquet off her arm, wiped the blood away, and bandaged herself with the scrap of silk provided her. She felt . . . peculiar and blamed this on the blood loss. Her menstrual flow had only just ended, and she knew she was low on iron. But the feeling persisted, a sinking dizziness that reminded her of a maudlum high.

She slid the bowl of blood to Lisavet.

The Countess raised it to her lips, took a small sip, and frowned. She withdrew a handkerchief from her pocket, spat the blood into its folds, and then crumpled and dropped it. She looked repulsed. "Ivor told me everything. But I could've tasted the truth."

Marion's heart plunged into her stomach.

Lisavet stood up. She took her plate and Marion's from the table, walked over to the buffet, and began to serve them, loading each plate with food. "You know, when I was a little girl, my father once told me that if you eat the weak, you'll never go hungry. I learned at a young age that love requires a kind of . . . dismantling. One learns to make the object of your hunger love you. Because when they love you, they'll do the emotional butchery themselves. It was you, Marion, not me, who cut open your own chest, reached into the wet cavern behind your ribs, cut your heart loose of its rigging, and offered it to me. I had only to take it."

"You make us love you," said Marion, but even as she said it, it didn't feel like the truth. "You manipulate us, so that we have no choice but to stay here."

"That's not true. I told you to leave when you had the chance. I gave you the choice and you said no." Lisavet set her plate down in front of her. There were two oysters, a charred slice of eel meat—the flaky meat shot through with prickly bones—and several mushrooms. The smell wafting off the food turned her stomach. "You made it easy for me, Marion. But I suppose all of you do. Cecelia, and Irene, the twins, Cora and the rest. So you see, it's only my fault in part. It's impossible not to take from you when you make yourselves so . . . prone."

"We don't make ourselves prone," said Marion, and in that moment all of the residual love she'd had left for Lisavet—love she now had no place or purpose for—curdled and turned to hatred. "We're broken into submission, by grief and poverty, long before we ever set foot in this House. And then we arrive, on the promise of the first kindness many of us have received in *years*, and you take advantage of our weakness. You cultivate it, to better exploit us. You torment people until they give up everything—their blood, their dignity, even their names. You're a killer, a *sadist*—"

"And you are a greedy street rat who left your brother for dead facedown in the shit-filled gutters of the slums to chase the dream of a fortune," said Lisavet. "So I would argue that the two of us aren't so different."

Marion froze. The room seemed to cant before her eyes, as if the foundation the House stood on had shifted. Marion half expected all the furniture in the room to slide to the far wall, crash against the windows, and plummet down to the marshes several stories below. But nothing moved.

"You know, after I first sampled your blood, I inquired about your brother. I wrote to the officers in Prane to ask what became of him. Apparently, he dragged himself into the streets, where he was discovered by two paper boys at dawn. According to them, a pack of stray dogs was in the process of making a meal of his corpse. They claimed that the hounds had so thoroughly devoured his face that he was beyond the point of recognition and the coroner was only able to identify him by—"

"I am nothing like you."

"But you could be. I see it in you."

"Stop it."

"You're not like the others. You're strong—"

"I said *stop*," said Marion, and she sprang from her chair with such violence that it clattered to the floor. "Where are my friends, Lisavet?"

"Marion, sit down."

Marion picked up the bleeding needle and extended it to Lisavet's neck, the tip lodged at her pulse, biting into the skin. A droplet of her blood bubbled at the needle's tip. Marion's hand shook violently, and she couldn't hold it fast no matter how hard she tried.

Lisavet smiled up at her, taunting. "Go on, then. If you have the nerve."

Marion's hand tightened around the needle. She tried to quell her shaking and summon the strength she needed to kill her. Tried and . . . failed. It had been different with Raul. She had never meant to kill him; at least that was what she told herself. She hadn't had time to think. She'd never been made to decide his fate. But this was something else entirely. If she killed Lisavet now, she would truly be a murderer.

Lisavet sprang in her moment of weakness, pinning Marion's wrist to the table in a movement so quick it was nothing but a sharp blur. She wrenched it, and the needle flew from her hand and skittered across the floor. With her other hand, Lisavet held a steak knife to Marion's throat. "I want you to listen to me very carefully. Right now, your friends are being led below. Their continued survival is almost entirely dependent on your cooperation. Nod if you understand."

Marion nodded. The point of the steak knife bit deeper, drawing blood.

"If you protest, put up a fight, so much as part your lips to cry for help, I'll kill them. However, if you allow me to escort you downstairs without protest or struggle—"

"You'll kill them anyway."

"Don't be difficult," said Lisavet, softly. "Do you want to see your friends, or not?"

Across the room, the House Mother stepped over the threshold. She looked very grave. To Marion's horror, she saw that Mae was with her, the woman grasping her wrist in a vise grip as though she feared she'd run away.

Marion wondered then if Lisavet ever mourned the girls who'd come before. Or if her feeling for them was no more than thin fondness, like that which the butcher harbors for the piglet born to be slaughtered.

Marion shifted her gaze back to Lisavet. "Take me to the others."

The House Mother sidestepped into the parlor, head bowed. Mae peered up at Marion, helpless, with tears in her eyes, as she and Lisavet brushed past. They entered the bedroom, and Marion stopped short, the tip of the steak knife biting deep into the meat between her shoulder blades. She barely registered the pain, or anything more than the corpse of a man lying facedown on Lisavet's bed.

"Ivor suffered a maudlum overdose this morning, shortly after your little card game," said Lisavet. "He died this afternoon."

"Y-you . . . poisoned him," said Marion, and it hit her fully then, a punishing high that seemed to rip her soul from the cage of her body. She staggered, attempted to catch herself on Lisavet's desk, but misjudged the distance. Her fingers swiped at a kerosene lamp. It struck the floor and shattered, and Marion felt herself break with it, as if the sum of her soul had scattered into so many pieces, sharp fragments that she couldn't arrange into a coherent identity.

She didn't feel like herself. She didn't feel like anyone.

A part of her was certain she was dead already. Gone to hell.

"Ivor had a reckless habit. Unfortunately, it claimed his life."

"Liar. You killed him . . ." she said, slurring; her tongue felt swollen and sluggish behind her teeth. "You poisoned him . . . and me. The bleeding needle."

"Ah yes, the needle," said Lisavet, sounding bored and far away, as if she were speaking from two rooms over. "The maudlum on its tip. Frankly, I'm surprised the high hit you so late. I made certain the maudlum was concentrated. You do have a high tolerance. Must run in the family. Like brother, like sister?"

"You *bitch*."

"Mind your tone," said the House Mother, still lurking somewhere behind them, Mae with her as what Marion now understood to be living leverage.

Dizzy, sick with despair, Marion braced herself on the desk, acutely aware of the knife tip dancing at her back. "How much . . . did you give me? Am I going to die?"

"Not yet. I gave you enough to disarm, not kill. But do try to keep a clear head. I know it's hard." With the tip of the steak knife between Marion's bare shoulder blades, Lisavet led her to the far wall of the bedroom, to that same velvet shroud drawn across the hidden door.

"Open it," said Lisavet, and Marion obliged her, pressing hard on the paneling until it gave beneath her palms and shifted slowly open. A darkness yawned open before them, the esophagus of the House, spiraling down to its belly, where Marion—like the other girls who'd come before her—would be digested. Consumed.

———— ◆ ————

IT WAS A LONG AND TREACHEROUS CLIMB DOWN A STEEP FLIGHT OF iron stairs that twisted first through the House, then down through the bedrock on which it stood and into the dungeon caverns beneath them. The journey was made worse by the continued effects of the maudlum high. The stairs seemed to ripple beneath Marion's feet—like the surface of a pond moved by the wind—and Marion struggled to descend without falling. Her knees felt as soft as bread dough beneath her.

As she descended, she tried not to peer over the stair rail. But when she did, she saw that the drop was at least as deep as the House was tall; the dark and her pervading high made it impossible to discern the true distance. With the tip of Lisavet's knife trained between her shoulder blades, Marion kept climbing down, taking every step with care, doing her best not to trip on the hem of her gown. A fall down those steps could easily break her neck. And a part of her liked that thought; she was tempted to throw herself down, headfirst, and be done with it. Better that than suffer in agony at Lisavet's hands. It was the memory of the girls that stopped her, kept her sane. They were depending on her. And she wouldn't let them down.

Lisavet led her onward and, perhaps sensing her mounting fear, attempted to distract her with vague summations about the caverns and the secrets they harbored. As it turned out, these passages were only a small piece of a larger labyrinth of catacombs that stretched beneath the House, connecting to a vast network of caverns that reached every corner of the island. She told Marion stories of flooded tombs and sprawling cave systems as large as villages, chambers so deep they connected to underground oceans whose waters had never been touched by the light of day. And then of course there were catacombs, their walls studded with the petrified skulls of Lisavet's oldest ancestors, and Lisavet warned that many a foolhardy explorer had died in a futile conquest to map them.

Lisavet shoved open an iron door and showed them into a small cavelike room, lit with lamps. It was so cold that Marion could see her own breath. Here the air bore the reeking fungal stench of mold and mildew, and Marion swore she could see spores circling through the lantern light like dust motes moving through a cone of sunlight. At the end of the stairway, another door opened out onto the dungeons. They walked past the wet specimen jars. Marion spotted a severed tongue among the assortment of body parts and wondered if it belonged to the jester.

"Where's Irene?" Marion asked, and her voice rang through the run of empty cells and echoed. She saw no one. Not even Cecelia. "Where are the twins?"

"Have patience," Lisavet said, and her grip on Marion's hand tightened. They walked on until they reached a part of the dungeons Marion hadn't seen before. It was lit by the wan glow of a single blood lamp that swung—left and right, like a pendulum counting the seconds—from the ceiling of the corridor. As it moved, on every second beat, it tossed a cone of light inside a large cell—illuminating the figures that cowered in its shadows. Evie and Elize huddled in one corner of the cell, shackled to the wall, their chains short. Irene was on the other side, crouched beside a heap of soiled rags, also chained.

Marion might've run to them, forced her arms between the bars of the cell, but she found that she couldn't bring herself to move. The girls, their backs toward Marion, craned over their shoulders and cried out to her, weeping. The rags beside Irene stirred and shifted as the Wretch, formerly Cecelia, raised its head. She had aged *decades* since Marion had last seen her, just a day before. Most of her hair was gone, and what little remained was gray and straggly. And she was emaciated, all slack skin, and muscle withering away from protruding bone. Her wrists—swollen and bulbous—were shackled together with a pair of rusted handcuffs, but she was the only one who wasn't chained to the wall.

"Oh my God," said Marion, sobbing. "*Cecelia.*"

The girl, the woman—Marion was not sure how to refer to her anymore—roused slightly, lifting her heavy head. The whites of her eyes were mostly red, filled with blood. Through a film of cataracts, she stared up at Marion, cowering in her nest of soiled rags. There was something in her gaze, the briefest flicker of recognition, there and then gone in an instant.

"Look at me," said Lisavet; she had her back to the cell, and she was facing Marion fully.

Marion didn't turn. Didn't move. Didn't pull her gaze from Cecelia's.

"I said look."

Marion only half turned, and Lisavet caught her, cruelly, by the chin, squeezing hard, her fingertips eating deep into her cheeks, meeting inside her mouth.

Lisavet advanced suddenly, pinning Marion against the opposing wall so hard her skull cracked back against the stone. She saw black and then a peppering of stars sparking to life, then dying into shadow. Her knees buckled, and Lisavet's hand dropped lower, encircling her neck, holding her aloft by the throat. "Stay with me, Marion. Pay attention."

Marion found her footing again. Her vision, still fuzzy about the edges, slowly came into focus. She watched as Lisavet opened her mouth, her jaw shifting out of its socket with a *pop* like the sound a bone makes when it snaps in two. Marion felt a pull within her, something akin to arousal, but in pleasure's place there was pain. And the pain felt . . . *good*. Then it changed shape, turned into outright agony.

Marion screamed, her mouth an open wound, life bleeding from it. Lisavet arched over her, jaw unhinged—devouring and digesting her years and life and youth. There was something close to fear in the young Countess' eyes, and Marion realized then that she was dying and Lisavet was every bit as powerless to stop it as she. The power within her, primordial, eternally starving, would never be slaked.

A hot slick of urine laced down Marion's thigh. Her knees buckled. She tossed out a hand to the cell bars in a futile attempt to reach for her friends. "Help me . . ."

The girls cried out in response, fighting in vain to free themselves from their shackles.

Behind Lisavet, Cecelia shrugged off her rags and pressed slowly to her feet.

The girl staggered toward the bars of the cage, swollen knees buckling with each step. She fell several times before reaching the door of the cell. But when she finally made it, she raised her shackled wrists high above her head. She reached through the rungs of the cell—her shoulders were so narrow that it was easy for her emaciated body to slip between them—then looped the handcuffs over Lisavet's head and dragged down hard, ripping her back and away from Marion, who crumpled helpless to the floor.

Lisavet staggered, crashing against the bars of the cell, the chain eating deep into her throat. She struggled, choking, as Cecelia dragged her full weight down on that rusted chain. The other girls shouted, screamed helplessly, fighting the shackles that chained them to the wall of their shared cell. Cecelia dragged down on the handcuffs harder, with what little strength she had left in her— wizened face contorting with the effort of her struggle.

Lisavet, lips blue, eyes alight, raised the knife.

Marion threw out a hand. "Cecelia—"

The Countess slashed blindly behind her, the knife tearing into Cecelia's throat. The girl, the Wretch, gave a throttled cry and crumpled to the floor of the cell, shaking and bleeding from the mouth. Gasping for air, Lisavet ducked her head beneath the chain, rubbed her throat. On the floor of the cell, Cecelia lay motionless, a puddle of red widening beneath her neck, her throat slashed open. The Countess glanced at Cecelia, expressing little more than disgust, then turned on Marion again.

Too weak to stand, Marion dragged herself across the floor as Lisavet approached. "You were right, you know. When you said we were the same."

Lisavet advanced, the knife raised.

"I've killed too. You said that made us kindred. And you weren't wrong."

The Countess edged closer, undeterred.

"If you let me live, I'll keep your secret," said Marion. "I swear that I will. I'll be loyal, just like you wanted me to be."

"Marion, no," Irene cried, struggling against her chains, the cuffs biting bruises into her frail wrists. "Please."

"I'm First Bloodmaid," she said, her eyes trained on the knife. "And you yourself said I was your match, your equal. As your mother was to your father."

Lisavet dropped to a crouch beside her. Her eyes were heavy-lidded; her pupils swelled, consuming the pale jade of her irises, then shrank to catlike slits in the span of a single heartbeat. She wasn't human, Marion realized then. She was something less . . . or more.

"Let me live," said Marion, and she peeled her gaze from Lisavet's. The other girls were weeping, screaming, and dragging on their chains. "I'll serve you with discretion. You won't have to be alone anymore. I'll be by your side, forever. I'll never betray you."

Lisavet slipped the dagger beneath her chin, forcing Marion to peer up at her once again. "At the very least, you could look me in the eyes while you lie to me."

Marion leaned forward then, even as the blade bit into her throat. Her lips met Lisavet's, and she hated herself for the way her body betrayed her, the way her heartbeat quickened, her lips parted, the yearning that throbbed like a pulse between her legs even after all she'd seen and suffered through. Lisavet kissed her back, open-mouthed, and hungry, *feeding* on her fully the way she had just moments before. But this time—as Lisavet drew from her youth and years—Marion was ready.

She caught the Countess by the wrist, ripped the dagger free of her hand, and pierced it into Lisavet's side, just above the dip of her waist. The Countess staggered back so quickly Marion's hand slipped from the hilt; Lisavet ripped the blade free of her ribs and turned it on Marion, with a vicious slash that slit the dark clean through. Marion threw an arm up to protect herself, cried out in pain as the blade's edge ripped through her sleeve and the soft flesh beneath it.

"You mutinous little cunt," said Lisavet, clutching her side, spitting blood with each word. But she was smiling, smiling wide like she was . . . *proud* of her. Blood filled the cracks between her teeth. The Countess staggered back, collapsing against the bars of the cell. She slumped forward; the knife rattled to the floor. In her moment of weakness, Marion sprang to action, slipping a hand into Lisavet's pocket, snatching the key to the cells. She scrambled to her feet, slipping on Cecelia's blood, or Lisavet's, she wasn't sure anymore. Panicked, she fit the key into the lock, turned it, and threw open the door to the cell. She unlocked Irene's cuffs first, and the poor girl staggered into Marion's arms with a little cry. Then she freed the twins, helping both girls to their feet as they wept and rubbed their bruised wrists. Cecelia lay on the floor motionless, eyes wide open.

"We can't just leave her," Elize sobbed, the gentlest among them. The weakest.

"We have to," said Irene, and she caught Elize by the arm. "If we don't, we'll share her fate."

Together, the four girls staggered past Cecelia's body, out of the cell and to the stairway that twisted up to the highest floor. As the other girls climbed up ahead of her, Marion faltered, turned to look at Lisavet one final time. But the Countess was gone. A smeared puddle of blood marked the spot where she'd lain just moments before.

From the darkness of the distant caverns, a voice: "Marion."

She faltered, her hand on the railing of the stairway.

"What are you waiting for?" Irene said, half-feral with fear. "Leave her."

Marion was tempted. But in that moment, she recognized a fate that had been made a reality the moment Lisavet unlatched her teeth from Marion's wrist and claimed her as a bloodmaid: Only one of them could leave that House. If this was to end, it had to be with Lisavet's death.

"You go on without me," said Marion.

"What about you?" said Evie. "We can't leave without you."

Marion nodded, a kind of peace settling over her that she hadn't felt before. It was the confidence that came with knowing she was exactly where she was meant to be, why she had been called to the House of Hunger in the first place. She had never been one to believe in fate, but she had been made a believer, and she knew that her destiny was entwined with Lisavet's and that only one of them would survive the night. She was determined to make it her.

"The night train should arrive soon," she said, grasping Evie by the shoulders. Elize stood frail and shivering beside her. Both twins began to cry. "You must be on the platform at that time. If I'm not there, go on without me."

"Marion—"

"Go."

Irene hung back, still unwilling to leave. "What about Mae?"

"I'll find her. Just get to the station. We'll meet you there. Quickly, we're running out of time."

At her bidding, the three girls escaped up the stairs of the House, leaving Marion alone in the caverns with Lisavet. Filled with dread, she stepped past the smeared puddle of the Countess' blood and followed the trail of droplets into the distant caverns, until the dark was such that she couldn't see them any longer.

"You knew, you must have known, that it would come to this

before the end," she said, calling out into the darkness. "All of these years, all of these girls. It couldn't continue forever."

No answer.

Marion braced a hand on the wet wall to guide herself as the darkness thickened around her. She felt as though the walls of the caverns, half-devoured by mold and fungus, were slowly collapsing, threatening to entomb her within. "Lisavet?"

A lantern sparked to light in the darkness, its glare near blinding. "I'm . . . here."

Marion staggered back, but not quick enough to avoid the vicious arch of the knife in Lisavet's hand. It slashed below her collarbone, tore clean through the collar of her dress. Shocked and bleeding, Marion stumbled back into a stake of stalagmite. Felt her knees go soft beneath her. Lisavet raised the lantern with her left hand, the knife with her right.

The blade carved through the air again, glinting brilliantly in the lantern light. Marion squeezed her eyes shut in wait of death, but it didn't come. The knife's edge faltered a hair's width from her throat.

"What is it?" Marion inquired, taunting her. "Can't muster the nerve?"

Emboldened by the insult, Lisavet drew back the blade to strike again. But Marion was ready. She dropped low to her hands and knees on the floor of the caverns, gathered her skirts, then pressed to her feet again and ran. Bleeding and blind in the darkness, she sprinted through the labyrinth of passages.

She could hear Lisavet rushing after her, see the lurching light of her lantern swaying like a pendulum as she ran. Desperate to escape her, Marion tore through the dungeons, through the caverns, until she reached the cells and the stairway in the caverns just beyond them. The Countess followed after her, emerging from the darkness. In her hand: a crossbow.

"*Fuck*," said Marion, frozen in place. How the hell did she get her hands on that?

"My father kept weapons hidden throughout these caverns," said Lisavet, as though she'd read her mind. "He liked to play games with the girls he kept down here. Shall we play one?" she inquired. The wound at her side was bleeding, but Marion could tell it wasn't mortal. "I'm going to count to six and you're going to run. When I'm done counting, our chase begins. One."

"Lisavet—"

"Two."

"It doesn't have to come to this."

Lisavet began to shake. There were tears in her eyes. "Three."

Marion faltered, torn between further attempts at negotiation and the slim chance of successful escape. She knew Lisavet was a wicked shot. She'd seen it firsthand during the hunt, and the dozens of taxidermied animals displayed in Lisavet's study were evidence of her prowess.

"Four."

"This won't end well, for either of us," said Marion, weeping now.

The Countess raised her crossbow to her shoulder, squeezed one eye shut. "Five."

"But if only one of us leaves this House, know it will be me."

Lisavet raised her crossbow and fired a single bolt that cleaved the air, sliced along Marion's cheek, and embedded itself in the cave wall. Stunned silent, Marion raised a hand to her bleeding face, gashed open by the arrow's edge.

Lisavet reloaded her crossbow and curled a finger over the trigger. "*Six*."

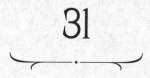

Desire is a kind of madness.

—CLEO, BLOODMAID OF THE HOUSE OF UMBER

GRIPPING FISTFULS OF HER skirts, Marion scrambled up the twisting stairway to the higher levels of the House and burst through the first door she met, tumbling into the darkness of a hall that was foreign to her. She thought she could hear Lisavet's footfalls echoing through the stairway behind her—slow and deliberate as though she couldn't even be bothered to properly chase her.

Panicked, Marion kept running, even as her lungs burned and her breath came in spastic gasps. She knew she had to make it back to Lisavet's chambers, find Mae, and help her escape if she had any hope of survival. She could only pray that Irene and the twins were safe at the depot and awaiting the night train, which would carry them to safety, regardless of whether Marion and Mae were with them.

The hall opened onto a wide and empty ballroom, on its opposing side four doors. Two dark, two with light beneath them. Marion turned to see that Lisavet had just entered the corridor behind her. The Countess was smiling, her crossbow lowered to her side.

"You're quite slow, Marion."

With a little cry, Marion sprang toward the second door, but it was locked and she was forced to enter through the third. As she turned the handle, one of Lisavet's bolts struck the marble floor at her feet.

Marion realized that this was a game to her. Lisavet was a good shot, a known huntress. She was merely toying with her at this point. Reveling in the joys of the chase, believing all the while that there was no way Marion could escape her. But she was wrong. Marion was determined to prove that.

She dragged open the third door and staggered into a large drawing room where the nobles of the court were gathered, under cover of a thick pall of maudlum smoke. All were in various stages of undress, lounging on chairs or bent on their hands and knees before the fire, losing themselves to the spoils of pleasure. Two girls, who Marion realized were Thiago's new protégées, were among them, in a tangle of limbs and grasping hands. The youngest sat on a chaise apart from her sisters, both arms extended to two nobles who were on their knees in front of her, drinking from her bleeding wrists. At the sight of Marion, her eyes came into focus. She called out to her with the voice of a child. Marion started to reach for her, but a bolt cleaved the air between them before she had the chance. Marion kept running.

Gradually the labyrinth of hallways gave way to the grand corridor, which Marion followed until she reached the adjoining passage that led through the empty kitchens. Here, the echo of Lisavet's footfalls faded, and Marion quickly armed herself with a brutal cleaver that hung on a knife rack above the butcher's station.

Marion heard a door open and close. Then the sound of footsteps on stone.

She brandished the cleaver—wheeling this way and that—as she edged through the dark bleeding parlor and toward the snowy courtyard beyond it. From there, she could cut through the greenhouse, unseen if she was lucky, and cross to the other side of the estate where Lisavet's quarters were located. She could let herself in through one of the garden doors, take the stairway up to Lisavet's private quarters, find Mae, and escape. The night was still young. She had time.

"Marion?" She wheeled to face Thiago. He stood lurking by the door of the greenhouse, a cigarette pinched between his knuckles. "What's wrong? What on earth are you doing with that?"

Marion, in her desperation, rushed him. Of course, *Thiago* could help her. He had tickets south. He had money. If he knew the truth of what lay below the House of Hunger, he would have no choice but to render aid. "I need you to get me and my friends out of this House, *tonight.*"

Thiago took a final pull on his cigarette, then stubbed it out on the heel of his boot. All that registered on his face was a passing look of . . . *pity?*

"Y-you know," said Marion, realizing the truth of his depravity. That the Taster she'd trusted was no better than the Countess herself. "All along you've known exactly what happens to the girls who are sent here to bleed. You know what becomes of them after Lisavet's favor wanes, and yet you sell them to her House anyway."

"Marion—"

All this time, Thiago had been supplying Lisavet with girls to replace the ones she drained and killed. He knew they would disappear; in fact, their disappearance was the very foundation of his business with the House of Hunger. He sent girls to Lisavet to be slaughtered, so he could replace them and line his pockets once more. "How much did she pay you for me?" she demanded, almost yelling now. "It was five thousand pounds, wasn't it? Tell me, Thiago, was the price of my head worth your soul? Or did you even have one to begin with?"

"Mind your tone," said Thiago. "A bloodmaid should never—"

Marion raised the cleaver. "Help me get out of this House along with every bloodmaid in it, or I swear on the bones of my mother I'll pen a letter to the *Prane Gazette* that is so thoroughly damning you'll never be able to show your face there again."

Thiago smiled just wide enough for Marion to see his gold-capped canines. "You know, the sisters I brought tonight are practically bred to taste, as close to born bloodmaids as any girl could be. They're the descendants of some of the most accomplished, sweet-blooded girls that have ever lived. Their mother, God rest her soul, was a beloved bloodmaid and they surpass her in both beauty and taste. But Lisavet seems, at most, bored with them." He paused to pull on his cigarette. "And then there's you, a lice-bitten little murderess from the grubbiest corner of Prane's slums who has somehow ascended to the title of First Bloodmaid. Lisavet fell in *love* with you. And tonight, in spite of that and everything else, you're still going to die."

Marion threw out a hand. "No. *Wait—*"

Thiago snatched a breath and yelled, "She's over here, near the courtyard."

Marion burst through the doors and let herself outside, stepping barefoot into a snowdrift. The cold was so stark it snatched the breath from her lungs, and the wind blew with a violence. Barefoot and shivering, she picked her way across the dead garden and let herself into the hothouse. There, the fog was thick—such that the light of the lanterns could barely shine through it. She could hear the whistling of crickets, though the talking parrots that occupied the hothouse were quiet, already roosting for the night.

"You know, Thiago was right. I did love you." Lisavet's disembodied voice moved like a wraith through the hothouse. "Perhaps I still do."

Marion turned wildly, the cleaver raised, trying and failing to discern where her voice was coming from. The fog made any attempt to see more than a few feet ahead of her next to impossible. "Is that what you say to all of the bloodmaids you slaughter?"

Lisavet emerged from the pall, her crossbow raised. "No. Just you."

At the sight of her, Marion turned and ran as fast as her numb feet could carry her, losing the trail and tearing through the garden brush until she reached the other side of the hothouse and searched for the door through the fog. Lisavet fired a volley of bolts, each one shattering the glass panes it struck. Marion climbed through one of the breaks, catching the underside of her knee on a jagged shard in her desperation to escape. Her gown tore, and she felt blood leak down her calf and lace around her ankle.

In a full run, she broke toward the door on the side of the House, opened it, and slammed it shut behind her. There was a deadbolt above the doorknob, which she quickly locked into place before starting up the nearby stairway, slipping a little on the steps—her left foot slick with blood from the wound on the back of her knee. She was slowing down, weakening rapidly. Her lungs were on fire, she'd lost too much blood and she hadn't had much to begin with, given the frequency of her bloodlettings. She wasn't sure how long she could keep running.

Still, she managed to limp to Lisavet's private quarters. She threw the door open to the parlors and called, desperately, for Mae. "It will be all right," she assured the little girl. "You have only to follow the sound of my voice. Come to me and I promise I'll make sure everything is okay."

Of course, there was no answer.

Marion burst through to the doors of the chamber. Ivor's corpse was still there on the bed, facedown, his stiff legs hanging over the footboard. On instinct she dropped to her hands and knees, and that was where she found them—Mae and Elize's cat, Theodore, huddled together in the dark beneath Lisavet's bed. At the sight of Marion, Mae's eyes lit up. She circled Theodore with one arm and dragged herself out from under the bed, ducking slightly to avoid Ivor's boots.

"Wait by the door," said Marion, and the girl obeyed.

Marion limped up to the bed, caught Ivor by the shoulder, and rolled him over with some effort. His body was stiff with rigor mortis, and he was beginning to turn colors, his cheeks mottled with large purple patches that made him look like he'd been badly beaten. She slipped a hand into his breast coat and was relieved to discover, in a silk-lined inner pocket, a pen and a slim, leather-bound checkbook.

Marion hastily smeared her bloody hands clean on her skirts and signed the check, then and there, filling it out for a hefty sum, forging Ivor's signature as best she could, based on her memory of it from the gambling salons that morning. She snapped the checkbook shut, capped the pen, and shoved both items into the pockets of her skirt before extending a hand to Mae. The girl took it with some reluctance before opting to grasp a fistful of her nightdress instead. She held a squirming Theodore, though it seemed the cat was taking pains not to scratch her with his claws.

Marion heard the grandfather clock in the parlor toll eleven.

"Come along," said Marion, leading the child into the parlor. "We'll have to be quick, and quiet . . . but I suppose you're rather good at that. The night train leaves at twelve, so—"

"Marion. That will be quite enough for tonight."

Horrified, she turned to see the House Mother standing between her and the door of the parlor. She was alone, no sign of Lisavet anywhere.

"I can't begin to express my grave disappointment, so I won't try. But I must now inform you that your tenure here has come to an end." The House Mother reached into the pocket of her skirts and drew from a narrow sheath the longest needle Marion had ever seen. "This is for your benefit. Your death will be more swift by my hand than Lisavet's." She motioned to a nearby couch. "Allow me to bleed you, once more, that this . . . bedlam might finally come to an end."

Mae peered up at Marion with tears in her eyes. She clutched Theodore to her chest a little tighter, half buried her face in the bloodied folds of her gown.

Marion turned back to the House Mother. "Where is Lisavet?"

"The Countess is no longer your concern."

"I want to speak with her."

"You haven't been summoned."

"If I want to speak to Lisavet, I will. I need not wait for a summoning. I'm not her bloodmaid any longer."

"The only person who can decide when your indenture ends is Lisavet. Until then, it's my responsibility as House Mother to attend to you." Again, she motioned to the chaise. "Now sit *down* and let me bleed you."

Something fluttered in Marion's belly, like a laugh she'd swallowed long ago. She smiled, giggled even, as she raised the cleaver. "I've bled enough tonight. It's your turn now."

The House Mother's expression softened from anger to pity. "It doesn't have to end this way."

"But it will." Marion stepped forward, raising the cleaver between her and the House Mother. Mae released her hold on her skirts. "Unless you let us go."

The House Mother moved with a kind of speed Marion wouldn't have thought her capable of. She struck her, a vicious backhanded slap across her gashed cheek that brought her to her knees and sent the cleaver flying out of her hand. Marion braced herself on the floor, a fresh flow of blood slicking her face and dribbling off the point of her chin—*drip, drip, drip*.

"It seems like such a waste," said the House Mother, as she produced a handkerchief and wiped Marion's blood from the palm of her hand, "to squander such talent. You might've grown to become a great bloodmaid. I saw the potential in you."

From the corner of Marion's eye, she saw Mae move through the shadows, edging toward the cleaver by the parlor's hearth.

The House Mother didn't notice her. She bent to one knee beside Marion, delicately peeled back the sleeve of her dress, and lowered the needle to the fat green vein in the crook of her elbow. "Despite my immense disappointment, it was an honor to bleed you, Marion."

Mae edged forward, dropped to a crouch, and slid the cleaver across the floor. Marion caught it by the handle and swung it in a sharp arc, the blade biting deep into the House Mother's neck. The woman buckled forward with a great and garbled cry, scrabbling at the cleaver's hilt. She collapsed, pinning Marion beneath her, thrashing and coughing and bringing up dark mouthfuls of blood. Her needle struck the floor.

Marion caught the cleaver by the hilt and tried to pull it free, but her fingers, slick with blood, failed to find purchase. Desperate, Marion summoned the last of her strength and shoved the woman off her and pressed to her feet, but not before snatching the House Mother's needle from where it lay on the floor. There was blood in her eyes—hers or the House Mother's, she wasn't sure—but it stung and made it difficult to see clearly. She scrubbed her eyes and staggered toward Mae as the House Mother lay twitching on the floor, trying to pry the cleaver free of her nape.

And then she went still.

"Get Theodore," said Marion, pointing to the hassock where the cat crouched, cowering.

Mae ran to collect him, wrapping him in a small throw that lay draped across the chaise. The poor creature looked traumatized, but Marion was determined to get him out of the House, for Elize's sake.

Together—Mae trailing behind her, holding a fistful of Marion's skirts—the two girls ventured down the hallway and back into the deep of the House. At first Marion retraced her steps back to the same stairway she'd ascended upon leaving the hothouse, but she thought better of it. That was the last place she'd seen Lisavet. She'd be looking for her there. It was a near-impossible decision, but she thought it better to take her chances in the House—where there were ample passages and places to hide—instead of out in the open where they could easily be spotted and overcome.

"Quickly now," said Marion, ducking down a narrow servants' passage and into a different gallery. Two noblewomen lay sleeping in this one, their mouths crusted with dried blood, a pale halo of maudlum smoke hanging about their heads.

Marion limped past them as quietly as she could and crossed into the same ballroom where Lisavet had first welcomed her, the night she'd become a bloodmaid. From there it was a short walk to the grand stairway in the foyer. If they were lucky, they could make it out the doors, row across the estuary, and reach the depot before the night train departed. They were so close now.

"Marion." She turned to see the Countess, standing on the other side of the ballroom, her crossbow raised to her shoulder . . . though it was trained not on Marion but Mae. "Not a step farther."

Marion moved to face her, deftly slipping the House Mother's needle into the pocket of her gown as she turned. "Lisavet. Please just let us go. We've come this far."

The Countess hooked a finger over the trigger of the crossbow and squeezed one eye shut. Mae began to cry, silently, into Theodore's neck.

"Come here," said the Countess.

Marion took a step forward, her wounded knee near buckling beneath the weight. There was no point in trying to run anymore. Somewhere down the hall, the clock tolled the half hour. The night train would soon arrive, and she knew now that she would not be there to welcome it. Her indenture would be the death of her, that much was clear.

But there was still Mae and the slim chance of her survival to fight for.

So Marion dragged herself—bleeding and weary—across the ballroom to the place where Lisavet stood. She stopped just short of her crossbow; the iron tip of the bolt kissed the soft hollow just above her collarbones. She extended both hands, cradling Lisavet's face, letting her fingers trace through the soft hairs at the nape of her neck.

When she leaned forward to kiss her, the bolt cut her. But Lisavet lowered the weapon, allowed their lips to crush together. Marion had waited her whole life to be kissed like that, waited her whole life to feel the way she did when Lisavet's arms encircled her and dragged her close. A weak and ugly part of her would have been content to exist in that moment for the rest of her eternity. But instead, she slipped a hand into the pocket of her skirts, wrapped her fingers tight around the House Mother's needle, and drove it up through Lisavet's throat.

The Countess staggered back, clasped a hand to her neck as the blood seeped through the cracks of her fingers. She smiled—in disbelief, or even with pride, Marion couldn't tell which—and then with a vicious yank ripped the needle free of her neck. She lurched forward, hitting the ground on her knees, but she was bleeding fast and her arms quickly gave beneath her.

"You wretched little bitch," she said, in a rasping gargle, still smiling as she lay on the floor, peering up at Marion.

The Countess whispered something more, but Marion couldn't hear her. When she dropped to the floor beside her and leaned closer, trying to catch her final words, Lisavet raised her head, parted her blood-slick lips, and fixed her mouth around the side of Marion's throat in a vicious bite.

Across the ballroom Mae cut a scream.

The Countess could have mauled her, could have drained her of whatever life she had left. She could have locked her jaw, wrenched her head, and ripped Marion's throat free of her neck. But her teeth sank just deep enough to get the blood flowing steadily, and Lisavet drank deeply of Marion's blood for the final time.

Then, with a gasp and whimper, the young Countess unlatched her teeth and slumped, limp, to the floor. Her breath came in ragged gasps. Her eyelids fluttered. She raised a limp hand, slick with blood, weighted by the thick signet ring on her middle finger. She slipped it off, took Marion by the hand, and pressed it hard into her palm, the sharp edge of the ruby biting deep. The stone in its center was worth more than the pensions of all the girls that Lisavet had ever indentured.

"Take it," she said in a blood-garbled whisper. "You've won."

32

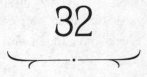

In the end there are only those who eat and those who bleed.

—LISAVET, COUNTESS OF THE HOUSE OF HUNGER

I T WAS FIVE PAST midnight when Marion staggered to the platform of the night train. Bleeding, she had limped through the mounting drifts and the half-frozen muck of the marshes until they reached the dock where the boat was tethered. The other one was already on the opposite side of the channel, bobbing with the waves. She smiled. Irene and the twins had made it to the other side.

Marion had helped Mae into the boat first, the poor child clutching Theodore tightly to her chest as he squirmed and clawed through her nightgown. Then Marion climbed in after them, took up the oars, and began to row them across, her shoulders burning with the effort.

By the time they reached the dock at the other side of the channel, the snow was falling hard. Hastily, they scrambled out of the boat and began to walk to the station, following the shallow, half-filled footsteps of the other girls.

The violent wind made each step a struggle. But Marion limped onward, head bowed, arms folded tight across her chest. Her feet were stone numb beneath her, far past the point of pain. As she walked, she kept her eyes on the distant horizon, where she could see the light of the depot. She followed the shallow tracks in the snow— turning back only to make sure that she hadn't lost Mae to the torrents of the blizzard—until she reached the deserted platform. Evie, Elize, and Irene were nowhere to be seen, and Marion's heart plummeted. Had they failed to escape the House?

But then, a voice: *"Marion! Mae! Theodore!"*

The three girls—Irene, Evie, and Elize—emerged from the tollbooth and rushed to embrace them. The bloodmaids clung to each other for a long time there on the empty platform, the snow falling all around them. Elize lifted Theodore from Mae's arms and wept silently into his fur.

"Come on," said Irene, herding her toward the tollbooth, where a teller sat behind a sheet of frosty glass. "There isn't much time. We only have enough coins to buy two tickets south. So the twins and I have decided to stay here. Marion, you and Mae go south. You can send help—"

"I'm not leaving you," said Marion. "Either we all go or we all stay. No one gets left behind."

With that, Marion limped up to the depot. She slipped the forged check from the pocket of her gown and set it on the countertop. She prayed the teller would take it. "Five tickets south . . . if you will."

The teller appraised her, his brows drawing into a frown. He was a large man, portly, with a thick beard and the dark skin of a southerner. He took the check, unfolded it, and studied the signature with a frown. And Marion saw it then, with a wave of dread: the rusty smear of a bloody thumbprint at the edge of the paper. The teller's gaze moved to Marion, snaring on her cut cheek, ripped open by

Lisavet's bolt, and the fresh bite wound at her neck. "You girls are bloodmaids?"

"We were," she whispered.

The man's eyes fell to little Mae. "I have a daughter at home. Not far off her age."

Irene stepped in front of the girl, as if to shield her from his gaze. The twins followed suit, ready to spring to Mae's defense, though they were so frail and weak they looked barely strong enough to stay on their feet.

The teller's eyes hardened. In the distance, the long peal of the train's horn.

Marion slipped her hand into her pocket and reached for Lisavet's signet ring. The value of its ruby alone was more than all their pensions combined. With it, they would have enough to start anew in the Isles. All that stood between them and their new lives was the teller. "Please, sir. We—"

The man took the check and slipped it into the drawer of his register. He then produced five tickets and slid them across the countertop. "If asked, we never spoke."

Marion's knees buckled. Behind her the girls began to cry.

"Th-thank you," said Marion, sobbing. "You don't know what this means to us."

The teller merely dipped his head.

Just then, with a wheeze and a huff of steam, the night train rounded a corner and drew to a grinding stop at the station. Hand in hand, the girls boarded the train, Marion claiming the same seat in the viewing car that she'd occupied the night she first arrived in the North with Thiago, all those months ago. Elize leaned against Evie, who folded herself into Marion's left side, and Irene huddled against her right with Mae in her lap, cradling a shivering Theodore in her arms.

Marion stared out the frozen window, and darkness edged into her field of vision. In the far distance, through the gathering shadows and the sheets of falling snow, she thought she could see the House of Hunger, its windows burning in the darkness. But before she had the chance to whisper her silent goodbyes, the train gave a violent lurch and charged into the southern night.

ACKNOWLEDGMENTS

I want to begin by thanking my brilliant editor, Jessica Wade. Her insight into my stories is uncannily accurate and I'm so grateful to her for working so diligently to make a space on the shelves for my books. *House of Hunger* wouldn't have been possible without her. My agent, Jenny Bent, has been such a force in my life since the day I signed with her. I couldn't have asked for a more honest, savvy, or supportive advocate. Alexis Nixon, my publicist, has created so many wonderful opportunities for me to share my work with the world and for that I'm so grateful. I also want to thank Katie Anderson and Lillian Liu for creating the Gothic horror cover of my wildest dreams and nightmares. I'm also immensely grateful for my publishing teams both in the US and around the world, with special thanks to Simon Taylor, Zoë Plant, Fareeda Bullert, Miranda Hill, and Amy J. Schneider.

I would be remiss not to thank my family, who have been a constant source of support through the writing of this book, which was, at times, a harrowing process. I owe a huge thank-you to my mom for always making sure I've had enough to eat and for caring for me so diligently. In the dedication of my first novel, *The Year of the Witching*, I said that I owe her everything and that still holds true. I want to thank my sister, Alana, for the dark humor and blunt (but necessary) feedback, and my dad for his steadfast belief in me. I also want to thank Alice for being my closest companion and confidant, and for keeping me grounded and semi-sane. I feel so lucky to have you as my partner.

I want to thank my friends for continuing to uphold me. I love you all. Special thanks to Genevieve Gornichec, Jennifer Duncan, Ronni Davis, Rachel Harrison, Rena Barron, and Ashley Hearn for making me feel less alone on this publishing journey. To the authors who've taken the time to blurb my books, share my posts, and support me, I appreciate you so much. To the librarians, booksellers, podcasters, bloggers, journalists, bookstagrammers, reviewers, and creators who've taken the time to showcase my work, I'm immensely grateful to you all.

Lastly, thank you to my readers who have been so kind, patient, and understanding. Thank you for reading my work, and thank you for the encouraging messages you've sent, the gorgeous fan art you've created, the recommendations you've made to your friends and family, and all of the reviews you've written. I'm eternally grateful. You keep the worlds I create alive and it's an honor to share them with you.

HOUSE
of
HUNGER

———— ◆ ————

ALEXIS HENDERSON

QUESTIONS FOR DISCUSSION

1. Who was your favorite character in the novel? Who was your least favorite?

2. This book is set in an alternate world, but it has similarities to ours. What did the time period, geographical locations, and fashions in the novel remind you of in our world?

3. Why do you think the author gave the book the title *House of Hunger*? What roles do food, blood, and consumption play in this story?

4. If you were in Marion's shoes—living in the slums, struggling to make ends meet—would you leave the poverty of Prane for the relatively unknown world of being a bloodmaid? What do you think Marion's fate would have been if she'd stayed in Prane?

5. How does Marion's relationship with the other bloodmaids evolve over the course of the novel?

6. Did the twists in the novel—like Cecelia's true whereabouts— take you by surprise, or did you see them coming?

7. At one point, Lisavet offers to let Marion leave the House of Hunger. Why do you think she does that? Do you think Lisavet truly loved Marion?

8. Do you think Marion truly loved Lisavet? Do her feelings for Lisavet prevent her from understanding Lisavet's true nature, or does Lisavet do a good job of hiding who she really is?

9. In the book Lisavet says, "If you eat the weak, you'll never go hungry." What do you make of that statement? Do you think she's right? Or is it possible to ethically enrich and empower yourself without the exploitation of someone more vulnerable than you?

10. What future do you imagine for Marion? Will her experiences at the House of Hunger help her survive?

ALEXIS HENDERSON is the author of *House of Hunger* and *The Year of the Witching*, a Goodreads Choice Awards finalist. When she's not writing, you'll find her tending to an assortment of houseplants or nursing a hot cup of tea.

CONNECT ONLINE

AlexisHenderson.com
🐦 AlexHWrites
📷 Lexish

Ready to find
your next great read?

Let us help.

Visit prh.com/nextread